THE BLOCKS
Karl Parkinson

Published in 2016 by
New Binary Press
Cork city, Ireland

www.NewBinaryPress.com

Cover image by Joanna Niec

This book is dedicated with love to all those who lived and died in the blocks, and with hope for all who are living there still.

A poet makes himself a visionary through a long, boundless, and systematized disorganization of all the senses. All forms of love, of suffering, of madness; he searches himself, he exhausts within himself all poisons, and preserves their quintessences. Unspeakable torment, where he will need the greatest faith, a superhuman strength, where he becomes all men the great invalid, the great criminal the great accursed--and the Supreme Scientist! For he attains the unknown! Because he has cultivated his soul, already rich, more than anyone!

—Arthur Rimbaud

PROLOGUE

11.02.1512 Bishop ODevaney kisses de hangmans noose, receives de hood, pale hands a-tremble as hes raisin dem te de grey Dublin sky, splintered by a red sun, momenterly.

De sun retreats. De rain washes away de blood uv de Bishops quartered body from de gallows. In view uv de sliced up saint a dyin man is healed, n de crowd strips relics from de corpse, dissolves.

Four n half centuries later a north-side Dublin block uv flats resurrects iz name. ODevaney Gardens n I grew der wit all de junkies, thieves, madmen n madwomen, sinners n singers, comedians n clowns. Wit de relics n de blood n de violence, n de beautifully deranged, de stories n de saints.

From de window uv me flat in de blocks I see de mountains exhale pink clouds, risin te de sky. I think uv de Chinese poet Li Po drunk under de grapefruit moon chortlin. He is long dead now, tho de poems er still alive n read.

Dese blocks wer Ive lived thirty five years. Dese blocks wer Ive fought n fucked. Been drugged, pissed. Meditated n made music. Wrote line after line after line. Read book after book after book. Loved like Byron n Blake n Bloom.

1

Anto waitll I get ya, Im gonna stab ya in de neck.
A scream in de street below.

De fat kids drink bottles uv coke wit der names on
dem n spit chicken bones on de ground. *Nike* n *Adidas*
signs er everywer, tracksuits uv indigo n concrete
grey, luminous yellow n glowin Dutch orange runners
on der feet

n dey know little uv poetry or Michelangelos
statues, tho poems er all around dem n deyve seen
many pietas in de cruel violet/black nights, blood n
music, music like cats burnin te death or long alcohol
pisses steamin n gurglin inte de drain.

Music like cats burnin. Music like saints dyin.
Music like motors rumblin. Dis is music. Dis notin uv
de sounds, uv de comedy, uv hours passin. Dis typin
uv words at de desk. Dis is de music I make. Listen.

Its 12:30 am n I write more lines. Line after line. I
make music here at dis desk. While de dealers n
children n cats er burnin outside in de blocks, burnin
wit hate, burnin wit desire, burnin wit love. I am
burnin. I am burnin wit de word. With de word I burn.

BLOCK A
CHILDHOOD VISIONS

*I havent seen yer face round, since I wuz a kid,
yer bringing back those memories of the things that we
did, yer hanging round and climbing trees pretending
to fly, dya wanna be a spaceman and live in the sky.*

—Oasis

In de beginnin I had no face. Dat wuz before I wuz born. Dat wuz de untime before de blocks.

De first block I lived in wuz de womb. De boom, boom, boom. De water. De sounds uv Ma, Da n Edel on de outside. Music; Imagine all de people, livin for today.

De womb, buh bum, buh bum, buh bum. Boom. Out wit a wail I came. OUT!
Like a drink uv water, me ma said.
Meanin it wuz an easy birth for her. Birth de origin uv trauma. Why did I volunteer te come back here again te be in de blocks? Kenneth Thomson, known te me mates as Kenny. Howya?

As a baba n a nipper I had a recurrin stomach problem. I kept puckin green, n somtimes green n yellow. Even den I spit de demons out.

Ballymun wuz de name uv de next block I had te escape from. Ball ey mun,
Balls uv moon, ballerman, de mun. We had two dogs. Laddy wuz a black shaggy little fella n Lassie a brown n white collie. Lassie disappeared, she ran away dey said. But really she wuz stolen by de Glooptings in de dark. I saw dem call her inte de tunnel. Poor Laddy, he got run over by a bus. Ma went away for de weekend, came back te find Da stoned n de dog dead.

I talked before I walked. I had conversations on de bus wit adults. Lit dem up wit stories n facts. Wen I did learn te walk, I started te run, round n round n round.

Zooooommmmmiiin round de table. Da n me Uncle Sammie blew hash fumes in me face te calm me down. De blocks er full uv smoke.

Lift me up Ma. Lift me up Ma. Lift me up Ma. Lift me up Ma. Dat wuz de mantra I chanted wen a boy. I didden like te walk out on de streets. I preferred te be carried or wheeled in de buggy. Sumtimes I wuz lifted up te de sky n flew wit doves. Deyd sing songs te me n Id sing along. A flock uv songs. Lift me up. Lift me up. Lift me up.

I stole teabags from de shop for me Ma n didden know why she gave out. I bit de head off a beetle on de balcony, n me sister Edel shrieked n ran inside.

Dats wen de bee first took notice uv me n decided te teach me.

Edel, dats me older sister. She wuz already in de blocks wen I entered dem.
She wuz a thin n lovin brown-haired little girl wit a demandin temperament.

One night two men in orange overalls wit helmets on came inte our flat wit a black pipe dat dey pretended wuz a gun n asked for De Money n Wers yer Da? I told dem te fuck off n said me Da wud bash dem wen he gets back.

Dey did fuck off n never came back.

De first time I saw de bee he wuz sittin in a field behind a wall.

He called me over n says Child uv de blocks, wot ya see here only a few can see. Tell me Kenny Thomson, why do ya think its okay te bite de heads off little insects hey? Ya know dats not good for ya or de poor headless mite. Ya see dat my head is too big te bite off, child. If ya wish te get back onside wit us, do me dis favour, scratch me back for me friend, wud ya?

I/ll help ya fuzzy bumbler, no bother I said.

It wuz a trick. He stung de fuck outta me. Inside me head der wuz a flash uv red n a sensation uv spinnin. I heard de sound woooghaa, woooghaa.

My advice te ya child, is be careful whose back ya scratch n whose head ya bite off in de future, see ya around young Kenny.

I came back around from de sting. I told Ma n Da n dey told me te stay away from bees n not te be silly.

BLOCKHOOD
A Nippers Tale Or
De Child Relates Iz Agony n Visions

One day a man fell out de blocks n splooshed on de ground. De Glooptings wer der n stood around de splooshed man, laughin. I gave dem de name Glooptings wen I first seen wunna dem. It wuz der in de lift, standin behind Da. It wuz black n thick like tar, but sorta ghosty like, aswell. I asked Da

Wots dat gloopy lookin ting der? He didden see nutting. He laughed it off. Wild imagination.

De Ballymun block wuz gettin outta hand. Buses runnin over dogs, me bitin beetles heads off, fellas jumpin off de blocks, bees stingin ya, glooptings laughin, men in orange overalls wit helmets on, lookin for money, n Da losin iz job n fallin asleep in de middle uv tings. We had te get out. So I called de white birds in de sky n asked dem te get us outta here, n dey sang de song uv movin, n we wer gone, just like dat. We wer gone, just like de birds go. But Ma n Da cud only afford te go te another block, one wer Da grew up. Dis block wuz ODevaney gardens. De grey place.

Ders Da smokin de rollies, de rollie, olees, de puff sticks, de cough bringers. Ma likes de longer smokes wit de brown bit at de end. De black birds flew over de blocks de first day we came.

Dey caw, caw, cawwwwwwed, in de sky.

Me sister Edel makes friends quickly. She always makes friends easily. I think its weird, becuz shes a headmelter te me, pokin, laughin, proddin. Loves me tho. Writes about me in school, draws pictures uv me. I love my brother Kenny.
I said te Edel Lovin is weird, lovin is mad. People love each other, n fight, n be all shoutin, n smashin up de place, wit love, like Da.

De Glooptings er here too. Did dey follow me? Do dey live in all de blocks? Gloop, gloopy, gloopers.

De banshee wails.

Like de screechin uv a feral cat. Shes sat outside our windowsill.
A bag uv bats, a shadow, huge, scary.
Awailin.
Edel n me in bed cowerin under covers.

Wots dat out de window makin dat noise?
Look at de big dark shade, in de corner uv de window.
Aggghhh, wots dat? Wots dat? Im scared.
Its a banshee I said.
A banshee?

Yeah, call Da, call Da.
Da, Da, Da.

Wot is it?
Der Da, out de window, its a banshee.
But as soon as he comes in de wailin stops n she, disappears.

Ders nutting der, its yer imagination, I told yiz about watchin dem horror films.

I swear Da, it wuz der, outside de window said Edel.

He walks over te wer Edel points n pulls back de curtains, not scared at all, Das a man, he has a moustache, hes not afraid uv anyting.

See ders nutting der, go back te sleep, its late.

Da musta scared it away, we thought.
But he didden, becuz wen he leaves, de banshee comes back. De shade n de wailin. Awwwooouuuugggghhhhhh!
Us kids huddled tegether in bed. All tru de night she keeps appearin, disappearin, appearin n disappearin. De banshee wailin… dis is how it begins.

Ders Da, smokin, puff, puff, puff, cough, cough. Sittin by de fire, hoggin all de heat, Ma wud say. Heres de old doggy, Shelley,

Hello Shelley belly, shes a good girl isin she. Shelley, Da n me all in de sittin room n de mornin, drinkin tea, eatin Cornflakes, drinkin de milk out de bowl, barkin at de postman, smokin de rollies, puff, puff, puff, cough, cough.

Mas gone te work in de sewin factory, wer she does de sewin.

Hole in yer trousers, no problemo, switch, switch, no holeo, in yer trousers anymoreo,

Cuz Ma sewed it all upoooooooooooooo!

Da says United er playin Arsenal in de cup later.

Go on United.

Da looks at me n smiles.

No one else cud see de bee, but it wuz der, it wuz real.

Bzzzzzz, ziiippp, flyin around de room, in de middle uv de night. I called for help.

Ma said she cudden see it, Da said yer imaginin tings again.

Dat youngfellas got a wild imagination.

Edel wuz laughin at me.

It wuz der, a big bee, de size uv a dog, flyin over me bed, its back again, de talkin bee dat tricked me.

I wont call out again, nuna dem can see um.

Wot dya want bee?

I want te get out uv de block... *Rrrought* said Shelley, n scared de bee away.

Me bed can fly. But nobody knows, cept me. Only at night wen everyones asleep.

I wake up, de bed starts movin, spinnin, woov, woov, woov. Faster n faster till it takes off. Den I fly tru de tunnel n come out te de purple place.

Mad purple mountains n de black sky wit shiny stars in it. I control de bed wit me head, I turn side te side. Its magic. Wen I want te go back home n go te sleep I just go back tru de tunnel. Den make sure dat de big bee is not around n pop off te sleepy-sleep.

I had a dream about a woman. She wuz in de nip. She had big diddies. I woke up, it wuz me birthday. Ma gave de presents te me. Da wuz der smilin. Cakes. Biscuits. Coke. Orange. Edel. Chocolate. Other kids. Shelly de dog.

Da again, in de sittin room. Blue, ragged hallowed housecoat, brown moustache, greyin hair.

Drinkin de tea, smokin de puff sticks.
Im an Indian I tellum.
Cool he says.

I got an Indian headdress, a bow n arrow. Im an Indian. Hey, ya, hey, ya, hey, ya, ho. On de plains, de

11

buffalo comes n I dance in a circle wit de tribe, Im an Indian. De buffalo speaks.

Kenny, yer de boy wit de buffalo in iz brain, yer de dancer on de plains, yer de shaman uv de blocks, spit de demons out Kenny. Buffalo n me dance in de blocks.

Me cousins live in dis block too. Sum over der, sum over here, sum down der, sum up der. I went out in de block one day n made friends just like dat.

Mad Mark Winters. Hes me best mate. Younger din me. Always tells iz Ma te fuck off.

Mark Winters, wait till yer Da gets home. Wait till yer Da gets home. Da gets home. Da gets. Da.

De banshee comes in de night. She comes tru de window. Her hands er bones, torn green dress, no face, just a black hole wit red eyes in it. She floats around de house; she has no feet just a trail uv yellow smoke. She tips Da on de shoulder n he looks around n sees nutting. She looks at me n a howlin laugh comes out uv her blackness.

De bee is in de backer flyin around. He sees me n flies at me, zoom, zoooommmmm. *Hello child, how are ya today?*

I tellum te fuck off. I run down de streets back te de block.

Child I must talk wit ya soon, forgive my sting, a lesson wuz learned, a lesson...

12

School, a navy uniform. Girls. Boys. I shit meself, it wuz on me shoe. I wuz left at de back uv de class wit de shit, n dey all went te de yard n stared at me on de way out. Holy shit. Holy moley, shitey shoe, Kenny Shitshoe.

Ma came te get me. Rescued me like a superhero. She gave de poor teacher a blast uv de tongue. Rarp, rarp, Im tellin ya, arp, rar, rarp, arp never again.

I shit de demon out dat time. I tried te spit it out like de buffalo told me but it came out de wrong end. I wuz hosed down n changed inte jammies. All wuz well again in de blocks.

De Glooptings wer hangin around in de middle uv de block one day. Havin a chit chat. Dat wuz de day dat de old woman died. Mrs Tracy. She went mad dey said. She banged on de door. Didden know wot she wanted. Ma looked after her. Dats wot mas do, dey look after tings. Hole in de trousers, no problemo, no more holeo, cuz ma sewed it all up o. Ma sewed up everyting dat needed te be sewed.

Old Mrs Tracy. Mad as a hatter. Mad as a puppy. Mad as a full moon. Mad as monsters under de bed. I saw de gloop on her back, whisperin, suckin on her head. I wuz scared uv dem Gloopers, n mad old women, knockin on doors in de block. But de buffalo wuzzen scared. Da wuzzen scared, hes a man wit a moustache. A man wit a shirt n jeans. A man wit

13

smokes n rollies, a man wit a blue housecoat. A man wit a job, a man wit no job, a man wit fists, a man who drinks beers n sings, a man wit a legalise pot t-shirt, a man who smashed up de gaff wen drunk, a man who went te jail, a man who wrote letters, a man who wuz hooked on a drug, a man who loved, a man who lived, a man whos in de blocks: Sittin on de armchair, hoggin all de heat, long legs stretched around de fire place. Heat hogger. Splif smoker. Garda dodger. Out de window n gone. De great escape. De shadowman flees in de night. Go on Da, go run, run, run fast inte de night, run out uv de blocks, run fast from de Gloopers n dat old, dark, creepy banshee n dem old blocks.

Im standin in de block wit Mark n sum other boys, in de sunshine. De seagulls er flyin n one comes n perches on de bollard n says
Its as good a day as any day for it.
For wot? I says.

For de meetin, de meetin uv de boy n de bee.

So, de bee is lookin te meet again,

I mused a minute.

Voices from de Blocks

Number: 1

Name: Gloopting.
Place: De shadows.
Year: 1983.

I am the scream in your nightmares. Muck! Filth! Dirt! Childhood abuse!

I am the chill in the room. Degeneration! Death! Bullies! Rape! Violence!

I put the urge in you to grab that bottle. Drugs! Bullshit! Disease! Horror!

I am your darkest thoughts. Fear of failure, fear of life, fear of death!

I am a deranged whisper. Lonely and decrepit! Vomit and depression!

We are the hidden ones. Shit! Poverty! Smoke! Nightmares! Shyness!

We who live in the cracks. Psycho TV! Society rules! Rats! Blood!

WE ARE FALLEN AND YOU ARE OUR PREY. Walls full of heads!

Drink it up. Smoke it up. Spiders and cesspools! Wolves devouring pigs!

Its safer that way. Piss in pants! Shit on foot! Curses! Hexes! Howling torture!

We are here for you and we have all the delights you need.

Monsters under the bed! Youths in flames! Weep tears of blood!

Wailing and moaning! The little ones will suffer the most.

Those who will love, those who can see, they are dangerous to us.

They must be watched with ardour. I am the priests cock!

I am the politicians tongue! I am the bullys taunts! I am the masters thump!

I am what I am. I have no choice. Fear of the void.

I am the lesson of the strap and cane. Hanging boys.

I am the teacher with a fist and boot. Bee stings and sickness.

I am the crying and the wailing of violence. Death masks and coffins.

I am the murderer under the stairs. Madhouse world in shackles.

I am pain and horror collected as a thing. Leap out window.

I am clinging to form. I am junk. Childhood martyrs of alcohol.

I want your spirit for a joyride. Condition by TV and family.

I am recruiting for the sickness. Snarls of misery.

I am the sorrow. I am the fear of the dark. Nightmares and filth.

I am at your side, feel my cold and hate in the blocks. Filth filth filth.

Death piss shit worms gunk vomit and gloop gunk death worms and gloop.

De bed starts te spin, wovh, woovh, woo, woo, woo wooooooooovvhhhhhhhhhhhhhhhhhhhh, n wer off, up, up n away. Ders Mark in iz bed asleep, I see um tru de window. I turn me head dis way, den dat way, anyway I want te go, yeeehhaaaaa.

Up over de blocks, Da looks out de window n says, Wots goin on here, wer ya goin on yer bed in de middle uv de night?

Im off out for a bit Da, dont worry, Im goin te de purple place, its safe, see ya in awhile yeah? Out de block n up tru de sky.

Wild imagination dat kids got, wild, wild, wild.

Den Da falls back inte de chair, aniz head slumps forward, iz chin on iz chest, inte de poppy land, wer de poor boys go te dream uv de noblocks.

Up past de moon I go, spinnin inte de gold web, push tru, inte de place wer de horses have wings n de beardmen walk on de water, n de blue Gods wit four arms dance, n all dat jazz n lights.

De purple place: Mountains made uv purple stone, pink water. Four moons, one blue, one green, one orange, one gold. No bee. No banshee.

De tree is massive n red n de leaves er golden n sliver. It glows n has a face like a woman. It talks like poems:

I am the tree, who comes to me,
Seeking solitude in the night,

17

Seeking the knowledge of the ancient tree,
Who is it that stands before me,
Who is it that took the sacred flight,
From out the blocks to learn to
Sing and set the world a light?

Its Kenny,
Kenny Thomson, from ODevaney Gardens, Dublin
7, Leinster, Ireland.
 I flew up here on me bed, I seek de sollll, solitude,
dats
 bein on yer own is it?

Yes, Kenny Thomson, solace in solitude you found,
In the flight of your bed to this hollowed ground.

Cool, wots yer name?

I am the tree.

De tree, okeey, dokeey.
 Wer is dis purple place? Dis is out side uv de blocks
isin it?

This is the land of promise, poetry, solace, song,
The noblock, the place of ideas, the land of
knowledge,
The place of the Indians, buffalos, Buddhas, angels
The place of no wrong, the place of dreams.

Cool. Dat sounds deadly. How come I can go here
n nobody else can?

18

You have the right sight, the vision is strong in you,
There are others too who can come here, who see
like you.

Vision, dats a nice word, I like dat word, vi si on.
I think I better go back now, its gettin late, n I need
sum sleepy sleep, see ya later miss tree.

Goodbye, goodnight little Kenny, and
Remember do not let de bed bugs bite.

I woovh off on me bed back te de blocks, n land
softly
in me bedroom n de room is full uv flowers, red
roses, n gold n pink ones.

Ah poor mad Mrs Tracy died n all de block started
te cry. She looked great in de coffin, better din she
had in years, dats wot de women said.

She wuzzen in de coffin tho. She wuz walkin
around de block, smilin, n she gave dat gloopting a
shove n she walked off down te de church n blessed
her self n flew wit de white birds in de sun n dat wuz
dat.

De white birds er seagulls, n other ones dat look
like de bird dat came back te Noah.
Ya know yerman outta de Bible, who built de big
boat, wots it called again, eh de ark, I read dat in de

Bible in Mas room, it has drawins in it uv Angels, Saints n Camels.

Mark n me n sum bigger boys er playin wit action men in de backer. Ders a war goin on. Its been goin on all day, fellas blown up n shot dead n injured. De war goes on all de way te dinner time, dat long.

On de way up te me gaff a girl grabbed me n tried te kiss me, I shoved her away n legged it in te de flat. Girls er weirdoes, like Edel, shes weird.

Music plays in de flat, Bob Marley hes me favourite, he looks like God outta de Bible. He says Rasta a lot. Hes a buffalo soldier, so am I.
I sing all de words n me Ma, Da, Edel n cousins er impressed, but dey laugh at me too n say Im a little mad yoke.

A little girl died in de block de other day. In an accident Ma said. De whole block wuz cryin n den it went real quiet, even de dogs stopped barkin.
I saw de little girl two days later in a dream, her names Louise, n den a gloopting n her wer in de backer n she looked at me, den dey disappeared in te de wall.

Sumtimes Im Bruce Lee, I watch every film dat hes in. I look at him n he looks out de telly n says Kenny, ya must train, ya must be like water.

I put on me Kung Fu suit n train n bang Im ripped, Im abs n I can beat anyone in a fight.

Me giant grey teddy bear stands up n looks at me n says

So Kenny ya think ya can beat me eh, ya think yer good enough?

Wen he says it, de words dont match iz mouth. De camera goes right up te me face n I say

Ya wanna fight eh? Lets go so.

He steams in n punches me in de face. I wipe de blood n shout

Hiiiiiyeeeeaaaaaggghhhhhh,

n kickum five times, bang, whap, crash, whack, crack. Den I jump onum n stand onum like Bruce does te yerman wit de scar in *Enter De Dragon*.

Ma says

Go easy will ya, de poor teddy hes in bits, I only sewed up dat hole in him yesterday. Come on get yer dinner, its yer favourite, coddle.

I change back inte meself n sit down for de aul bit a coddle, loads uv sausages in it, n a slice uv Brennans Bread.

Me cousins dat visit de most er Gina n Danielle de sisters. Dey live up in another part uv de blocks called de small balconies. I live in de long ones.

Gina is small n pretty. Danielle is bigger but younger n responsible, Edel n Gina sumtimes call her a rat. I dont think shes a rat tho, she hasnt even got a tail.

Me, Edel n Gina er dancin te Madonna n Michael Jackson songs in de bedroom. Danielles de DJ, so she duzzen dance.

Dey make me learn de moves n we turn n twist n sing wit hairbrushes for mics.

Sumtimes we play make up games, we pretend te be adults who go te de pub n bring back food from de chipper. We pretend te smoke n drink n fight. Edels always de Da. We play doctors n nurses wit teddies n dolls, we play hide n seek, I hide in de closet, I climb right up te de top, Im der for ages, n ages, dey cant find me n wen I come back out, dey laugh n say yer deadly at hidin Kenny, we cudden find ya, ha-ha. I dont think its funny. I think der dopes.

Ma n Edel er out shoppin. Da n me er in de flat. Woo, wooo, woooeeee. Is it de banshee, in de middle uv de day? No, its de army barracks beside de flats, Da says

Its war son, its war, der gonna come n drop de bomb soon, quick we have te hide, go hide in yer room quick, Im goin in here, n he went inside de kitchen cupboard n locked de door. I want te get in der witum, but I cant de door wont open. Hes in der

22

for ages, Im gonna die, I start te cry n just den de bee flies in te room n says *Stop cryin child hes lyin hes up te no good in der wit de brown powder, de poppy dream powder, ya know de nudge n wink stuff?*

Wot er ya on about, brown powder, wink, nudge, fuck off, me Da hasnt got any powder, hes not up te no good, hes good, ya prick ya.

Child I tell no lie, Kenny Thomson keep yer eyes open, child.

Da came out grinin, wipin spit from iz chin n said it wuz all a joke. I didden think it wuz funny.

Not funny atall, atall. Neither did Ma wen I told her.

De banshee is walkin around de hall, shes tall, long black hair full uv knots n bugs, long dirty yellow nails, a broken comb in her hair, cryin. I run inte me bedroom n jump inte bed.

She comes tru de wall like vapour n stands over de bed, looks at me n says,

We cant take ya boy so dont worry.

Den floats slowly up tru de ceilin inte another flat. Shelly barks de place down. Shelleys another brown n white Collie, wit a bit uv Alsatian mixed in dat makes her a good scraper n biter.

Das gone on a holiday te a place wit big gates made uv steel, in a scary lookin block. Ma gets me up for school n puts de cereal n de milk in de bowl n makes de tea. Ma smokes a lot.

Ma likes de telly. Ma makes dinner. Ma looks after people. Ma pays de bill. Ma gives me hugs. Ma makes me brush me teeth before goin te bed. Good night Ma, x.

Voices from de Blocks

Name: Little Louise.
Year: 1985.
Place: ODevaney Gardens.

Me Mammys cryin again.

She always cries at dis time on a Thursday.

She comes in here te me room n looks around n sits on de bed n picks up Teddy n den starts cryin until I go over n sit beside her n say dont cry Ma, Im here, Im here beside ya.

Den she stops cryin n goes back out te make Das dinner or wash de floor. Me room is always tidy n looks de same since I fell out de window, but de window stays shut now all de time.

Fallin out de window hurt a lot. It wuz like bein a bird for a bit in de air den smack it hurt me a lot n den all de blood went woosh n splooshed outta me everywer.

But den I got up n just looked at meself n all de people runnin out de flats n Ma wuz on de ground beside me screamin n miss Peterson grabbed her n pulled her away n everyone in de whole block wuz cryin n screamin n runnin around like mad tings. I wuz callin Ma n pullin at people but dey cudden see me or

25

hear me. A few felt me. Den de shady black tings came for me n said,

Come here with us we can help you child n one a dem keeps me safe now, dats wot he says anyway, but dem shades er very bold sumtimes, whisperin in peoples ears n gettin dem te drink beer n smoke n all dat stuff.

Dey sumtimes get me te do tings I dont like te do, get other kids in te trouble n hide tings on people. But wen I get inte me own gaff dey never come in, de leave me in der wit ma or Da for a bit, but den dey call me wit der song n I cant help it,

I have te move out te de song n go te de block n play wit de kids or play tricks on dem.

One little boy looked at me for ages n waved at me. I think iz names Kenny.

De last while dey made me be friends wit a little girl who calls me Lorna, but dats not even me name, me names Louise but she cant hear dat wen I tell her, de shade said dats te confuse her so de adults wont hear me name. Her Ma says Im an imaginary friend, but Im not imaginary Im real, Im real but Im dead, Im dead but Im alive, Im alive but not like de people in de block er alive n Im dead but not like de shades er dead, der like nasty dead.

I keep lookin for God or Mary or Jesus but I cant find dem yet. De shades said dat I shud forget about all dem, wot did dey ever do for ya? Wer here for ya.

I seen dat boy Kenny again de other day lookin at me n den I seen him tellin wunna de shades te fuck off, I laughed me head off at dat, hes brave n a bit mad.

I think he might know how te get out uv de blocks, cuz I seen him one time flyin on iz bed in de sky, hes magic or sumting like dat.

But de shades keep me away from him n say hes bad n now de one who stays wit me is around me all de time nearly, but its not Kenny whos bad its dem shades whos bad.

***

I run real fast in de night time inte de block n hes chasin me n hes singin de song but I just put me fingers in me ears an run n I take off, I dont know how but Im runnin in de air real fast, I go right in tru de wall inte Kennys bedroom n de shades gettin very angry, he grows bigger n hes spittin out black phlegm n tar n smoke but I jump on te Kenny in iz bed n stick te him on iz back n he wakes up n coughs n de shades der lookin at him n ders light all over de room it blasts de shade out uv it n it goes flyin tru de block n lands over in de backer n is cryin like a little baby, n Kenny is coughin n coughin n den a real loud cough aniz face is red n I go tru him n out iz chest aniz mouth n fly up like a rocket on Halloween night, out tru de light out de blocks up te a garden wit pink flowers n roses n lilys n a woman in a white dress grabs me n she says

Its alright now.

Im alright now cuz ders no block here n no shades, only flowers n animals n de woman n music I hear de music now, lovely music n water, green water.

In de new school Im wunna de smarter ones. We learn te write n read n sing holy songs n make our communion, eat Jesus n drink iz blood, own up te de priest dat we said fuck n shit. Say prayers n get money off aunts, uncles, n grandparents. I have two grandas, me big granda n me little granda, de big one is me Das da, de little one me Mas. Mas ma died from cancer years before I wuz born.

So Ive one granny, she stays in de kitchen a lot wen we go der on Sundays for dinner, even after de dinner. She brings Granda de brown sauce. De men n boys watch football on de telly. De women smoke n talk about dresses n hair. Den de men n women go de pub except me granny, she baby-sits. Grannys gaff is in de blocks too, in ODevaney, around de next block from ours.

It smells like cabbage n potatoes. Granda always sings dis song dat goes, yum, yum, pigs bum cabbage n potatoes, while rubbin iz fat belly n me n all me cousins laugh atum.

Me little granddad lives in a house wit wunna me mas brothers. He has bent up hands, n looks very old, about a hundred. He gives ya money te go de shop te get iz smokes wit de picture uv de sailor on dem n sweets for yerself, hes a kind old man. I love me Grandas n Granny.

I saw a Gloopting in little Grandas house one day, crawlin on de floor n den it went inte iz room. Iz house is near de park just around de corner from

29

ODevaney. De bus stops der te take ya te town, te go see de Ghostbusters in de cinema. Popcorn n sweets.

In de blocks we play kick de can n red rover n chasin. Mark n me play football in de backer, its every stadium in de English league, its Wembley, its Anfield, its Old Trafford, its Highbury, its Goodison Park.

Its de F.A. cup final. Marks in goal, hes Bruce Grobbelaar, he kicks de ball out, high, down de pitch, it comes te Ronnie Whelan, he takes it down, Im Ronnie Whelan, he passes it out left te John Barnes, I run down de wing, I beat two players, I whip in de cross, de ball hangs in de air, its headed down by de defender, comes out te Ian Rush, I hit it first time, whack, Mark dives, de ball goes under him, hits de net, Rush, scores, Rush scores, wot a goal, its one nil te Liverpool, de crowd goes wild, I run around de pitch, slide on me knees, me team mates on top uv me. In de Kop is Marks Uncle Billy, lookin out iz window, hes smilin at us and cheerin for de goal. Sumtimes other boys come n ruin de game. Sumtimes we play world cup wit Marks cousin John n our older mate Wayne Handy n sum other block boys.

Da came back from iz holidays. He didden stay too long tho.
One day, ma said,
Yer Das goin te live sumwer else.
Why?
He just is, cuz hes on drugs, dats why.

No, da, no, dont go, its not fair, I hate ya Ma, I hate ya.

But I didden hate her for long. She cooks me dinner. She pours de milk on me cereal. She sews up holes. She stitches up Teddy after a kung fu fight or wrestlin match.

Da, wit iz bags, iz skins, iz rollies, iz moustache, iz holy blue housecoat, iz works, iz Bob Marley records, iz *legalise pot* t-shirt, iz banshee, iz overcoat, iz heat hoggin long legs, iz jokes, iz oxtail soup wit de bit uv milk in it, de way only he cud make it. Iz anger n addictions. Iz heart broken. Gone out de door.

Bye Da.

Im in Mas bedroom. She has a big double bed. Its just de right size for a wrestlin ring. Here comes Teddy de tank.

He walks in te de ring, six foot ten n weighin two hundred lbs n tonight he/ll be squarin off against de titan uv terror, de beef uv de street, de one de only King Kenny de crusher. Im seven foot tall now n two hundred pounds. Teddy comes in wit de kick te de groin. I go down, he stomps me, he elbow drops me. He tries te pin me. No way, I push him off just before de three count. De curtains in de room er drawn, n de windows open. Down in de backer a crowd uv kids er der; Danielle is wit dem, dey look up n see me n Teddy in de ring. Dey start te chant, Kenny, Kenny,

31

Kenny, Kenny. Go on Kenny killum. Deyre all smilin n laughin.

Im up now. I grab hold uv teddy. Headlock, punch, punch, DDT, stomp, stomp, pick him up off de ropes, dropkick, body slam, n now de big finish, off de top ropes, de crowd below is awestruck, dey hold deyre breath in anticipation uv de death-dealin move, I jump, I soar tru de air all seven feet n two hundred n eighty pounds uv me n come crashin down on poor teddy. One, two, three, hes out. De crowd er jubilant, cheerin, chantin me name. I am de Champion still n always will be.

I look down in te de backer n see de kids pointin up, smilin, confused now.

I shut de curtains n go te sleep.

Da lives in grannys gaff now. I see him on Sundays. But sumtimes hes not der, den he goes missin, no one knows wer. He lives in iz sister Pams flat now, she lives across de block from Grannys.

Ma has a job, den has nun, den has one, den has nun. Der used te be an Easter Bunny n Santa Clause, den der wuzzen. But ders still Easter n Christmas, still chocolate eggs n presents n new clothes. Sumtimes de electricty gets cut off, we have a spare fuse te put in de box outside te make it come back on, hah up yours ESB.

Im walkin home from school. I sense sumting behind me, I look, its de bee.

How are ya Kenny Thomson? I see dat yer Father has exited de buildin, for iz misbehavin, wit de powder, hey?

Im ok. Shut up, dont talk about me Da like dat.

Okay, child calm down, I speak no ill uv him, just de truth. I have a proposal

for ya, a job for ya te do for me.

A job, wot job? Hold on now, last time ya tricked me n I got stung, fuck off.

Help me n I/ll help ya.

Alright, wot is it, wots de job, wot do I get for it?

I need ya te take me te de tree, in de purple place, dat ya go te on yer bed, I need te speak te her, shes my friend, child ya have de necessary vision n power te get me der, if ya do dis for me I/ll help yer father wit iz powder problem, wot say ya Kenny Thomson?

Ehhhmmmm, yeah, ok, ok, But ya have te help me Da first den I/ll help ya, deal?

Deal it is so, deal it is indeed my child.

Right so, buzz uv now n sort me Da out.

In me bed at night. A gloopting, sits beside de bed, lookin at me, its got a nasty feelin off it. It just looks. Its black, human like shape. De bottom half uv it is smokey. Like a solid cloud. De top half is thicker, molasses like. It talks in English. It smells. Its tall. It has no feet. It glides. It whispers in ears. It drinks pain. It eats sufferin. It likes heroin n beer n violence. It bathes in tears. It wails. It moves tru walls. It clings te de body. It welcomes de sirens. Its a poor old

33

wretched ting dat knows not wot it does. Poor Gloopy bastard.

Da walkin around wit a junkie, me da a junkie, a robber. Dey score, n go te a flat, typical den type place. Cook, works, bang up. Heads fall back like every junkie does in every Hollywood bangin-up scene. Goofin in de place uv noddin n noblockin. Tries te light a smoke wit de wrong end uv de lighter, tries te put it in iz mouth but hits de nose. De junkys like a baby, sleeps, shits, cries, feeds. Wer did ya go Da, in dat poppy dream? Did ya calm de anger? Did ya float out uv de blocks? Did ya meet yer dead brother Clive? Did ya sing wit de Rastas n fly wit de doves? Wer did ya go Da?

Da got sick, twice. Once he had a ting dat makes ya go yellow for a few weeks, n de next time he looked like sumone who had a fight wit Bruce Lee n lost.

We went te de hospital te see him twice. Drips, nurses, clean beds. Smokin, 7up n fruit.

De bee came n told me dat it wuz him who turned me Da yellow. He said he got inte de barrel uv de works n swam inte de vain n stung de silly fucker good. Gave him de aul yellow fever te teach him te leave dat powder alone once n for all. But da didden leave it alone. So de bee tricked him. De bee came in de night n sang a song in de ear uv a girl n she went te look for Da, n got him te get de powder for her, cuz she wuz too young te get it, but she didden look too young n she had a nice face an all.

But her brothers didden like her doin de powder n dey wer big n mean, n dey had te teach Da a lesson.

No lads, I swear I didden know she wuz only sixteen, fuck sake she duzzen look it, n she told me she wuz twenty one, for fuck sake, lads, I didden make her do it, shes strung out, she wuz lookin te score n so wuz I, dats it, says Da.

Sorry Gary, but we put de word out, anyone sellin te her or buyin for her, is gettin it n dats it, anyone Gary, so dats it mate.

Da jumped on, dragged te de ground, he puts up a fight best as he can, too many uv dem n der big bastards, de batterum wit punches n kicks, den a wooden bat belts de side uv iz head n hes out. He wakes up dazed, bruised n bloody.

De bee said dat shud make him give up dat powder for good now. But it didden. Da still liked iz powder. He went missin again after he got out uv de hospital, for longer dis time, nobody knew wer he wuz.

Gary Thomson, strung out, goin from junky pads n shootin gallerys te mates gaffs n dealers dens. Shop liftin n stealin from cars, n cookin up n shootin up. Goofin n droolin on iz chin. Wanderin around Dark Dublin lookin for a fix, lookin te score. Gary Thomson me Da.

De bee flew in iz ear n went right in te iz head n made him dream about iz brother Clive n about iz Ma

35

cryin, n me n Edel wen wer older n we take tablets n get drunk. Wen he finally came back he went te a new block, a block down de country, wer people who used te like de powder but dont any more, go n live der until dey hate de powder n dey love smokin n drinkin tea only. We visit Da der, we get on a big bus wit other familys goin te visit other blokes who er havin trouble wit de aul Brown powder. One time we wer playin ping pong n Edel fell n broke de table in half.

Da n me laughed our heads right off, dey rolled on down n out de block n like Helium balloons floated off up te de sky wit de gulls n, wings grew out wer our ears shud be, n our noses became beaks n den we wer white birds n we flew high up in de sky. Da saw a Garda n shit on iz head, den I shit onum too, we laughed our heads off. We saw ma n Edel back down on de ground, Edel wuz cryin n Ma wuz stompin n hollerin, get back down here, de two uv yiz. So we swooped down n landed. Our heads wer heads again n rolled on back up te our necks, n Da picked up Edel in iz arms n she stopped cryin n Ma quit her hollerin n stompin n drank her tea n smoked her smoke. De table got put back tegether. We headed home back te de blocks n Da wuz at de window, wavin, n wavin, n tears wer in iz blue eyes.

Da left dat block after a few months n moved inte a flat on de North Circular Road just around de corner from ODevaney. He gave up de powder now for good, just like de bee promised.

Da n me er watchin de world cup final n Maradona is playin Germany.

Diego Armando Maradona wins de world cup n Da n me cheer n celebrate him. I put a picture uv Maradona on de wall beside Bruce Lee, n Jesus on de cross, its a small black cross wit a silver Jesus on it. I draw pictures uv Batman n Superman n armies fightin wars n robots from de future. I read comics, Spiderman n Judge Dread. I watch Star Wars n Rocky n Rambo n Predator.

I dont like bikes n everyone thinks its funny. I tried te learn but I fell off, I dont like it, I dont like sittin on de fuckin bike even, Ma cant understand, she tried her best te get me on it, te teach me te cycle.

I walked away n left her der wit de bike n dats dat. I/ll walk or run or fly but Im not gettin on a stupid bike.

Da n me go up te de park n play football, Da keeps lettin me score by divin de wrong way. I tellum I dont like dat, I want te score by meself, not him lettin it in, I want te be good at football really, not pretend good.

De bee comes te me at night, he flies in tru de opened window n says

Well child, I did as wuz promised. So now ya have te keep te de deal we made n bring me te de Purple place.

Ok, lets go den, land on de bed, if yil fit ya big fat yoke.

De bee n me squashed on de bed tegether. Woovh, woovh, woo, woo, woo, woovvvvvvvvhhhhhhhh, wer off, up, fast, far, high, on n on, up n up, out de blocks, over de moon tru de tunnel n inte de purple place.

We land on de purple dust ground. De bee, flies off de bed.

I climb down n stand der, lookin at de mountains n moons.

De tree appears before us, tall n swayin in de breeze.

Why has this bee come with you to hear the tree?
He said hes yer pal.
The tree knows not any dog, cat, bird or bee,
A trick, a trick, has been played on thee,
Little Kenny.
A trick, wha..?
Do not worry, child I had te trick ya again, but Im free now, free uv de blocks, for good, no more buzzin around, hidin in de shadows, appearin te kids, teachin lessons te man, woman and child, stingin folks, free n its all thanks te ya, Kenny Thomson, me good friend.
Wha de fuck er ya on about? Free, wots goin on?

38

Den de bee lands on de dust wit a thump, shakes n hollers, iz body shrinks aniz wings turn inte arms aniz legs become a mans legs aniz fuzzy body turns from yellow n black te pink n now he is a man.

De tree says
A man he is and not a bee, a man sent into the blocks to teach and learn and feel the pleasure uv the life of an insect,
For he was once a rotten man, a stingy man, and so the gods did mock,
And turned him into a bee, to pay for his shame and debt.

Fuckin hell, dis is gettin weirder by de day, men turnin inte bees n bees turnin inte men, n trees talkin in poems.

Do not worry me friend, I shall trouble ya no more in dis life. Im free n off I go te de river te bade n on te de next life, so long, n remember de lessons I thought ya child.
N he wuz gone n I never seen him again just like he said.

Back on de bed n back te de blocks, cuz I wuz tired now, after all dat messin around.

Seconds, minutes, seconds, minutes, seconds, minutes, days, nights, days, nights, days, nights, months, months, months, months, years, years,

39

years, breakfasts, dinners, suppers, games, school, movies, friendships, Easters, Christmases, Halloweens, toys, eggs, fights, hide n seek, kick de can, red rover, banshees, school days, Shelley de old dog barkin at de post man, barkin at de coal man, Ma sewin de holes, Edel growin up n out, long hair, Da lost de moustache, aniz hair went all grey, yea hey, Im an Indian, Im a buffalo, Im Bruce Lee, Im de king uv everytin, Eh wots up doc, da, ah, da, ah, daa, dats all folks, ek, ek, ek wers me Olive. Im a buffalo soldier, Im a dread lock Rasta, Im Ian Rush, Im seven foot tall n two hundred pounds n still de champion uv de world.

De banshee wails, ahhhhwooooouuuuugghhhhhhhh, de dark shade on de window sill at night, de Glooptings in de blocks, under de beds uv kids, de sing songs uv drunk grownups in de sittin room, Diego on de wall, Jesus on de black cross, de backers grass growin n gettin cut, de bed flyin te de purple place, de tree speakin poems, Coddle n stew in pots n bowls, Madonna, Michael Jackson, Edel n Gina n me dancin, Mark winters tellin iz ma te fuck off, Keith Connors ma shoutin over de block, Get in here now or I/ll smack ya so hard yer face will be on de other side uv yer head, de Garda sirens, old woman dyin, lookin great in coffins, batter burgers, Sky channel, DJ Kat show, new neighbours, old neighbours, gloop, gloopy gloop, puff, puff, fire lighters n briquettes, coal n fiiiirrreeelogs, heads n volleys, world cup, Kung Fu movies, tea-cakes, birthdays.

One day, Teddy wuz wearin a bra n knickers, n wuz a woman wit tits n a fanny, n she said
Hey baby, ya wanna come play wit me?
An I said, Well miss teddy-bear ya look ravishin tonight, I wud love te play wit ya.
N we did play a new game.

Ma got a job in Bradleys restaurant on Parkgate Street beside de pub. We got free sausages n chips. Ma has a boyfriend, iz names Gem, he drives a big lorry, hes Scottish n tuff, has big arms. He let me sit in de lorry n steer de wheel.
Edel has a boyfriend, den she hasnt den she has one, den she hasnt, den she has another one, most uv dem er pricks, dat tease me n slag me, so I throw water on dem, or tell Ma, or get a stick n whack dem wit it, de pricks. Older boys ask me all de time, Is Edel Thomson yer sister? Shes a fuckin ride she is.
Den she gets wit one who she loves n dey see each other every night n kiss on de balcony, ugghh. She comes in drunk n pukes on de floor, smells like rotten apples, Ma slaps her n puts her te bed. Edel n Gina left school n work in de sewin factory on Gabriel Street, beside me school, de same one Ma used te work in.

Im not gonna work in de fuckin sewin factory no way, Im gonna play for Liverpool n Ireland, or be in movies or sumting like dat, ya know?

Ma n Edel go out tegether now te get drunk. I stay in Das flat n watch telly or play wit toys dat I bring wit me. Da still smokes de rollies n listens te John Lennon n Bob Marley songs, n drinks lots uv tea. He asks me if I like Mas boyfriend Gem, n I tellum,
Yeah hes cool n he let me drive iz truck.
Well Im yer da, remember dat, pal, ok?
Ok Da, yer me Da, I know.
Da lights iz rollie up n puffs on it, lookin at a spot on de wall wer nutting is n I see de banshees ugly shape at de window, n hear her laugh in de darkness. De moon shines real bright n de face on it is sad like Das.

Its winter time in de blocks, cold n grey, fires blaze in de fields wer winos sing n piss, n fart n drink. Gargoyles perch on de roofs uv de blocks, watchin, silent, fanged n winged. De doves dont come out for too long now. De Gloopers roam, sniggerin, whisperin evils in de halls n rooms, de statue uv de virgin weeps n prays for us all.

Ma n Edel er out. Gem n me er in de flat, hes drinkin a can uv beer n Im playin wit sum Star Wars figures. A knock comes te de door. Bang! Bang! Bang! Bang!
De guards always knock de same way says Gem.

42

I go te answer it. Two tall Garda, dey ask,
Is your mother home?
I say No.
Is anyone else home with ye?
No.

Dey say dat its about me Da, hes not in trouble er anyting, but dey need te chat te sumone, an adult. I tell dem dat me granny n granda Thomson live in a flat around de next block. We drive around in de Garda car. Im in de back uv de blue car, in me pyjamas, sum older boys er lookin in te see whos after gettin nicked.

One Garda goes up de stairs te me Grannys flat n de other fella stays wit me in de car. Dey drive me back around te me gaff n say goodnight. I wonder wot Das up te?

Gem tells me I better go te bed, dat me Ma/ll be back soon.

I go te bed n I dream about de banshee, shes combin de knots out uv her hair n sittin on de window uv Das flat, her green dress is blowin in de wind and de rain is lashin down.

Shes just combin her hair n wailin, cryin, she turns her head in tewards de window, n throws her comb at Da, he picks it up n starts te combs iz hair n turns te me n says,

Go on now Son, go back te sleep, I/ll see ya again soon.

In de mornin ma wakes me real early, n she says Kenny, yer das in de hospital, he, hes goin te die.

No hes not I say.

He is Kenny, Im sorry, hes still alive now, but hes gonna die soon, we have te go up te see him, come on, cmere, I love ya, Im sorry.

Ma hugs me, I cry, its cold in de blocks, its winter.

De hospital: Da, hooked up te machines dat bleep. White bed, white sheets, white walls, all white, an awful white. Da, eyes closed. Da, grey hair, Da, sleepin, Da, still.

Adults all around, relatives, nurses, doctors. No 7up dis time. No yellow bee fever.

De banshee is dressed as Death now, smokin a cigar. Fuckin Glooptings on de ceilins, droolin, inhalin all de rot n tears, n one grows a black rose from its head, plucks it n hands it te me, it withers instantly, de black rose. Den we all say goodbye te Da n he cries, just one tear comes out uv iz unmovin body.

Its all dark n dull n forgetful for a while after dat.

Black cars n black suits, gettin sick in de car from de gloopting dat tried te cling te me, like dey do te others, but I puked him up n out de window uv de car, dirty black sick. Da, cold wen I kissed him. Dats not Da I said. Dats a body. De church, de cryin, de wailin, de prayers, Jesus on a big fuckin cross made uv wood. Ireland qualified for de World Cup, John Aldridge scored two goals against Malta, n me Das in

44

de dirt. He wudda loved te see Ireland in de world cup, but he cant hes in de dirt.

Fuck dat. Fuck dat banshee. Fuck de Gloopers. Fuck de blocks. Fuck yiz all.

Two weeks later Im walkin from de football pitch in ODevaney. Goin down towards Thor Place n across de road I see a man. Hes Das height, hes wearin Das brown leather jacket, Hes got Das grey hair. Its Da, its Da. I follow him around de corner. Da wer ya goin Da, its me, Da yer not dead.

Da.

He stops, turns iz head.

Wot son, wot is it?

Wer ya goin, yer alive, I knew it, Ireland qualified for de World Cup.

I know son, I know, but I am dead, Im just havin one last look at de blocks, n I came te say goodbye te ya, I have te go sumwer else now, ya cant come or visit, I/ll see ya sumtimes in dreams or visions, ok? Cmere n gimme a hug, gimme a kiss, Im not cold anymore, Im not in de dirt anymore, I love ya son.

He hugged me n I said goodbye. Den he put iz arms up wide n white feathers grew out uv dem, iz hands even turned inte feathers n he arched iz back n put iz legs together aniz body wuz full uv white feathers n he changed iz whole shape aniz face became a beaky bird face n he wuz a giant white bird, a dove.

I finally found out de name uv de other white bird, its a dove, me Da became a dove wen he died, n he

45

flapped iz huge wings n took off n flew up high, n flew out uv de blocks forever, up towards de sun.

Another Man said te me

Ar ya alright der son? He wuz wearin a brown leather jacket n had grey hair. I didden answer him I ran home te de flat, n dat wuz de end uv all dat wit Da n I/ll be twelve soon n leavin primary school te go te secondary school, so I think I/ll get rid uv me toys now.

De block is cold. Its winter. De walls have names sprayed on dem.

De shell uv a burned out car is still smokin on de pitch.

De kids in de block er singin:

A ring a ring a rosie,
A pocket full uv posies,
A ring a ring a rosie,
A pocket full uv poems eh?
A pen a pen for Kenny, iz pockets full uv poems yeah!

BLOCK B
ADOLESCENT BLUES

Dont cry, dont raise your eye,
        its only teenage wasteland,
teenage wasteland, oh yeah
        its only teenage wasteland.

—The Who

After all dat de banshee wuz never seen again She went wit Da.

Teddy finally had enough, had one too many Kung-fu fights n wrestlin matches, no more dressin in drag, had one too many holes, n Ma stopped sewin him up, poor bastard wuz punch drunk n fucked, he went in de back uv a rubbish truck.

I stopped flyin in me bed n de purple place n de tree dat spoke poems faded inte memory. I wuzzen Bruce Lee or Ian Rush anymore. Mad Mark aniz family moved out uv ODevaney, n went te live in Finglas.

De Gloopers faded from me sight, only a flicker here a feelin in de belly, a whisper on de pillow.

De Sea-gulls, Pigeons n Crows still flew but de doves disappeared. Me legs n arms grew n so did me dick n hair grew on me balls n every mornin I wuz hard n sumtimes wet n little kiddo Kenny who spoke te bees n flew on iz bed n whose Daddy died became Kenny de teenager.

Ma started te go out te de pub a lot more n got drunk n fought wit her friend Maggie from upstairs, dey drank n fought n sang n hugged n drank n fought n worked tegether in jobs.

Gem aniz lorry wer gone as quick as dey came, a few years later we heard he done em self in by suckin on de exhaust fumes uv iz motor. Edel anner fella Frankie wer in love n fought n drank n hugged n loved n fought n drank n made up n so on.

De blocks never changed. De blocks er de blocks.

Georgie

I met all me best friends in de summer time, n I met wunna de best uv all in de summer I turned sixteen. Me big Granda died dat Summer, me Da aniz Da died uv de same ting, a brain aneurism, so did iz brother Clive aniz Sister Adel. Me little Granda died not long after Da died, had a heart attack on de bog just like Elvis only he wuzzen de King uv rock n roll, he wuz de King uv fuck all so nobody but iz family cared.

He wuz sixty five, nower near a hundred.

So it is death-in-life n life n death n de search for meanin n friendship, yeah friendship dat meetin uv minds dat says

Hah, yeah dats wot I think too,

n dat wuz de summer I met Georgie.

Georgie Teeling, a strange lookin character, five foot two inch tall wit wild curly hair n squintin eyes. Clutchin a stick for reasons known only te himself, bobbin as he walks. Football brought about our meetin, block football, street football, games dat went on for two, three hours sumtimes wit no break or maybe a break wen sumone has te go in for dinner cept in de case uv David Newman who wud be called te go te de shop for iz parents at regular intervals tru out de game, first for smokes, den eggs, den potatoes, den firelighters instead uv writin a list n have him get it all in one trip. Weed all complain te um, te no avail. Georgies Da wud watch us from de balcony uv de top floor, drinkin iz cheap cider n yellin inaudible commentary. Das n drink, Das n drugs, Das n fists, Das n death, Das n sons in de blocks.

Georgie lived in de top blocks also know as de luxuries. Dese wer flats dat had individual balconies front n back. I lived in de long balconies wer ya shared a long communal balcony wit yer neighbours. Neighbours on top uv ya, each side uv ya, underneath ya. Weird single men wit beards n stinkin hallways, dirty curtains not washed in ten years, windows always gettin broken. Small grey concrete pram-sheds wit wooden doors dat held bikes n prams in dem, sum turned inte pigeon lofts n dog sheds n smoke dens n sex dungeons. Steel poles wit rope tied between dem, washin hangin from de line. Hopscotch squares painted on de ground. Tall streetlamps bent a bit te one side from been made inte swins by children. Small stone bollards, vicious dogs barkin n fightin. Young couples wit young kids. Families who had four flats in de same block. Sisters, brothers, aunts, uncles, cousins.

De next block, we spoke uv it as if it wer another part uv de city n not just a minute walk. But each block had its own feel te it n changed truout de years, cept for me old block dat remained de same, quieter din sum uv de other ones, more communal. Tho still it had its feuds, tragedies, fights, loonies n mad dogs. Other blocks had much worse reputations. Wunna dem wuz known as H-Block:

Its like bleedin Beirut up der.

50

Georgie lived in de same block as iz cousin Shaun n Me cousins Gina n Danielle. Gina n Danielle had two other younger sisters, Nelly n Sandy. Der Da wuz me Mas Brother Tony.

Georgie lived wit iz Da, iz sisters aniz younger brother Jimmy (Dey looked like each other, both short, dark hair, Jimmy wore a little ronnie sumtimes, wuz more confident n quick tempered).

Georgie had just left school dat summer n wuz fifteen years old n mad for gettin high or drunk. Most uv de men in de Teeling family wer uv dat same ilk, alcohol a river uv sufferin flowin tru de family bloodline. All small men, tho tuff, n brave in a bust up, never afraid te get stuck in if needs be.

De first uv de Teelings I knew wuz Shaun, a short, mousey brownish blonde-haired, blue-eyed, good-lookin guy. We wer in de same class in secondary school at St Pauls CBS on Brunswick Street, an all-boys school run by Christian brothers. Shaun wuz good at any sport he put iz hands or feet te. Had a charm n a roguish gleam te um dat worked on de girls as much as it did on de guys, so dat he wuz never short uv male friends or female girlfriends unlike de bashful Georgie n de sumtimes frigid, sumtimes fussy me.

Gargoyles perched on de edges uv de blocks watchin over us as we sat on top uv pramsheds at night talkin under de stars about our future lives.

Georgie says Psshht, I wont be livin te dat age.

A dark prophecy. I shuffled awkwardly.

51

So I says Ah shut up, yil meet a good woman n have kids de whole lot, I betcha.

Yeah right, Georgie said in a cloudy mood.

Wer did de clouds come from? De clouds came from rage at de Mammy who slipped out for bread n milk n never came back. Rage at de Da who morphed inte a monster under de poison uv drink. Rage at de poverty uv welfare n bein so small n so strangely black-lamb-woolly haired n far-sighted n acne-ed n horny for sex witout hope uv gettin it. Rage in de blocks uv iz mind. Rage at de shyness dat made him blush in de face wen questioned by strangers n sumtimes familiars n only Tipex, hash, vodka, butane gas, lithium n cider n blueys n yellows n heroin cud make dose clouds lift n music n our friendship did for awhile.

Ah Georgie.

Georgie fell in love fast n easy. Dis most likely stemmed from feelin a lack uv love from iz Ma. Made him become obsessed wit any girl dat showed him any real tenderness or affection. Der wuz Patricia Doolan, she lived across de block from me n wuz a friend uv me sister Edel. Wuzzen much older din Georgie n me but a lot more experienced. Slim, sad, peroxide in her hair, sand-colour skin, small breasts. Her Da wuz abusive anner Ma wuz an agoraphobic. Sheed all dese little weird scruffy sisters who wer years younger din her. Dey wer like little mice scurryin up n down de stairs afraid uv everyone. She had a Boyfriend who wuz a tuff pit-bull uv a guy, a kick-boxer n feared street fighter, Mike Tyson build n Mexican face. He wuz in me class at school for a bit, he wuz older but had been kept back. Hes dead now. Got murdered in sum gangster bullshit. But back den he wuz still very much alive n kickin n wud kick de shit out uv Me, Georgie n all de rest uv us. Patricia wuz back livin at her Ma n Das place while de corpo sorted out a flat for her, her boyfriend n Daughter. So it wuz summer n she wud come over n have cans wit Edel n me Ma n Georgie n me started te have a few cans wit dem. Over a few months friendship developed between Georgie n Patricia.

He fell madly in love wit her, doted over her n she knew it. She felt good bein loved n lusted, treated like a lady even if it wuz by an awkward dwarfish scruff. Heed get her cans out de fridge, walk her across de block, deyd be chattin away te each other. Edel n me wud tease um, not gettin our cans for us Georgie no? Even wen she got de new flat n moved in nearer te de city centre, he wud walk her home. Iz small, fat hands tryin te rub gently on her shoulder but only becomin a drunken grope. One night dey kissed. Patricia had a fight wit her fella n wuzzen seein him for a week or two dis wuz de rationalisation for it. De flattery, de attention, iz kindness n drink all mixed in te produce a kiss. Georgie got it in te iz head dat dis wuz it, love, boyfriend/girlfriend. But uv course it wuz just a one off ting, a mistake even? For Patricia.

Ya see ya dont just leave sumone like Patricias boyfriend. Dey wer back tegether two days after de kiss. Georgie cudden take dis, he went inte a bad depression n so it wuz wall punchin, goin off on iz own for hours, nobody knowin wer he wuz, slashin at himself wit blades, naggins uv vodka supped from de bottle n de empty bottle flung te de ground.

Georgie Teeling sits under a tree in de Phoenix park at night huddled n shiverin.

He began te be a pest te her, writin letters, followin her home, weepin. De boyfriend found out. He stopped me on de street one day

Kenny wunna yer gang, Georgie de little fella hes got a bit uv a crush on Patricia n its startin te get out uv hand...

Hold on now, its not my gang, Im not de boss uv anyone, wer just mates.

Wotever Kenny, listen, all Im sayin is, he needs te back off, now, hes a nice young-fella, n I dont want te have te hurtum ya know, so it wud be better if ya advised um, ya know wot I mean?

Yeah, yeah, I know wot ya mean, I/ll letum know dat, dont worry.

Good man Kenny, look after yerself now.

Will do, cheers, see ya.

So, dat wuz dat Georgie had te give up de game or we wer all in trouble.

He did n went inte wunna iz classic dark periods for weeks. Den one day he comes back in happy as fuck like he just took a bath in liquid lithium or sumting.

Ah Im over her.

Great den wer all safe from de pit-bull says I.

We laughed n rolled joints n threw darts at de board.

Georgie wud go up te de park on iz own sumtimes te brood or rejuvenate himself, escape de blocks. We used te go up der for a game uv heads n volleys, te de football pitches wer dey had full-size goals n grass on de pitch. Georgie wud come wit ball in hand. Good size five leather one borrowed from a cousin or neighbour. Georgie all flighty n bouncy, cap on, navy jumper n hand me down jeans. Jimmy n Liam follow um. I get ready: T-shirt on, hair done, jeans, football playin runners old ones so not te wreck new ones.

Make up a few joints for de walk up te de park te smoke hash n play football in de sunshine smokin our lives away, smokin till we greened n flopped on de grass, sweaty, dreamy n nower goin in de park.

Georgie comes te me in a vision n says
Write dat book pal, tell de story, tell de truth.

I/ll try Georgie. I will Georgie. I am Georgie.

So here comes Georgie te me door in de blocks:
Ma answers. Hes still in bed.
In bed? At dis time? De lazy bastard.
I know. Go on in te um George.

Me in bed: Not really sleepin but half dreamin, half

wakin, plannin wot drugs te get, who I owe money te, who Id like te fuck, wot de girls across de block look like in de nude? Wot wud it be like te fuck so-n-sos sister? How much hash is left in de box? Ar der skins? No...shit...used de last uv dem last night, half a joint in de ashtray. Georgie enters.

Ar ya up?
Gettin up now.
He takes de darts out uv de board n throws dem.
Ah, shite score.
Ya know ya cant play wen yer sober.
Yeah, any hash der?
Yep.
I/ll get a joint tegeth...
No skins.
Bollix.
Ders a half a joint in de ashtray.
We quietly smoke de little half splif den Georgie says
I/ll run up te Brendans shop n get skins.
Right I/ll bum a smoke off me Ma n make a cuppa tea.

Georgie whose Ma ran off n Da drank, who bought every Bob Marley album he cud, who cried out for love, love for iz little confused n broken body, love for iz tender soul. He roamed around at nights high on vodka n hash n punched metal street lamps n walls till iz hands bleed n swelled up.

He took razor blades n slashed at iz wrists n arms.

56

He fell in love wit any woman dat gave him de slightest attention or nicety or a kiss, wow a kiss! A walk home in a haze uv love sickness. Heed stalk dem, wait outside der house, across de street, offer te walk dem home, be a gentleman. It never lasted; dey led him on for reason known te dem? He scared dem, he got de message all wrong for reasons known te him or not?

Heed sit on de balcony outside me flat all de time even if I wuzzen der, waitin squintin te see who wuz dat comin inte de block, mistakin dem for sumone else.

Georgie started te wear a baseball cap aniz hair curled under it, wore a red n navy hood, black faded jeans or pale blue ones, old runners. Navy n yellow Liverpool F.C tracksuit. Didden care too much for fashions or wot others thought uv iz clothes or so he claimed.

Its me n Georgie walkin up Infirmary Hill tegether. Heads bob up n down n around in all directions. Lookin at trees, de sky, de road ahead. Lookin menacin, moody n eager. Georgie walks a little behind, iz short legs juttin a step every few he took, tryin te keep up wit de long legs uv iz friend. Hes got a stick uv wood in iz hand dat he found on de street, he taps on de ground as he walks. Hes got a crazy rhythm goin wit de stick n de juttin. Hes whistlin *Rat in de kitchen* by UB40. We reach de top uv de hill n turn right towards de blocks. De blocks, four storeys high, corporation built blocks uv flats. Three hundred flats n thirteen blocks. Families boxed n stacked n stuck on concrete shelves.

Ive te go up te de gaff n pay me ma, before I go up te Beatzer, yeah.

Cool, yeah. He/ll be up der all day anyway.

Ders enough for a joint up der we/ll smoke dat before we go up te um.

Ya gettin more off um today?

Yeah.

Dya wanna get a quarter n I/ll go half on it, pay ya on Friday?

Yeah cool, cool man. Datll do us for a few days.

Is dat Tommy standin on yer balcony?

Yep its Doyler alright well spotted for a blind cunt. Georgies face turns a little red at dis remark.

I can see tings far away mad isin it?

Yer fuckin mad, dats whats mad, hah!

Georgie n me walk up de stairs dat have names n love-hearts wit initials n plus signs inside dem. A smell uv grease n vinegar in de air. On de balcony,

Tommy Doyle is standin waitin for us.

Wats de story Doyler?

Alright Tommy?

Alright lads?

Why didden ya not knock, me ma wud uv let ya in?

Ah, just thought Id stall it here I knew yiz werent der cuz ders no music.

Come in n smoke a joint wit us wer goin up te Beatzer after it.

Yeah, nice one lads, Beatzer up in de pitch as usual yeah?

Yeah.

Yeah, ha, ha.

Alla us enter de flat, rubbin hands, scratchin necks, whistlin, happy in anticipation uv de joint wer goin te smoke together.

Georgies arms er criss-crossed wit blade marks. Iz face is contorted, iz glasses steamed up. He takes dem off n looks at de bath, de water looks green but he knows it isnt. He undresses slowly iz short hairy body is numb, he climbs inte de bath n takes de blade, he might hit an artery dis time, he might get de wish, he might leave de blocks for good dis time.

He thinks about Beatzers face in de coffin, how he looked happy n as good as he ever did. A dark gloopin shade is salivatin in de bathroom wall. Its de scream in a small bathroom uv a flat in de blocks. Its art dyin in water. Its as dull as a soap opera sex scene.

Georgie Teeling, sits wit a gang uv Gargoyles n Glooptings in de blocks. Iz hair shabby, iz face worn, iz relationships cracked n broken. Iz body weary. Spirit chained te de walls, chained te de concrete uv de blocks. Georgie goes n scores a few bags uv gear from de dirty hands uv a faceless man. De money is wet from sweat. Georgie skips n trips n falls on de ground. He vomits white witdrawal all over de place an old man passes by n harrumphs at him. Georgie spits a gob in de blokes direction n grins. Its cold de air has ice in it. Georgie gets up wipes iz face n lips. He looks for a pub toilet te wash iz mouth out n looks in de mirror, sees iz face full uv spots n scabs, he wears iz glasses dese days, has no choice, hes eyesights fucked. He sees a shadowy blur around iz head n back, swerves around but its not der, shakes it off n leaves de pub on Manor Street. Walks on by de bookie shops, Chinese take aways, video shops n newsagents, traffic trudges down de road.

Georgie n de gargoyles in a small cold flat in de blocks get it tegether wit de works n sliver spoon, a bummed cigarette n a lemon for de acid.

Ready te ride de worlds again.

De brown powder blooms in de veins, swims tru de small weak body n hits de broken heart. Georgie blue in de face, foamin at de mouth. Rockin n moanin on de ground. Glooptings stroke iz face in wonder. De door gets busted down by another junkie in need uv de flat te shoot de shit dat swims in de arms uv little George Teeling. De junkys skinny yellow hands turn Georgie on iz side, kicksum in de back wit tattered Nike foot. Calls 999 n fucks off te another cold, dirty room, full uv butts n barrels n shadowy beins. Georgie in de back uv an ambulance eyes rollin. Georgie in me shirt. Georgie hands bruised. Georgie lookin at himself n sayin

Wot a dope.

Georgie in n out uv iz body. Georgie on de hospital bed. Pumped out. Breathin heavy. Georgie back in iz body in de Mater hospital. Drips n machines dat bleep. White bed sheets n white walls, white everyting cept de shades n shadows.

Georgie half-awake. Stumbles from de bed. Spittle on iz chin. Georgie unhooks de drip n gets off de bed topless, shoeless, no glasses. Georgie, de great escape from de Mater hospital, avoids de security. Georgie heads for de walls, de damn fuckin walls uv de blocks. Georgie staggers inte a gallop. Georgie leaps on de wall, go on Georgie get out, run Georgie, leap Georgie. Georgie Teeling a hero uv dis book, slips shoeless n stoned on de walls uv de blocks n falls, iz neck catches on de barbed wire, iz hands so small n fat grab n tear at de wire, swingin n spurtin, chokin on blood, iz face blue, bluer din its ever been, iz lips white, breath gone, eyesight at last perfect, he looks n sees de stars glowin in de sky n hears music, like sumting from an old movie like Ben Hur n hes gone. Georgie Teeling hung der on de barbed wire. Crucified by love n drugs, hung by heroin. Glooptings below pointin n laughin, floatin up n all around de body, lookin for a fix, a pack uv nightmares. De Gargoyles flew away te de top uv de blocks n lowered der heads in silence for de night. Poor Georgie Teeling hung on barbed wire in de blocks turns inte a Francisco Goya Etchin.

Martyr uv dis book. Georgie Teeling dead at twenty-one n free from de blocks. So long buddy n so long wuz de weepin uv all de characters in dis tale.
In de church Christy Dignam sings

Its a crazy world, how can I protect ya in dis crazy world?

De stain glass Jesus looks like a sick joke te me. Me eyes hurt wit de salty tears.

Me Da is in a haloed shade uv whitish grey sleepin in coffin, pale, cold te de touch uv me child selfs lips. Georgies Da is tryin te hold it tegether in de church but de tears flow. David Newmans Da wore a wig n painted on iz eyebrows wit mascara te conceal iz alopecia. A sad comedy it wuz, for all te see, de wig tilted too much te one side. Me Da became a dove wen he died. Georgie became a dove wen he died. We all become doves wen we die.

David n Dan

Its summer n David Newman, Dan Carr, a fat fucker called Liam White, Georgies younger brother Jimmy n me er playin football in de backers.

Sumtimes we hung around in de blocks wit a blondy little youngfella named matt aniz tall pal Mikey who wuz a few cans short uv a six pack, but a decent footballer.

From dis bunch uv boys aged between ten n sixteen de teams wud be made for long football matches uv three or four a side. Played like a cup final; kickin, screamin, celebratin, controversy n glory. Whistles in mock referee, wen sumone committed a foul, loud shouts uv YESSSSSSSSSS wen a goal wuz scored, de wallop uv de ball as it hits de balcony uv one uv de bottom flats n rebounds back te de pitch, de crash uv two bodies as dey collide in a tackle from a hospital pass, de holler uv instruction from de top dog player,

Hit it long, play it wide ya dope ya, agh for fuck sake wot wuz dat?

Many other head-de-balls pass in n pass out. Shauny. Deco. Chicken. De unforgettable Dickey de kicker, who grew up te be a Georgie Best livealike n almost became a pro, even had a few games for Coventry City reserves but wuz back in Dublin two months after he went over te England. Mad Dog Maddox, ya have te letum play or eles he/ll kick de bollix outta ya. Various block boys lookin for a kick around or punch-up or both.

The Backers—Our makeshift pitch, wer me bein paly wit Georgie kicked off. A friendship dat lead te drugs, music, violence, love, other friendships, poetry, death, tears, survival, dis book.

Dan Carr n me wer stayin de night in David Newmans. It wuz de holidays so we stayed up all night playin video games on Davids Nintendo, Super Mario Bros had alla us addicted, includin Davids Da Dick.

It wuz about four in de mornin, n Dan had fallin asleep face down on a batterd brown sofa dat looked

like it had been stitched tegether out uv discarded
corduroy.

David wuz sat on a cushion on de floor n Dick n
me wer sittin on de armchairs. I wuz startin te drift off
wen de familiar beeps n surreal music uv de Mario
Bros game woke me, n Dick sayin
Yes boys, I did it level ten here we come.
I opened me eyes n looked across at Dick; he
looked strange n funny te me, de bad wig, de painted
on eyebrows n him totally engrossed in de video
game, while iz wifes in bed n de kids er half asleep. I
rubbed me eyes n looked at Dan, asleep, droolin on de
couch. I looked back at Dick n he wuz passin de
controller te David.
Here son, have a go, I cant seem te focus on de
screen.
He began te rub iz eyes n turn iz head back n forth
from de TV.
Ar ya alright Dick? I asked.
Yeah, I just cant seem te focus on...
Iz arms shot out in front uvum n went rigid, iz fists
closed so tight iz knuckles whitened as if de bones wer
about te pop right tru de skin. Den iz whole body
began shaken violently n de wig slid off n wuz hangin
from de side uv iz head like a run over cat.
Da, Da, wots happenin?
I wuz startled. It wuz like a possession. De first
thought I had wuz te run inte de bedroom n get Davids
Ma, Tammy. I burst inte de room witout knockin n
Tammy stared at me wit her green eyes, wonderin wot
I wuz doin.

Tammy, Dicks havin sum sort uv fit or sumting, quick,
quick I dont know wot te do?

She pulled back de covers n sprang from de bed, naked, her pale plump body, saggy breasts, rodent-like bush. She threw a parka on n we sprinted inte de sittin room. Hands te her face at de sight uv Dick slumped over in de chair, wig like a cat across iz face, lips foamin like bubble bath n David bawlin n panicin. De sun had come up n light shone inte de room as de Mario bros theme tune looped around de room, frazzlin me head.

Go upstairs te de Brezlins n tellem te ring an ambulance, quick.

Dan woke up n seein me runnin out de door, thought it wuz a fire or sumting, n just got up n ran after me. I banged up de Brezlins n dey called for de ambulance, Mr. Brezlin said

Its an Epileptic Caesar, im tellin yiz, dats war it iz.

Dan n me stood around outside in de block waitin till de ambulance got der, n dey took Dick out on a stretcher, put um in de back n drove off in de creepin-burglar-temptin-mornin-half-light.

Mr. Brezlin wuz right.

It wuz an Epileptic seizure brought on by de Mario Bros game.

Afterwards I just kept thinkin te meself, shit man, I just seen Dick wit iz wig hangin off n Tammy in de Nude, first vagina I seen dat wuzzen an accidental glance at a cousins or even worse seein yer Ma gettin out de bath, or in a picture in a sticky paged passed around imported porn mag, it looked kindda scary. I also thought, fuck dis is gonna be awkward next time I see dem.

Dick Newman is wunna de blocks tragic comedy Das. Iz eyebrows painted on wit one bigger dan de other, iz non-stick Beatles wig knitted from de hair uv old dead cats. Iz muscleman arms, iz workmans hands, mechanic, painter n decorator, carpenter, smacker uv iz kids wen iz football team got scored on. One uv dose oddmen who did oddjobs in the nineties. Called te everyones gaff every now n den, fixin de sink, unblockin de jacks. Turned up in a lot uv British porns, wit a step ladder n a horn for a billboard. Had all these facts dat turned out te be waffle wen ya looked dem up.

Full uv mad anecdotes n superstitions n silly jokes n opinions about people, Blacks n Pakistanis n de English, dat wer ignorant, but he believed te be de gospel.

Once Tammy went out te de balcony durin an Ireland world cup match te get away from de tension n Ireland scored, in Dicks mind der wuz a connection der, sumhow? So anytime Ireland wer behind in a match, poor Tammy got told te go outside on de balcony n de odd time dat it worked, Dick wud say

I told ya, I told yiz it wud work.

Totally ignorin all de times it didden work. If ya knocked on de door lookin for David n by chance iz team got scored on, wen he went back inte de room, heed scowl contemptuous n shake iz head in disgust, sumhow yer knockin at iz door in a flat in Dublin had effected de flight uv a ball a on football pitch in Manchester England, Butterfly wings an all dat, eh?

He wuzzen too bad tho, he tried te look out for us boys n done iz best, just iz best like most uv de blocks Das, wuzzen enough te stop us gettin inte trouble, Dick n Tammy Newman er still alive, de wigs shrugged off, bald n proud dese days. Still football lunacy goin on no doubt?

David ended up on de gear. Last I heard he wuz still in dat on it/off it stage. For a short time, we wer very close, I had love for de guy n he me, but it didden last, I wuz three years older, Dan n de others wer older din um too, n he had dis way uv getin up peoples nose, cudden take losin or slaggins n it wud end up in a fight, a fight dat he wud always lose, bein so small n weak, but he wudnt give in till he had a busted nose or black eye n den yid look at um n feel guilty.

I hope hes ok now, I hope dat Dick, Tammy n de other kids er ok, I hope dey get out uv de blocks safe.

De Sounds uv de Blocks

Garda cars n ambulances, sirens wailin n infants cryin, n couples screamin, n mangy dogs barkin, n de crack uv bones, n de smash uv windows, n ahhhhhhhhhhhhhuuuuuuuuuummmmmmmmmmm de moan uv orgasm.

De jazz brush uv wind against de stele, the wind tearin at the concrete, de blocks.

A Shaken baby feverishly dreamin uv snakes. De blocks er teemin wit de sounds uv joyridden Honda Civics n hoots n wild yellin from teenage boys, *Fuck you! Old Bill er scum.*

Mas callin for der kids te come in for dinner. Girls skippin rope n chantin *In, out, in, out, shake it all about, ya do de hoky koky n ya turn around.*

Boys screamin YEEEEEEEESSSSSSSSSSSSS as de plastic street football sails inte de top corner uv de goal. De flicks uv lighters flamed te burn hash inte joints or burn heroin from tin foil or burn young mens arms or burn up de body uv a junkie on de goof.

Children singin *Queenie i oh who has de ball, is she big or is she small?*

Hear de screams uv Leonda Brown as her boyfriend, Billy *de dirt* Mooney, punches her face, takes her by de hair n smashes her head against de wall.

Hear *Labour uv Love* by UB40, hear DJ Pressure, hear Erasure, hear Black Sabbath. Hear de banners n rockets. Hear de Christmas crackers n aul fellas singin De Dubliners n De Wolf Tones songs. Hear de yowl uv the stab victim in de blocks at night. Hear de mother wail for her dead child. Hear a window smash n de scarperin uv feet. Hear an Ice-cream van play *Popeye de sailor man*. Hear neighbours call each other cunts n bastards n hear dem shout yeah baby give it te me good. Hear hopscotch rhymes. Hear kick de can n red rover. Hear de hum uv de laptop n de tappin uv keys as I play de song uv dis book in yer ear, dear reader.

De crack uv bones.

De cryin babies.

De barkin dogs.

De drunks singin n fightin.

De girls chantin.

De boys screamin.

De banners n rockets.

De music.

De mas callin.

De sirens wailin.

De childrens games.

De notes from a cheap guitar muffled by de dreary Dublin wind.

Dis is how de blocks sound n its nutting like de sea, *Glenroe, Fair City*

Bray or De Angelus.

Memory block

Edel had a baby for Frankie.

A snow haired boy named Charlie, tho we nick named him Charlo.

He starts te kick a football as soon as he can walk. Punches people in de balls for fun n runs off sniggerin. Wants te be wit me all de time.

Is monkey mad n loud from de day hes born. Not as loud as Edel tho.

No man or woman alive is as loud as Edel wen she gets goin. A voice dat wud bring down Jericho on its own, a voice dat wud score ten on de Richter scale. Edel n Charlo in de back bedroom, shoutin n cursin at each other, a ping pong match uv insults.

Ma still single in her double bed. Me in de small room at de front.

De balcony shoot on de wall outside. Banged by neighbours tryin te stuff down cardboard toy-boxes n bits uv broken stools n black bags full uv empty beer cans n cider bottles.

Ouija board

Georgie n Shaun, told me te put me hand on de Ouija board.

Were sittin on de floor on de dirty green carpet in Georgies dinky bedroom, laughin at each other n makin eyebrow gestures n head tilts. Dey stopped laughin wen I put me finger on de coin n it moved wit super-natural speed.

Ar ya movin it?

Me? Its yur fuckin board, yiz made de ting n asked me up te try it out, fuck off wud yiz n stop messin.

Wer not movin it, swear te God.

It wuz a home made board, just a bit uv cardboard wit letters n words n a star uv David all done in blue ink. Deyd planed te play a game on me, te try freak me out. But dey didden think it wud move like it did. Dey didden count on the touch uv de other.

It hadden worked for dem earlier or it inched towards a few numbers n letters, spellin de name Tom or Pat, n both uv dem wer convinced de other one wuz movin de coin.

It moved wen I played de game.

It flew along, spun in rapid circles round de board, spellin out not just names but entire sentences. It wuz as if our fingers wer stuck te de coin. Our bodies even started to rotate in rhythm wit the coins magic movements.

We asked De Sprit sillyboys questions about girls n wud we get married n have kids, n den we got braver n tried te cast a curse n asked de spirit if it wud cuz wunna de teachers in our school, Mr. Murray, te have an accident, not te killum, just break iz leg or letum lose a finger. We got a bit freaked out n excited wen de coin spun n stopped dead on de yes mark on de board.

We stopped playin wit de board den, n Georgie folded it up n put it under iz bed. De lads wer lookin at me hard, reverance n nervousness mixed in der eyes, I cud tell dey wanted te know why the ting worked so good wen I wuz der n not before wen dey tried it first, but I didden fuckin know, n I wuz a bit wierded out by de whole ting n I went home.

Wen I got home, I told Ma, Edel n Frankie about it. Dey broke der shite laughin n said de lads must have been windin me up, so I made a board from a ripped up *Corn Flakes* box n drew de letters n symbols on it wit a red pen, I used de top uv a hairspray bottle for de cursor instead uv a coin, so we cud all fit a finger on it. We sat around de wooden coffee table wit de board on it. Ma n Frankie wer smokin *Benson n Hedges* cigarettes. Charlo wuz in bed asleep.

Again dey guffawed, until once again de supernatural spinnin happend wen I put me finger on de top n called on de spirit n asked if anyone wuz der. De bottle top swished under our fingers dat once again felt glued te de cursor, de laughter turned te open mouthed slow breaths now.

The spirit responded te me questions. Me promptins. It said it wuz Da n dat he wuz in a place he cudden speak off, dat he wuzzen allowed te tell about.

Ma asked him for de *Lotto* numbers, as if dis wuz an important ting te ask de spirit uv a dead man, cud he even tell de future? He gave one number, it wuz six.

It came up on de lotto dat week, lucky guess?

Frankie wuz a big tuff guy dat a lot uv people in de inner city feared, but he wuz shittin himself n wudden walk home on iz own dat night n had te stay at ours for de first time, soon he wud move in te de back room wit Edel n Charlo. Manoeuvred by de spirit?

De room had an unreal feelin te it, like we wer in a simulacrum. It wuz blurry at the edges n cold in de air. De Glooptings grinned wit yellow canine smiles n reappeared in de corners n cracks uv de blocks.

Wuz it Da? Wuz it a hoax? Wuz it mumbo jumbo? Wuz it a spirit or spirits? Wuz it De Spirit?

Ma said it wuz de devil n burned de board.

I didden go te school de next day, thank de Spirit, n Mr. Murray didden break iz leg er lose a finger, thank de Spirit.

First drink

Id just turned sixteen in July uv 1994, n completed me Junior Cert in school, I done well, four passes n three honours, made me Ma n teachers happy. Ma bought me de *Mortal Kombat* game for me *Sega Mega*

Drive, dat n *Fifa Football* wer the games we played dat summer, wen we werent out playin ball in de block, or rounders or catch n bash or sum other street game.

Id never had a drink or done a drug up te dat point in me life, n me first drink wuz at Edels 21st birthday bash in de Park Lodge on de North Circular Road. Me, David Newman n Dan Carr sat at our own table, watched closely by Dick Newman from under de wig n fake eyebrows n me Ma peekin over her pint uv pills. We started out by gettin pints uv shandy, n it took us an hour te finish one pint uv the sugary beer. All de family wuz der, Aunts, Uncles, Cousins, in-laws, n neighbours, Yonkers ONeil n Tazzer Ward de demented duo dat sum times hung around wit Frankie n who he used for der endless supply uv recreational pharmaceuticals n assorted head candy, n a few uninvited fuckers who end up at every party, weddin n funeral, one uv dem wuz nick named follow de hearse, after iz habit uv endin up at every funeral wake in Dublin 7, 8, 9, 10 n 11.

Sittin der in de smoky hall, birthday balloons n streamers on de walls, dressed up in our white polar necks, black jeans wit red patches on de arse uv dem n white *Adidas* runners. Sippin on de pints n watchin de girls dance in de lights, lookin at tits in low cut tops n long legs comin out uv short skirts n tight arses n big perfect round arses that we day-dreamed uv bein in bed wit n shaggin all night.

We went on te de lagers secretly, pretendin dey wer shandys te de adults. We got Frankie to go te de bar n get us three pints uv *Heineken* n we went n got a bottle uv lemonade n poured a sip inte each pint just in case Dick came over te test de pints.

After one more round, we wer sweatin n bleary eyed, de courage te dance n chat growin in us. De alcohols bitter buzz wound its way tru me nervous system pumpin intoxicatin flavour n brash machismo inte me body n mind.

De DJ played all de party songs, *Rock de Boat, Timewarp, Jive Bunny, Stevie Wonder Happy Birthday* n de hits uv de day, *Here Comes De Hotstepper, Bump n Grind, All That She Wants.*

Finally at de end uv de night we got up on de dance-floor, full uv drunk sexy girls, aulones who wanted te kiss ya on de cheek, old lads doin de side shuffle, blokes out uv de head throwin all sorts uv shapes n smackin each other on de shoulders, n we done our best or worst rave moves, while gawkin n grinnin dumbly at de girls, gettin nower except high. But it didden matter, we had de buzz, we had strobe light fever, we had each other, fuck de rest uv dem.

After de party we went back te me gaff, wit a take away uv three cans between us n a big lump uv birthday cake wrapped in tin-foil. Walkin home I kept thinkin if anyone started on us, Id smash a can off der heads, de pricks. I felt confident in meself as a goer all uv a sudden. Id bein in fights as a kid, won more din I lost, but I wuz never aggressive, but now I felt like a fight cud be excitin, like it wud be de next best ting te a ride.

Ma wuz locked n went te bed, Edel n Frankie went inte a nightclub wit der mates n Charlo wuz in Frankies sisters for de night, me uncle Jake aniz boyfriend came back wit us n gave us Champagne, Dan puked orange n yellow sick on himself n all over de bathroom floor, wen I went in he wuz asleep in a ball on de floor face down, we got um up, washed his face, took off iz top n put um down on de sofa for de night wit a duffle jacket over um. Dan wuz always gettin himself inte troubles, n accidents.

I woke de next mornin in bed wit all me clothes on, an rank beer breath, witout any hangover, wonderin wot all de adults wer on about? I decided den dat I liked bein a little drunk, I liked de feelin I had de night before uv bein a bit braver n cocky. It opened up sumting masculine in me dat I felt I needed te survive at dat time. A Grizzly bear wuz born in me den.

First drug

De first experience I had wit drugs wuz wit Georgie, Fat Liam, n Dan.

We wer standin in de porch uv wunna de blocks. Der wuz nutting te do n we had enough football for de day. A bunch uv young boys wit hats, gloves, n hoods on, we wer a pack uv wild dogs, snarlin n waitin for sumting te happen, waitin for sumting te do. Waitin for sum spark te strike us.

Georgie suggested we get drunk n asked if anyone had money?

Nope wuz de answer.

Well, not enough te get de amount uv alcohol it wud take te get us all drunk.

So he asks if anyone has ever done any solvents before?

Solvents wots dat? asks Liam White.

Tipex n gas, ya sniff it n ya get out yer head on it, its deadly said Georgie.

I heard about kids dyin from dat stuff, I said.

Georgie says one in a million, done dem loads uv times n I didden die yet.

A part uv Georgie longed for death. So wit a mix uv nerves n adrenalin runnin tru us, de rest uv us agree te Georgies plan.

We only need te get two pound up between us te get a bottle uv tipex n Liam has de sandwich bags in iz Mas Flat says Georgie.

Yep says Liam.

We scrape up de two quid n dey elect me as de person te buy it as I look de oldest n Im tall n can put on de act uv nice young man who needs tipex for school.

I went up te de park shop n bought de tipex wit no bother from de shopkeeper, Back te school next week.

De four uv us go te Liams, iz Mas in work, no Da livin der aniz younger brother Shane is out playin in de block wit de other scrufs.

In de sittin room, Liam gets out de bags n gives dem te Georgie, n he shows us wot te do, a mad teacher uv desperate tings for mad n desperate times wuz Georgie.

He puts sum tipex in de corner n puts de bag te iz mouth n starts te inhale de fumes in long slow breaths, talkin te us in between breaths,

Come on, do it, come on will yiz, its fuckin class.

Red faces, high brains, weird auditory hallucinations uv football commentary n cheers from de backers, deep voices, mad laughter, purple light in de eyes.

Georgie holds de bag der for de longest n goes inte a little trance, pushin at death, trapezin de worlds, a cracked Brujo uv de blocks. He goofs off for a bit.

Wer all feelin good about de experience, whoopin n hollerin, makin jokes n takin de piss, mostly at de expense uv Liam, I look at Liams head n it looks like a giant cherry wit fluff on it n I say dis out loud te de rest uv de lads, dis puts de gang uv us inte a ten minute laughin fit, dat leaves us sore n happy n glazed over.

We open de balcony door n go out n look at de backers, de kids playin, n de dark clouds above de blocks, n we spit over de balcony inte de grass below, n witout sayin anyting for a minute or two we all feel n know dat sumting we cant fully understand has happened between us, n for de next few months we looked for anyting in a tube or canister dat had on it, *do not inhale* n bought it n done wot we wer told not te by most, but wer told by de spirit uv danger n fallen youth in Georgie te do n do n do as wuz our want n need.

Drug memory block

Night time in Dublin in de blocks. Its autumn. De cold is a presence.

Georgie n me er standin in de porch, de walls er full uv names n cock drawins. Wer puttin pennies tegether te get a can uv butane gas te get fucked out uv our heads. We need Liam te get it for us becuz Ive been te all de shops around de area over de last few weeks n cant go back in for a few weeks. Georgie dey take one look at n say no.

So we write up a letter supposed te be from Liams ma sayin *Can you please give my son a bottle of Lighter gas, as Im not well and unable te go te de shops, thank you* and sign it wit a fake signature.

Liam walks out de shop n turns de corner slowly, iz big frame made even bigger by de Liverpool FC overcoat hes wearin, Georgie n me er standin in de cold, mist blowin out uv our mouths. Eyes dark ringed, shufflin from side te side, hands pocketed.

Did ya get it?

Yeah, just gave her de note n it wuz no problem.

Lovely stuff.

Right, wer we gonna go do it?

Cant go te mine cuz me Das in de gaff.

Not mine either.

We can do it in mine, me Mas gone te bingo.

Cool, lets go so Liam, we do it in yer room yeah?

Yeah, yeah, come on.

Liams room: Clothes strung on de floor n de backs uv chairs. A personal computer (Before anyone had one in de flats), bed, Liverpool F.C posters on de wall.

Its warm inside, we take off our coats n hats, n get de gas out. Georgie grabs it sticks it in iz mouth n sprays de toxic fumes down iz throat. Iz face turns bright red n he starts te laugh, iz voice altered by de gas, sounds like a bad Darth Vader impression. Liam n me giggle n say look at iz head, ha-ha de colour uv it.

Wer passin de can around n takin turns te get a blast uv it, its a disgustin taste n cold feelin in yer mouth n throat. Im suckin on de can n inhale a big gush dat sends me inte a mad trip, for a moment I cant see anyting except burnin red light in me eyes n forehead, a whoopin, whooshin sound swirls round me brain n tru me head, I feel like Im out me body n spinnin around de room, I think Im gonna die, I throw de can on de floor n scream Agghhhhaaahhhh n just get up n run out de room n right out de front door n down de stairs.

I can hear Georgie say Wot de fuck? But it sounds like

Wwwwhhhhhaaaatttttt
dddddddddeeeeeeeeeeeeeeeee
fffffffffffuuuuuuuuuuuuuuuucccccccckkkkkkkkkkkkk.

Wen I get half way down de stairs I snap out uv it n Im back te normal n think, oh right, cool Im back, Im me, Im grand.

I walk back inte de room like nutting happened n

Georgie n Liam er in fits uv laughter at me.

Wot de fuck happened te ya? asks Liam.

I thought I wuz gonna die for a minute der, but Im grand now.

It gave me a hell uv a fright tho n put me off doin de gas for awhile.

I lay on de bed.

No more for me tonight boys.

Den I went tru a comedy performance scene I wud do for de lads, wit Liams small toy dart board throwin de darts pretendin te be playin in de world championship finals, while doin de BBC commentary.

Here he is now, dis youngman from Ireland from ODevaney gardens, look at him so slim n pretty, throwin for de set. Bristow beatin by a boy, hes done it, world champion. De kids de champ uv de world.

Georgie finished off de last uv de gas suckin on it till it wuz completely empty, even standin on it te squash de sides in, te get de smidgin uv a bit left in de bottom.

Wotll we do now lads?

Think I/ll go around n get sumting te eat says Georgie,

Im gonna get a shower n Ive school in de mornin, so… says Liam,

Right, Im gonna go home so.

Its dark in Dublin n Im at home thinkin uv wot te eat for dinner.

Dinner memory block

De sittin room is navy blue n mahgony brown. Blue wallpaper, brown table, brown wot-not stand n picture frames. Das face in a frame, Little Grandas face in a little frame. Little sky blue n white statues uv aristocratic lookin ladies n gents, a 3 in 1 Hi-fi wit a glass door.

Charlo is playin wit a small yellow n black sponge football, hes wearin a nappy n a Batman jumper, no shoes or socks, stocky legs.

Edel: Peroxide blonde, figure like an underwear model, sprayin her hair wit a massive bottle uv *Pennys* brand hair-spray, de fumes go everywer.

Ma says Can ya not go n do dat in de bedroom, dis is wer we eat, like ya know?

Im sat on de gikna-pigeon grey sofa wit a plate on me lap, eatin chicken burgers, chips n beans. Charlo, gets up n sits beside me, Ma gives um iz plate n he looks at me n starts te eat. De telly is on, *Eastenders.*

Edel makes a face n fusses around in de kitchen, fixin her -finger in de socket- hairstyle, poutin in de mirror.

I say te her

Yeah, will ya give it over, sprayin dat shit wen wer eatin.

Charlo says Ye, Ma, stop dat, do wan dat on me chicky buurers.

Edel curls her bottom lip up, grrs at us all, n den

83

stomps out de room wit brush n hairspray in hand. Off te complete de four hr ritual uv hair, make-up, try on differant outfits till she gets de right look, four glasses uv vodka n coke, handbag n shoes dat match, just te go out for de night wit Frankie te a dive uv a pub in Parkgate St.

Charlo n me finish dinner n I make tea for Ma n me, Charlo gets a glass uv Blackcurrant juice n choclate Bourbon biscuits. De tea is drunk, de Friday night soaps n *Top uv de Pops* er watched.

Charlo wit tomato sauce on iz face n biscuit crumbs on iz lips says te me

Ya play football wit me Kenny?

Come on so, come out te de hall, Nannys watchin her telly.

Agh yer not playin in de house er yas?

Yeah, its lashin rainin outside, dont worry its only a sponge ball, Ma.

Omly a spun ball, Nanny, is rainin out says Charlo lookin at Ma n den at me.

Only a ball made uv sponge, only hairspray in de air, only a middle age woman watchin telly, only a boy playin wit iz uncle, only an average night in a corpo flat in de blocks. Only de Tao playin peekaboo wit its self.

Bedroom memory block

De bedroom is a cramped box, double bed wit black manly covers, two old green posh second hand armchairs, a bookshelf full uv old Super Hero comics n *Match n Shoot* football magazines, a thirty year old varnished wooden chest uv draws full uv clothes wit a framed picture uv Bruce lee n a paintin uv Darth Vader on top uv it.

Georgie Teeling, Dan Carr n me sit on de sprin protrudin mattres uv de bed tegether, we take out a small block uv hash, red *Rizla* rollin papers, n a box uv *John player blue* from our pockets n place dem on de bed.

I take an old *Incredible Hulk* hardback annual from de shelf n put it on de bed te use as a flat surface te make de joint.

Do ya know how te do dis Georgie?

I think so, ya get three skins n stick dem, den put in de tobacco n burn de hash inte it.

Wot way do ya stick de skins tegether?

Dats wot Im tryin te remember.

Georgie takes out a bunch uv skins n starts te stick dem tegether in different formations, till he finally cracks de code uv joint makin architecture.

Ahh, got it, yep dats de way it goes.

Good man, good man, now can ya roll it, hah?

I/ll give it go.

Georgie sticks, pours, burns, spreads, licks n rolls n gets a big fat cigar shaped joint tegether n lights it as Dan n me look on intensely.

De room fills wit thick smoke, n Georgie starts te cough. He puffs n passes de joint on, de three uv us keep hittin de joint, takin long slow pulls, swallowin de smoke, blowin fumes in de air, coughin, laughin our bollix off. Slowly I get me first joint together; it turns out te be just as good as Georgies. I feel proud uv it. De joint uv pride n youth gets ceremoniously smoked n we giggly. We put a Bob Marley tape in de stereo, press play n drift n lie back on de bed n float on de wave uv hash n music up over de blocks n even de doves have dreads in dis dream.

Den de front door uv de flat opens, n Ma n Edel come in wit shoppin bags full uv messages n Charlo in de pram. I jump up, pull back de dark curtains, open de window wide, grab a bottle uv Lynx n spray it in big archin gusts around de room.

Georgie grabs de paraphernalia n puts it iz pockets. Dan hides de ashtray under de bed, kickin it wit iz foot. I go te de bedroom door te meet Ma, Edel n Charlo before dey can get te de room.

But Edel smells de air n says
Smell uv hash in here n pushes de door open, n wen de Lynx hits her, she smells a cover up.
Deyre smokin hash in here Ma, deyre after sprayin Lynx te try n hide it.

De dirty rattin fucker! I go inte complete denial mode.

Wot er ya on about, get out uv here ya dope ya.

I turn te me nervous mates n ask Wer we smokin in here, tell her will yiz?

Dey both say NO simultaneously. Georgies face blushes red.

Charlo yells out Smell in here, whas dat?

I tell Edel te fuck off n say te Ma

Im goin out, see ya later, come on lads.

De boys get up n walk out de front door quick as de can n try not te look me Ma in de face; I lock de bedroom door, put de key in me pocket, smirk at Edels rat face n follow de boys out de flat.

Georgie, Dan n me sit at de bottom uv de stairs, high n wild, n flighty.

Fuck, nearly got caught der boys, ha-ha.

Shit, we/ll have te find a better place, be more careful.

I think yer Sister n Ma know wha we wer up te.

Fuckem, just gonna keep denyin it, no proof, no crime.

Sniggers n nudges, we walk on up te de top blocks.

I fell in love wit hash right den, I felt like it wuz exactly wot I needed, it filled up a hole inside, de sacred smoke. N I dropped de gas n tipex. It wuz safer, easier te get, didden leave ya wit spots n scabs on yer face, nobody ever died from a hash overdose, n we wer grown up now, it wuz time te do real drugs not

87

sniffin outta bottles n plastic bags like kids on de corner. It wuz time te get serious.

Heads & Volleys

Heads n volleys is an Inner-city football game played in all de blocks uv flats in Dublin.

Ya can only score wit a header or on de volley. Der is no limit te de amount uv people who can play.

It wuz de game dat Georgie, Jimmy, Liam, Me, (n anyone else in de block dat came by n wanted te join in) played. It didden matter wot age ya wer, even Charlo wud play wit us at de age uv five, n de odd time, wunuv de adults who wuz decent at ball in iz day wud join in, till he wuz fucked n breathin like a pregnant woman climbin stairs.

Each player starts wit an allotted number uv points, say twenty each. Every time sumone scores a goal on ya, a point is deducted from yer score. If ya hit a shot n it goes wide or de keeper catches it witout de ball bouncin first, den ya swap places n yer in goal. Wen a player is on zero deyre out uv de game, de last point can only be deducted wit a header. Dis continues until ders only two players left.

De overall winner is decided by a penalty shootout between de two players, who must act as both goalkeeper n penalty taker durin de shootout.

Heads n volleys is a high velocity, muscle bustin, shin brusin game te play, in a block wit de porch uv de stairwell bein used as de goal. People walkin up n down de stairs or goin te de bin wit rubbish.

Hold de ball for fuck sake.

89

Watch de baby, will yiz.

Occasionally sumone gets a belt uv de ball n calls us wankers. De people who live on de bottom floor beside de porch come out n shout
Fuck off wit dat ball, Im tryin te go asleep.
Or old smelly Neddy wit de comb over n newspapers for wallpaper, wud come out n threaten te kill us or stab de ball wit a steak knive, de fuckin loon.

Sumtimes we ignored dem as we wer just too inte de game, havin too much fun.

Bein in goal wuz de worst part uv de game. Nobody liked it, n whoever wuz in wud shove, cheat, dive on de concrete, do anyting te get out uv goal n back on de pitch(street). Der wud be shots comin from all angles, low toe pokers, ambitious lobs, scissor kicks, n risky on yer back overheads, sum cunt wud belt it at yer face, yer hands wud sting from de hard shots ya had te save wit no gloves on, yid make a tremendous effort te make a save, only te lose yer footin n fall out on yer arse, n sumone wud chip de ball up in de air, n another one taps it over yer head as ya lay der watchin de ball sail in slow motion in te de goal, like in sum shite sports movie.
Wen ya got out uv goal ya blessed yerself n went at it wit a fierce energy. Goin out wide te de stele rails round de block, whipin in crosses for de other boys te get on de end uv, smashin shots at full power dat hit the wall uv de porch n bounce back n hit a little youngone goin by, divin headers in te de top

90

corner, fallin on top uv de keeper as ya try te knock him n ball inte de goal. Dodgin de washin line poles in de middle uv de block as ya chase down a big hoof uv a pass dat goes way over everyones heads. Gettin in de face uv another player, for callin ya a selfin cunt for taken too many shots, *Leave it out boys, its only a game, give over will yiz.*

It wuz murder but ya loved it at de same time. Most uv de time we used a plastic 1:99 *Cup Champion* ball made te play on de street. De odd time sum poor fool wud be cajoled inte bringin out de hand stitched Gary Lineker leather size five ball, dat iz Da told um wuz only te be used on grass. De ball we loved most wuz de indoor football from de community centre on Augrim Street.

While wer playin a match in de centre wunuv us throws de ball out de side door n goes n tells de attendant dat it got stuck up in de rafters, dis wuz plausible as it did happen, ya cud see de ball stuck up der stranded like Robinson Crusoe. Wen wer finished n payin for de hour, wunuv us sneaks out de side door n gets de ball n meets de rest uv us around de front.

De indoor ball wuz a rare commodity n held in high regard in de blocks becuz uv its luminous yellow/green colour n unique texture; it also bounced unusually high givin it a different feel te play wit.

Wen it rained it wuz fantastic te play wit, de fluffy, fibrous texture soaked up lots uv water, n it cud get real heavy n dirty. Havin one uv dese alien balls gave ya standin in de blocks, fellas wud knock-up te yer gaff lookin for a loan uv it te play a match, n ya get invited te play wit dem, uv course if ya wer a weedy kid or lackin courage, de ball cud be just taken from ya by sum other robbin bastard or bunch uv robbin, shit kickin cunts.

Wen ya took de ball on yer chest or headed it, it felt like a ton weight hittin ya, thumpin off yer body. A big brown rain soaked blob on yer shirt or forehead, water drippin down yer face, dirt in yer eyes. Fuckin deadly it wuz.

Georgie, de boys n me, soaked, stoned, jubilant in de rain, down in de block wit a nicked-green-indoor-football, playin an all day long game uv Heads n Volleys, not givin a bollox about de world or sex or money or nefarious deals.

I watched her ass in white jeans walkin up de Road

De 2nd time I went te a pub wuz de first night I had sex. I wuz sixteen, n had ten pounds in me pocket, a five spot uv hash, a packet uv skins n three smokes. I went down te Parkgate Street te de *Judge n Jury* wit Edel, Frankie aniz mate Keith. Edel sat drinkin wit de girls out front, while de guys all went inte de pool room, wer we smoked joints, shot pool n took de piss. Two small wooden tables, stools, a big mirror, n a blackboard wit chalk te write de list uv players names.

Pool gets bornin n de talk uv football, bad bets, drug deals, n one night stands gets dull after awhile. I had three pints uv *Carlsberg* inte me n a heap uv joints, n wuz feelin like a fuckin man.

A girl named Natalie wuz sittin wit Edel n de other moths. She wuz about two years older din me, had black hair n a nice figure. She wuzzen pretty lookin, but had a great ass n pert tits n I wuz as horny as man cud be.

I sat beside her n Edel n Frankie, n we chatted a bit. Bad 90s music wuz playin: Dr Alban, Snow, 2unlimited. Middle age woman drinkin shots n big bellied men slurpin *Guinness* n belchin. We smoked a joint tegether n me head spun, me stomach churned, I cudden hold it in n I got sick inte an empty pint glass I grabbed from de table. I filed it up wit brownish

93

yellow spew. Frankie n me went te de toilet n washed de glass out n I cleaned me face.

Wen I got back out she wuz still der. I didden fuck it up. A few minutes later she kissed me, she kissed me even tho I just puked inte a glass in front uv her. She kissed me even tho me breath stank uv vomit, beer n smoke. A long, tongue trashin, sloppy kiss. I knew right den, dis wuz it, I wuz goin te finally get te fuck a real woman.

I watched her ass in white jeans walkin up de road as her n Edel walked ahead. I ate greasy chips n talked wit Frankie, he wuz givin me tips for de bedroom, iz best moves n wer n wen te lick, de importance uv foreplay, I noted it all down in me head.

We got te de flat n Charlo wuz snornin little snores under a Power Rangers blanket on de sofa, while Ma wuz drinkin cans uv beer n watchin late night Saturday TV movies about murders n rapists. She wuz surprised by me comin in n introducin her te dis girl. Nataile n me said goodnight n left tegether for de bedroom.
I showed her inte de room. De walls wer full uv dead rockstars n topless woman n a few amateur drawins I done. I went n brushed me teeth n washed out me mouth. Fresh n ready te lick her out. I looked in de mirror, smiled n said
Lets do dis man, lets fuckin do dis.

I took out de condom Edel gave me n left it on de

94

locker beside de bed. De lights wer off. Natalie n me got inte it den. I quickly got naked, took off me jocks n flung dem across de room. I struggled wit de bra like a cliché under de sheets. Natalie undid it herself. I slid off de knickers. I kissed her all over n went down for de black bush, der it wuz de pussy, de gee, de snatch, de fuckin doors te paradise dat Id been dreamin of for a long time. Dat I watched in poorly filmed pornos wit friends n wanked off te in der toilets. I cud smell its intoxicatin juice, I cud tongue its erogenous flesh at last.

I fumbled, fingered n licked. Remembered de tips from Frankie n de moves uv de porn stars wit de massive cocks. She grabbed me cock n flipped me over n sucked it slowly n pulled on it, n sucked it n pulled it in a faster rhythm, den she straddled me n rode up n down me cock n grinded on me, den I flipped her over n me cock fell out, so I stuck it back in wit her help n lashed in te her for all I wuz worth n I came, n me thin body shuddered n it wuz all over in a few minutes uv drunk animal ruttin. It wuzzen much but it wuz a relief, I felt good, I felt like Id achieved sumting, I thought I wuz a fuckin man now.

We chatted for a bit as we lay tegether in de bed, her in de wet patch, n she told me how she hated her brother, dat he smacked her around, she got emotional n started te pen up about her hopes for de future n she said I wuzzen half as quiet as Edel, Frankie n Keith told her I wuz. Dat I wuz a dark horse n I wuz smarter din de average men she knew. Dat I had it in me te get

95

a good job or do sumting wit me life. All dis she got from a few pints, a joint, chips n a drunkin ride.

I didden want te hear any uv dis about her brother or her hopes for de future or me gettin a good job, truth is I wanted te have more sex n we did n it wuz even more sloppy n dumb, den I rolled over, faced de wall n went te sleep before she had time te start gabbin again.

In de mornin I hardly said a word, it felt weird lookin at dis girl I hardly knew but had had sex wit de night before n man she looked rough n so did I. I made her a cuppa tea. We smoked a joint n said fuck all te each other. I let her go witout a kiss or thanks or see ya again. I watched her ass in white jeans walkin out de door. I didden even walk her out de flats. Acted like a right dickhead. Like a sixteen year old boy from de blocks who thought dat gettin iz hole wuz easy, dat he wuz de big fuckin deal.

De girls, de woman uv de blocks have such cruelty put on dem, its no wonder most uv dem turn vengeful n full uv wrath n anger.

Did she think we wud be boyfriend n girlfriend? Lovers? Friends even?

I saw her a few weeks later in de same pub n tried de mooch. She let me walk her up te her neighbourhood n den she turned te me n said
See ya, Im goin te a party.

Dis wuz te spite me. I gave her no reaction; I smiled n said Ok, see ya around.

I walked back home te de blocks pass de all-nighters on de pitch, pass de spray pained walls, pass de holy grotto wit de Virgin Mary lookin at me, her head bowed in disgust, I gave her de finger n walked on pass de small fire burnin at de pramshed wall. I got inte me gaff, made sum toast, rolled a joint, smoked it, had a long satisfyin wank n remembered dat me bed once flew te a purple place wer a tree spoke in poetry, n wondered how n wer I wuz gonna get de money for hash tomorrow as I fell inte erotic dreams uv Natalie n de Virgin Mary n me.

Career guidance

I turned seventeen a few months after Natalie broke me in n wuz in fifth year in school. I hated school n de teachers wer all cunts.

More adults full uv rules, hate, sarcasm, failure, dey reeked uv oldman.

I got on wit a meagre bunch uv class mates, n de rest I detested der faces. Der names wer like paper cuts te me skin. Me real friends wer me block friends.

I only stayed in school becuz it kept me Ma happy n I really had no idea if I wanted te go te collage, learn a trade, work a dead end job, nunuv em jumped out at me as excitin or interestin, n I wuz from de blocks.

Career Guidance teacher: So Kenny, wot do you want te do wen you leave school?

97

Dont know.

You dont know?

Em, a plumber (Fuck off, ya nosey bastard).

A plumber, ok.

I cud have said Id like te sit around stoned, smokin massive lumps uv strong hash from a giant bong Sir, wit a bowl uv whiskey, a crate uv Scrumpy Jack cider -delivered te me each day- beside me, n a harem uv girls, Asian, Black, White, big tits, small tits, blondes, red-heads, brunets, short hair, long hair, te have all manner uv sex wit, anal, oral, threesums, foursums. Ya know, de type uv stuff dat runs tru me mind wen Im day dreamin instead uv listenin te ya pretend te give a fuck about wot I do after I leave dis fuckin life suckin hole uv a place ya wanker.

Sir, it will be great if I dont go on fuckin Heroin. Sir, I aim te stay out uv prison. Sir, not killin meself by immediate or slow suicide will be fuckin tops if I manage it. Sir, me Da died wen I wuz a child, before dat he wuz strung out on gear n me Ma threw him out. Sir all me adult role models er thick thugs, sad junkies, terrible thiefs, awful alcoholics, demented drug dealers, lovable lunatics.

Sir, do ya know ya look like a cardboard cut-out uv a man, a drip fed asshole? Every word ya say is meaningless te me, in-fact I hate ya n I hate everyting ya stand for. Fuck yer guidance, fuck yer classroom, fuck yer accent, fuck ya n de likes uv ya all over de world. Fuck all teachers, advisers, guides, rule makers.

Sir wud ya like me te come around n have a look at yer pipes, ya fuckin horrible cunt! Sir can I fuck yer wife wen I come over, can I bend her over de washin machine n stick me cock up her hole? Sir, Im from de blocks, nobody has a carer, or cares about collage ya fuckin dickhead, just send me up te de fuckin dole office now will ya?

But I didden I just said Plumber n he left me alone. De Mars red clouds came upon me too. Georgie n me beclouded in a hashish dream, fightin te see de sun over de blocks.

Buyin drugs on de pitch

Pitch made uv tar, white lines painted on it. Goal post at one end, de other toppled, a robed car crashed inte it. Names in yellow spray paint: Anto. Damo. Noddy. Yup Yup. Hendo. Beatzer.

Georgie n me er scorin hash from Beatzer. Its 5pm its cold. Beatzers wearin a t-shirt, black tracksuit bottoms, gloves n a baseball cap. Hes flanked by Yonkers ONeil whos wearin a white *Nike* shell suit, white *Air Jordans*, n has a thick gold chain around iz wide neck, iz face is dotted wit acne aniz hair is streaked bleached blonde n mousey brown. N Tazzer ward whos wearin a pair uv de same *Air Jordans* n a Red *Arsenal FC* shell suit, wit a *New York Mets* basball cap on over iz skinhead.

Story lads?

Wots de craic boys?

Any hash for sale Beatzer?

Yeah, Ive score blocks, lovely ones, nice bit a meat on dem, n its lovely blow, best soap-bar around lads, I tell yiz one ting boys, yer millin de blow out uv it dese days, hah!

Fuckin boys smokin it up everday, wha? Says Yonkers.

Yeah, cool, give us two will ya? Fuck all te do round here is der?

Yer right der boys, fuck all te do cept get out uv it, two, no bother lads, forty blips, yeah?

Tazzer yells out

Dats it boys, smoke till ya fuckin croke, yeaaaahhh!

Beatzer twists iz head at Tazzer,

Will ya keep it down ya mad ting ya, tryna do business here ya know like?

Ahh yeah, sorry Beatzy, sorry pal, only buzzin like.

Money n drugs change hands. De meaty tinfoil wrapped blocks er tucked inte inside pockets n de cash is put in a sock.

Georgie n me perk up n sprint back te de flat, leavin Beatzer, Yonkers n Tazzer te der nights work n play, wer rushin te get inte de bedroom te skin up, light up n smoke our brains out in de blocks. Two lost losers. Two heads te get mad out uv it. Two bodies te chill. Two boys te sing reggae songs.

Robbed car in de block

A silver ford mondeo screeches round de corner uv de block at eighty miles an hr. Inside er two sixteen year old males, Billy, skinny n sallow skinned n Trevor a pudgey, blonde haired boy, deyre not de owners uv de car. De owner is tucked up wit iz wife in der four poster bed in der home in Castleknock.

De boys er tearin it up. Dey feel de elation uv de ride, de car, de road n der bodies one entity, man/machine/road. De Guards will be here soon te spoil de fun. Billys drivin, Trevs in de shotgun, shoutin instructions n encouragements while puffin on a joint.

De car reaches de pitch, Billy rallies it up n down pullin handbrakers n doughnuts for de cheerin crowd uv youngsters dat have gathered around. Wot a show wer puttin on here de boys think.

De Garda car comes in fast from de opposite end uv de pitch dat de robbed car is at. De crowd whistles n shouts SCETCH te alert de boys. Wot a show.

De chase begins. Billy uturns de car n speeds out uv de pitch n on te de road, de Garda in pursuit. Both cars er at accident speed levels now. De crowd legsit out uv de pitch after de cars te see de climax uv de show. Billy whips a sharp left turn onte de North Circular Road n doubles back inte de blocks, de Garda up iz arse. De boys plan: Get te de pitch, dump de jammer, take it on toes, spider-scale de army barracks wall n hide in de long grass in de dark, face down till te pigs fuck off, den bale out uv de back uv de barracks te freedom. Wot a fuckin show.

Billy n Trev in de Ford Mondeo, de Garda squad car in Jaws pursuit. De white mondeo, head lights off, rockets onte de pitch, smashes inte a bollard, spins out uv control n crashes inte de community centre wit a tyre track screech n a battlefield bang. Trevs seat belt jerks n whiplashes him back n forth in iz seat, Billy isnt wearin iz seatbelt, de machstick bodys hurled head first against de windscreen, de neck snaps, de tragic figure lands on de dashboard, a limp bloody mess. Wot a show.

De Guards smash de side windows, n open de doors uv de death carriage, Garda OHara unbuckles Trevs seatbelt n drags de boy out uv de wreck, slaps de little gurrier face off um, cuffs um n puts um in de back seat.

Garda Murphy checks Billys pulse, nutting, radios for an ambulance n calls in de death te de Garda staion. De shows over. De crowd er dispersed.

Tomorrow de myths will be told. In de schools, in de papers, in de blocks.

Wot a fuckin show.

Exit Dan n David

Poor Dan Carr, he had a year long period wen he became a dumb show uv accidents n teen-age dramas.

He broke iz big toe while playin football in-doors wit David n me. We wud take de sofa in Davids sittin room n push it on te its front n it became a mini goalpost frame, n we had a childs size sponge football.

102

Dan tried te take a shot at the sofagoal n walloped iz foot on de wall, breakin iz toe. Another time we wer playin football at night in de block n he wuz chasin down an opponent n ran neck first in te an unseen clothes line dat wuz tied between two poles, whipped backwards n belted de back uv iz head on the stone ground, givin himself a concussion.

On Christmas Eve he stretched for a box uv Roses te go wit iz cuppa tea n tipped a kettle uv boilin water down on te iz unshoed foot, scaldin it. He wuz playin a match in de seven a side football tournament on de pitch in ODevany n had iz ankle broken by a nasty tackle from de Sheriff St teams hatchet man Bingo Walters, n wuz back on de crutches for a few months.

He strolls inte de block one day, Georgie, Jimmy, Liam n me er loungin der. He shows us dese singles n albums hes got: Outhere brothers, UB40, East Seventeen, n he tells us dat he stole dem from HMV music shop in town. Nunuv us believed him, he had money aniz parents wud buy um stuff if he wanted it, why wud he rob CDs?

So I sez te um,

Tell ya wot, I/ll go inte town wit ya tomorrow, we/ll go te HMV n ya can show me how ya done it, stroke a few more CDs yeah?

He agreed, instead uv ownin up dat he just wanted te look cool or impress us.

So wer in HMV on Henry Street. Dans goin around pickin up CDs n shovin dem down de front uv iz tracksuit bottoms n tuckin iz top over dem, n Im sayin

Here grab dat one, take dat one, great song dat.

But Im not stealin anyting, fuck dat. Hes taken CDs like he owns de place, like dis is iz private collection, like its a fuckin free gift store n hes doin wit such nonchalance dat I start te believe dat he might be a master shop-lifter after all, Dan Carr de big time stroker. De thought quickly exits me mind as we stroll out de shop, n a big arm uv a huge security guard comes from behind us n takes Dan by de shoulder, nicked, dragged back inte de shop by de scruff uv iz neck. I keep on strolin out de door, real casual, seen as Im not a dozy cunt who picks up CDs and walks out de door without payin for dem, like. De silly fucker got a JLO for iz foolish stunt, aniz Ma n Da wer called inte de shop, a total fuckin embarrassment for dem.

Another time, Sam Kelly a girl from de blocks he wuz mad about, n pestered all de time, sendin letters, askin te dance at de disco, but shes always got a fella on de go, so he cant get anywer wit her, one day she agrees te meet him n den hes off wit her every night for two weeks, deyre goin off around de backers, in de pramshed, de park anywere dey can. one night Liam says

Duzzen she go out wit Dennis Clarke?

She did but Dennis wuz on holiday in Santa Ponsa wit iz family for two weeks. Wen Dennis got back, Sam just went back wit him like her n Dan never even spoke te one another, like she didden even know Dan existed.

So wer perched on de balcony uv de block n we see Sam n Dennis come along lover linked on a romantic walk, neckin each other, loved up te fuckin eyeballs.

104

Dan strides down de stairs n goes over n starts tryin te claim dat Sams iz bird now n tells Dennis dat Sams been suckin iz cock for de last fortnight, shes havin nunuv it, says Dans full uv shit, de two boys square up for a bit like two stags, we go down n grab Dan n Sam takes Dennis by d arm n takes um out uv de block. Eventually Sam ownd up, but claimed dat it wuz only one night n she gave inte Dans persistent cajolin n harassin, dat she wuz lonely n she imagined it wuz Dennis wen she had Dans cock in her mouth n dat Dan kept at her for de rest uv de time Dennis wuz away, dat he wuz a stalker, uv course Dennis believed iz girl.

It ended badly once again for unfortunate Dan, Dennis n him had an arranged fight te sort it out, up in de park, which ended wit Dan havin a lump on de side uv iz head, a busted lip n a black eye, as he ran at Dennis, flailin wildly n throwin air punches, Dennis picked him off wit five or six good clean shots n dropped Danny boy te de deck n finished de fight wit a kick te de face. Den Liam n me stepped in n put an end te de beaten, Hes had enough, leave it out Dennis, no kickin wen sumones down, cmon now. Dennis backed off n him n Sam kissed n walked off tegether.

Dennis had nutting but a sore hand from punchin Dans poor thick head. We took Dan home, iz Ma answered de door, What now, Jaysus sake Dan, look at ya, get in der n get cleand up.

Altho we all found Dans misfortunes funny in our teenage boys way. Georgie, took pleasure in dem, he found it hilarious dat Dan got beaten up, said he deserved it for bein a tick cunt anyway. He resented Dan for havin, two parents, a Da who worked, for havin money n new runners n girls dat wanted te suck iz cock.

Maybe we all wer a little jealous uv Dan? Georige n Jimmys Ma had fucked off, my Da wuz dead, Liam never even met iz Da, n we shared de bond uv a one parent family home, a bond Dan didden share wit us.

So, by de next summer der wuz a split in de gang n we no longer hung around wit Dan.

Georgie convinced uz dat Dan wuzzen wunna us, he didden live in de blocks, he lived in a house beside de blocks. Pure bullshit uv course, it wuz still a corpo house n Dans Mas family wer raised in ODevaney. Dan took it on de chin n moved on te new friends dat suited him better anyway.

We seen less n less uv David too, he hooked up wit a girl dat lived out in Clondakin n spent most uv iz time der n soon fell in wit a new crowd uv friends, n he fell in love wit de youngone n she got pregnant, dey wer both sixteen years old. Weed see him now n again, heed call inte smoke a splif wit us but he wuz no longer wunna de main players uv our gang. It wuz Georgie, Jimmy, Liam n me for now.

School ends / Adult stirrins

I wuz allowed te drink alcohol n smoke hash in de house by Ma now. She cudden stop me if she wanted te, anyway.

Me bedroom became de centre uv our lives, de meetin spot. De hangout area. De place wer we left de hash n drink. I hung a dart board up on de wall, n we had a monster sized two hundred card deck uv cards dat wuz made up uv many decks, n we played our own nuts version uv switch, wit so many twos uv all suites n five kings uv hearts, sumone wud be on der last few cards n den a two goes down n bang, bang, bang, bang n its Pick up thirty five. Jimmy wud often come in wit a King uv hearts or a Jack stolen from a deck belongin te a friend or family member.

De winter months went like dis: Georgie, Jimmy, Liam n me, gettin stoned, playin cards n darts, listenin te music every night. Georgie n me gettin drunk wen we had de chance te on a Friday. Shauny wud drop in on occasion pissed, a bag uv cans under iz arm te share wit us, askin everyone te take turns gettin um in a headlock te see who cud holdum der de longest or heed be on de dry n wud come in all fidgety, a ten spot uv hash for de room te smoke n heed role joints wit shakin hands three or four in quick succession, talk serious talk about work aniz bird. On an even rarer night David wud visit, iz hair gettin longer aniz face thinner each time he called in. Football durin de day if it wuzzen too cold or too wet.

Standin around de blocks lookin at girls. Waitin for a robbed car te come on te de pitch n watch as it screeched up n down de pitch doin handbrake turns at reckless speeds. De Garda wud come roarin in, in der high powered cars, n everyone wud leggit te different

107

hidin places or scarper home, if de Garda caught sumone-even if dey wer only watchin de car- deyd get a good kickin n brought down te de Bridwell station for de night. Other times weed play sum video games on me Sega mega drive or Liams PC. Saturday wuz football day, listenin te it on de radio, n watchin *match uv de day* on *BBC* at 10:30 at night.

Music became a massive ting for us n we wer huge Bob Marley n Oasis fans. Bob had always been der since I wuz born n every workin or lower class boy in de world knows n loves Bob, hes de Black musical prophet uv de underprivileged de world over, iz image as present as Christ or Buddha. Oasis wer our band, hard, cocky, loud, young n new. Brash n up for it, n we belted out songs like *Shakermaker, Cigarettes n alcohol n Supersonic* wen we wer high. Soon de winter turned te summer.

I got out uv school -witout too much damage done- after sittin de leavin cert n got a small time job fillin petrol n washin cars at an *Esso* station in Amiens St.

I wuz paid two pound an hour n tips, I stole bars uv *Cadburys* chocolate te make up for de cheapness uv de bosses. Most uv de time I sat on me hole on a wooden stool outside de shop, day dreamin about sex n more n better ways te get out uv me head, listenin te music on a *Sony walkman* I bought dat Summer. It wuz a borin as hell job, waitin for cars or trucks te come in te fill or wash, most uv the other guys dat worked der wer so uninterestin dat I wont bore ya wit der names or generic faces or bland personalities.

I spent most uv me wages on hash n cans for Georgie n me (he said he wuz waitin te get on de dole n had no intention uv ever workin). Sum people, includin iz own relations said dat I shudden keep buyin him cans, dat he wuz a bum, but fuck dem, dey knew nutting uv friendship or Georgie n me, I wanted te get drunk wit me best mate, dats dat n we did at least three nights a week n always on a Friday n Saturday.

I stuck at de job for a few months, got sum new clothes: *Adidas* tracksuit tops, Levi jeans, white n black trainers. N a ticket te see Oasis live in Cork, I went wit a few guys from school dat I thought wer alright, dey wer me posh friends on de side, two brothers, Ken de fat one wit a mouth full uv spit wen he spoke n Edward de thin one who wuz prematurely bald, a short dark wavy haired good lookin bloke called Tim from Dorset St flats n Matt Dooley a six foot two ginger bollox always makin jokes n cud drink all day n night n stay standin up. Dey wer fun guys, n had good taste in music, went te de pub, chased girls wit confidence, me block friends didden go de pub, never had de cash, or looked too young or too wild te get in.

De Oasis concert wuz in Paric Ui Chaoimh in Cork. We got de train at 8:30 in de mornin, I had a small plastic money bag wit twenty joints n ten one skinners in it, a small block uv hash, a bag uv Fosters cans, a rucksack wit clothes, money n a ticket te de gig.

De train wuz full uv excited, rowdy teenagers n early twentys boys who wer all dressed like de Gallaghers or Damon Albarn from Blur, de girls wer mostly wispy wit tight clothes, sum had short indie hair cuts or bigger girls wit cleavage on show, der wer lots uv guitars, Oasis n Beatles songs played n sung along loudly, *Adidas* clothes n trainers n lots uv booze n drugs n crisps n sandwiches.

We pitched our tents for de night at de campsite n we proceeded te get smashed off our faces wit a gang uv other fans, chattin up any girls dat came our way n we fed ourselves on fast food n packed ham sambos. We strutted n strided our way tru Cork City wit thousands uv our own generation uv hip, young, sexy music lovers, all tegether te hear n see our band play live on a stage in front uv us, fuck Woodstock n fuck shite Boybands n EuroDance hits, dis wuz wer de cool fuckers wer. I felt de movement uv us all like a wave uv cock sure energy, me eyes kept fallin on more n more beautful people, slim ones n stout ones, tall ones n small ones, drunk n stoned ones, mad ones, friendly ones, stropy ones, posh ones n common ones, all uv dem a fuckin gorgeous mass uv lovers, n it wuz a blazin hot day, I had a can uv *Fosters* in me hand n a spilf hangin from me lips, it wuz fuckin perfection n de scene spoke te me wit a wink in its eye sayin

Come on lad, get wit it, feel it inside ya, know wot ya want, now take it.

Finally de concert came n it wuz a blured rush uv tunes, alcohol spllin, screamin songs, bad dancin, n in de middle of it all I went off wit a girl who tasted like *Wrigleys* Spearmint chewin gum n Tim wuz wit her mate n she tasted uv de same gum. We danced n sang wit de massive crowd all uv us swayin, arms around each other, in awe at our manc-mad for it heroes, de climax, Liam Gallaghers voice shrill n cool as fuck, singin Shake a long wit me, shake a long wit yoouuuu. N we shook n sang, n puked n swaggered full uv dreams n hash n burgers n mint gum tastin girls n guitar riffs, n ringin in our ears, te our tents in de hot n humid summer night in Cork n slept like lambs under de moon.

I turned eighteen a week after de gig, I left de job n went on de dole like a good block boy. I still didden know wot de fuck I wanted te do or be. I didden want anyting except te get stoned wit Georgie n de boys n wake up at two in de afternoon n wank off n play music loud n watch football n play games on Charlos *Playstation* wit him. But der wuz a stirin in me from de streets uv Cork n de Singer on de stage.

De metamorphosis uv Beatzer

Iz right shoulder has a tattoo on it dat says *100% Irish Beef.*

Left Shoulder has a scar from wen he fell out uv a robbed jammer.

Six foot two inchs tall, lean n muscular like a middleweight boxer.

Face square n bony, eyes er brown, forehead wrinkled.

Topless, another scar across iz stomach, got stabbed in a fight.

De pitch is full uv glass n piss stains, de remains uv fires.

Hes got a bag uv deals in iz underpants, tucked under iz sack.

He drinks from a two litre uv *Old English* cider, belches loudly.

De pitch is surrounded by dark energies, ghosts uv dead boys who crashed cars n motorbikes in de flats, junkies dat OD/d, Beatzer cant see any uv dem,

but feels de grime, loves de grime in iz hair n bones.

Smokes a joint, blows Os in de wind, throws stones at de goal post.

Dances te iz radio, house music.

De pitch is dirty, empty cans, dog shit, spit, blood stains.

He walks up n down, callin out te passers by, whistles, looks for people dat owe um, he might bash wunna dem if its been too long.

Beatzer de king uv de pitch.

Kids play football, he watches dem, hes at every party dat ends der.

Its iz Garden uv Eden, hes de Jehovah uv de pitch.

Beatzer, grew der like a stinkin flower, loves it der.

Beatzer n de pitch, heed fuck it if cud, heed make it iz queen.

Fuckin hell I wuz outta me box last night. Fuckin great night. On de pitch, radio out, tunes pumpin, bag uv cans. Smoked a lump uv blow n ran around in me nip for a bet, twenty blips in me sky rocket yup yup. Remember bein de last one on de pitch outta me bin, lyin on me back in de spinners.

Ive sum head on me now tho. Only ting for dat is a little jog around de pitch, do about twenty laps, just te get de air in de lungs den a hundred press ups. Me bag uv cans, crack wunna dem, batter burger outta de chipper, few chips, loads a salt n vinegar, all set te go for another night on de pitch. Fuckin love it I do, I mean wot else wud ya do, watch fuckin telly, me bollix, get a job, fuck dat, go de pictures, too far, birds, do yer fuckin head in. Im not a fuckin faggot or anyting, anybody start sayin anyting like dat, have te, give ya de slaps, ya know me, I dont let anyone get smart wit me, who de fuck am I even talkin te? Wer am I? Awh yeah, Im Beatzer, Im on de pitch, Im de fuckin king uv de pitch, yup yup yup!

Beatzer on de pitch, its winter, its freezin, he has no top on, hes wearin de same tracksuit bottoms since spring but he duzzen smell, he drinks a can, smokes a joint dat never burns down or goes out, does five hundred press ups, eats a batter burger from de same brown bag every time. Beatzer on de pitch, its Summer now n he still wears de same bottoms, he still duzzen smell uv sweat.

He sees Kenny Thomson, walkin by n shouts at him

Kenny, wots de story wit ya bud?

Kenny looks around n rubs iz eyes n shakes iz head, *Beatzer?*

Shakes iz head again n looks right tru Beatzer, walks over te de pitch, looks around. Beatzer is standin right in front uv him

Kenny, ya dope, wot de fuck er lookin around for? Give it over will ya? KENNEY YA PRICK, I/LL FUCKIN MILL YA, YER FREAKIN ME OUT! Beatzer swings a punch, it goes tru Kenny n he feels a shudder, pretends its de wind, walks away.

Beatzer runs after him but he cant get past de white lines uv de pitch/he panics/he screams/a Gloopting puts iz arms around him. *Come now Beatzer, back to the pitch, drink your cans, eat your burger, dance to the radio, remember youre Beatzer the king of the pitch.* De can drops from iz hand, he crushes it wit iz foot, picks up de bag uv cans throws dem over de railins uv de pitch, on iz knees, hands turn black, fingers grow long n swarm about like vipers, feet fall off, legs stick tegether n became one, back arches torso husks, a black hood sprouts from de back uv iz neck, shrouds iz head n face, eyes turn red, voice becomes a whisper. Beatzer drifts across te de other glooptings n forgets dat hes Beatzer in de night in de blocks. De block is dark, walls dark n oozin a black goo. A gang uv youths drinkin cans n bottles uv *Budweiser* n smokin Joints. Wunna dem pours a sup on de pitch for Beatzer de old king uv de pitch.

De bloom uv art

One day I wuz submerged by a dank wave uv no money, no sex, no idea uv wer I wuz goin, wot I waned te do, wot I cud do. Music wuz de ting dat

114

made me feel truly alive. It wuz religious, it took me deep inte duende. I had dis urge te rise out uv de drownin dankness, prompted by Georgie n me goofin in iz bedroom one day listenin te de radio n diggin de music n de words uv *Slide Away* by Oasis n he says

I wonder how do dey write a song, like how do dey do it?

N in a moment uv supreme confidence n knowin I replied,

I wudden say its dat hard te be honest.

Georgie burst out laughin at me n I smiled at de absurdness uv me statement, but again I said,

Nah man, Im tellin ya, I dont think it wud be dat hard.

I realised later on dat night wen I thought about it, dat we wer talkin about de words uv de songs more din de music.

So wit dis feelin dat for me at least it wudden be dat hard te write lyrics/poems, dis feelin dat wuz insistently bangin on at me since I said wot Id said n de stirn uv de voice in de street in Cork. Den dis urgin from witin n from outside simultaneously, dis feelin n dis urgin, insistin n pressin, throbbin n pulsatin in me n at me, I went n bought a copy n pen n headed te de Phoenix park te write n climbed up de steps uv de monument n wrote a little poem about de nature surroundin me, me feelins, about music n how I wuz sumhow bein thought sumting about life that had previously been unknown te me. De otherworld wuz breakin tru. A theophany called Art!

I felt a release, a spontaneous rapture, de dank n pain had just been taken out uv me body n lifted away. I felt powerful n renewed by dis act uv creativity n de Sea-gulls n doves appeared in de sky in a huge flock squawkin a song n swirlin in mad mystic patterns n glooptings shuddered in de dank regions n de gargoyles roared all inte de night at de moon n de blocks quaked in der foundations n love flooded me body n I wuz hooked on dis here pen-work.

I filled up pages n pages uv copies n notebooks wit sentence after sentence. Poems n song lyrics n dey came out uv me in great reams full uv anger, lust, joy, melancholy, angst, confidence, wild insights at all hours uv de day n night, n after a while dey started te sound good te me ears n Georgie n me one night de two uv us wer der drinkin, sittin on de armchairs n I said te um once again in a moment uv sheer confidence n assurance dat it shocked me dis time,

I think sumday a lot uv people er gonna read dese words I write, ya know?

N he didden laugh or snigger or balk n he replied wit a sincere heart,

Yer right, dey will, Im tellin ya man, yiv got talent, really ya have?

So I wuz hooked even more, I had so much te say n it all came tru me again brilliant torrents uv it, I cud hardly get de pen te move fast enough.

Pages n pages, line after line, copybook after copybook.

Not one page or line uv dose days is left now, tho

116

pages I still fill. Dese pages. Dis book, for you Georgie, n for you too up der, sweet reader, dis is for you.

Thanks Georgie for lettin me know I wuz good.

Voices from de Blocks

Name: Georgie Teeling.
Year: 1998.
Place: Stairs uv wunna de Luxury Blocks, ODevaney Gardens.

Its always de same, always de fuckin same, life, shite, all bollox n shite!

Ya get a kiss n think yer gonna get more. Walk us home Georgie. Get us a can Georgie. Den she takes dat wanker back n its fuck ya Georgie, dont come near me Georgie. Ya need te geta job Georgie, I dont wanna a job, I hated school, I can hardly buy sumting in de shop witout bein paranoid. Im no good at anyting, Ive no ambitions either, fuck all dat I just want te be happy for fucksake, just get sum girl te love me n fuckin get drunk tegether n have sex, pssshhtt, yeah right, I cant even get dat, so fuck it, so wot anyway, nunuv it matters, so Im gonna sit here on me own n get wrecked cuz ders nutting else te fuckin do in dis world, all dis shite!

I wudda looked after her, done anyting, shes gorgeous, love, bollox, supposed te be great, yeah right, it makes ya worse.

Wot a life, Ma fucks off, Das a drunk, Im short n half blind, ugly, weird fuckin curly hair, I hate it all. Another can so, pick up dat razor blade, Pain rush, takes de pain outta de head, cut me arm, feel de razor, der ya go Ma, der ya go Da, der ya go world, der ya go bitch, der ya go fuckers, der ya go world, fuck ya. Im gonna drink dis last can, den go down de road wer all de snobby pricks live n smash sum rich wankers car up, see wot she thinks about dat, see wot dey all think about dat, den Im gonna get sum Vodka, drink dat n head for de park for de night, lets see if anyone actually cares, cuz I dont, I dont fuckin care wot happens te me anymore in dis life, shite n bollox te it all.

Rooner in n out

Summer time again.

I wuz a long term dole boy. Me hair wuz a shaggy mop uv curls; I looked like Richard Ashcroft from De Verve n peacoked around like I wuz in de video for *Bittersweet Symphony*.

De next great friendship came wen I met Luke Rooney. It came tru drugs. I wanted sum he cud get dem. Jimmy wuz in *FAS* wit Luke. Der wuz a drought on n all ordinary suppliers in de blocks wer out uv hash.

Except for Heath, a skinny, ginger, ascetic, Doberman faced guy, not originally from de blocks, a blow-in. He wuz a paranoid coke n valume taker. Had dis elaborate set up wit de few people he wud sell te in de blocks.

Yid ringum up, n ask

Have ya any uv dose T-shirts?

Heed say Yeah, how many do ya want?

If ya wanted a five spot yid say five, a ten spot ten T-shirts n so on.

Rooner cud get dese T-shirts. I had cash n wuz just mad for a few new T-shirts.

So Jimmy n me went around n asked Rooner te get us sum T-shirts n said weed throwum one for himself, wink, wink. Dat wuz how Rooner became wunna us.

Rooner lived wit iz foster family de Browns. He wuz found sleepin on de stairs uv de blocks at de age uv fifteen. He ran te de blocks. He ran from a Da wit quick fists n steel toe capped shoes n a Ma who cudden get out uv bed from de pain uv beatins n de shame uv wine.

Iz collar bone smashed, iz brothers n sisters separated n housed around de country. Luke Rooney a slim, mallet headed, limb swayin comedian, a maelstrom uv anger n fear, an artist uv sufferin n madness. A survivor. A thick browed philosopher uv pain n glee. Luke Rooney, who appeared on de stairs uv de block wit an aura uv dark energy n flame uv blue light. Came from Tallaght te ODevaney.

De brown family wer a typical blocks family: Da n Ma who thought dey wer still teenagers n liked te smoke blow n do Es, have big parties wit der son Jimbo aniz mates, DJ decks n house music pumpin. Had a menagerie uv pets: Dogs, cats, a lizard n a cockatoo. De Da, big Jimbo, played de guitar badly n told stories uv rock n roll dreams. Liked te believe he wuz a tuff guy, dat he wuz dead wide te life, dat he knew how te a kill a man wit a blow te de windpipe or a secret judo rear choke, dat iz pot belly n flabby arms wer muscles. He wuz a good soul underneath all de bravado n bullshit. Loved iz wife n kids. Worked at shit jobs all iz life te pay de bills. Shared iz drugs wit iz mates. Took in thick browed Rooner n tried te be a surrogate Da te him.

Rooner wuz happy te have a bed n food n smokes, but complained all de time uv unfairness, uv bein treated differently din de other kids, dishes te wash, messages te do, drugs te buy, beds te make, dogs te be brought for walks. Rooner n de family brown. De flat wuz ever noiseful, barkin, meehowin, guitars, beats, fights, all mythical in me mind now.

Rooner is in de kitchen uv de Brown flat, big hands in de warm water washin dishes indignantly.

Wash de dishes Luke, clean de toilet Luke, go on a message Luke, here Luke heres yer twenty pound for yer birthday, here little Jimbo heres yer fifty pound. Its not fair, dey get paid off de government for me, *for* me, its my money, its not for hash n cans. State uv dat guitar dey got me, a piece uv shit, Jimbos one is well nicer. He duzzen know dat I play it wen hes out n I learned te play *Wonderwall*, hah, cant wait te see iz face wen I play te whole song, ya have a better guitar but I can play mine, ya cant play a fuckin note, hah!
Soon as Im done here Im goin around te Kennys, get stoned wit de lads, listen te sum tunes, get out uv dis gaff, I hate dis gaff.

Fat Liam is in iz Bedroom, a boy in a man size body, beached on iz bed, eatin a hot-dog, countin iz money.
Lovely, enough te get a twenty box uv *Superking*. I/ll keep dat two pound for popcorn later, munchies. I hope dat Georgies in a good mood. A bit uv cards, darts n a smoke, ahh yeah, den back up here for eleven or me Ma/ll go mad, school in de mornin, ahh summer hols start next week, cant wait.

Georgie n Jimmy amblin side by side, twin like, heads down, stick in hand uv Georgie, smoke in Jimmys.
Is dat a smoke or joint?

122

A smoke ya blind bastard.

Only askin, ya little prick.

Im only tellin ya, ya little sap ya.

I have te pay Tony wot I owe um.

How much do ya owe um?

All uv it.

All uv it? Ya owe um yer whole labour?

Yep, well Ive a tenner, enough de get cans for tonight n tomorrow.

Jimmy shrugs iz shoulders n laughs.

How much hash did ya buy dis week?

Not much, only me whole *Fas* money, hahahaha.

Hahahaha, Kenny shud be finished iz dinner now.

Get in n get a joint n a game uv darts. I/ll follow ya around after I get me cans.

Im sittin on de worn green armchair, drinkin tea, smokin a joint, n readin a poem I wrote, I hear de knock on de window n know its time for de ritual te begin.

De walls uv de bedroom er covered in posters uv rock stars: Oasis, Bob Marley. A huge wunna John Lennons head, long hair n a full beard, Yokos head is at iz shoulder *Dey look just like two gurus in drag, Sid Vicious* in black n white, chest slashed n bleedin, pretendin te play iz bass, Alicia Silverstone posin topless, hash leaves chained te a wall, a slogan underneath: *Free de weed.*

Behind de posters ders weird white wallpaper turned yellowish brown from smoke, it has little red, blue, yellow n green spots on it. A thick cannabis cloud uv smoke fills de room.

Im puffin on a rasta sized joint n throwin darts at de board. An enormous poster uv Liam n Noel Gallaghers heads covers one side uv de wall. Ders holes dotted about der faces like acne from all de bad shots uv darts dat have struck dem.

Georgie is sat at de top uv de bed wit a pillow propped against iz back, readin an old beat n yellowed book uv Bob Dylans lyrics, underlinin de names uv de ones he likes best.

Doyler is sittin at de end uv de bed smokin a joint n playin cards wit Jimmy whos sat at de edge uv de bed waitin for Doyler te throw down a card n pass de joint te um.

Ders a fat black stereo on top uv a pink painted wooden stool, De Doors album *La Woman* plays loudly. Doyler n me turn n look at each other, joints in hand n sing in a Jim Morrison voice *Mr. Mojo Risin, Got te keep on risiinnnggg*, simultaneously we take long drags from de joints n den hand dem over te Georgie n Jimmy. Ders a knock on de window. I pull back de curtains te see who it is.

Its Liam.

De Big lump says Georgie.

Liam comes in, a big silly grin onum,

Alright boys.

Alright, Liam.

Wots up ya big lump?

Liam sits down on wunna de old green armchairs, iz fifteen stone body crashin inte it. Have ya any smokes Liam? I ask as I throw darts hittin de twenty each time.

Yeah, a fresh twenty *Superking* large.

Ah lovely, weve a quarter we got off Beatzer, wer sorted for de night so.

No wer not, weve no skins lads, Doyler says.

Ah Prrrriicckkk says Georgie puttin down de Dylan book as he does.

I hold de darts up te de light n say

Only one ting for it so lads, game a darts te see who goes te de shop for skins, Round de board, yeah?

Everyone gets ready te play hopin its not dem who loses n has te go te de shop on der own in de bitter cold te get skins.

Round de board is essentially a trainin game, aimed at gettin de player used te hittin each number, includin its double n treble, te know de board.

Each player begins at de number one, n as he hits each number he moves te de next, den de doubles, den de trebles, n finally te finish he must hit de ring n den de bulls-eye. De player throws three darts in an attempt te hit iz number, if he hits de number dat hes on wit iz third dart he gets three more darts, if he misses on de third, de next player enters te throw. De top players in de gang wer Shauny if he wuz der, den Jimmy n me, Georgie dependin on iz mood aniz alcohol intake, too much or too little aniz throw wud be off, Tommy dependin on iz drug intake, at de bottom wuz Liam n Rooner n invariably it wud be one from Georgie down who had te go de shop or make de tea as loser, on rare occasions, wunna de top dogs wud have an off round n have te take an underdogs place, wit de other tops laughin n ascertin der superiority in de room.

De game dat night went in its proper order, Jimmy n me round n hittin de bull first, smirkin n raisin brows te de rest, den smugly sittin in relaxed posses on de bed. Georgie comin in third wit a squint at de bulls-eye n a yerrhoo.

Tommy wit a yes, n hard luck te de other lads, n a grin te us, safe n tru te de sit-down. Only Liam n Rooner left, in a two man shoot-out.

Both get down te de ring n de bull at de same time, Rooner first up, throws iz first dart it pings de steel uv de ring n bounces back off de board n lands on de floor, makin everyone flinch. De second dart lands in de ring.

Rooner clenches iz fist n mutters hee-hah. De third dart flys n lands wide uv de bull.

Liams throw. First dart bang hits de ring. A dopey smile. De second dart, ring again, everyone leans forward te see, Rooner gets up close, followed by Laim,

No. Last dart, soars n nestles between de others right inte de bull. Game over. Liam gos red, n screams inte Rooners face Yessssss. Everyone laughs, except Rooner, he grins sarcastically, n says threw iz teeth

No bother, I/ll go de shop, its only down de road

anyway, bitta exercise ya know what I mean Liam Huh? I/ll make a five skinner n light it up soon as Im back, not too bad really, heh-heh.

Rooner burned like a bonfire, iz eyes wer *Chainsaw massacre* slasher movies. Rooner beaten by iz Da, on de floor in tears. Hospitalised, homeless, n broken. Thick browed. Iz mind a tornado uv razors. Iz body a train crash. Rooner jokes in de blocks. He knows its a dream. A narcissistic Buddha in de fields uv de backers. A maestro on de guitar. De greatest musician Ive ever know or seen play in de flesh in front uv me, still te dis day n I seen a multitude uv dem, n not sum big ol rock star a million miles away up on de big stage, huge above de masses, wer ya cant see wot de hell der playin, n its all just big drunken hysterical gropin n strainin, no, Im talkin in front uv ya, der wit breath slow n loud as dey play, sweat on der top lip, de sermon delivered wit delicacy n rapture. Rooners de greatest I seen or heard like dat. De greatest.

Rooner, sleepin under bushes, sleepin on stairs, sleepin in detention centre, hard mattress bed, held down n beat for bein different, not a delinquent like de rest, just thrown in der becuz der wuz nower else te put him.
Poor Rooner. Mad Rooner. Anger spewin from iz street preacher mouth, Ahab like in iz doldrums. A poet/philosopher who never read a book,
I just cant do it, I dont know why Kenny, sumting, sum block, wont let me read books, I cant sit n

127

concentrate on dem, its music for me man, music is de key?

Rooner, walks like Liam Gallagher, smirks at anyone who duzzen. Flips out in great reams uv tragicomedy scenes, eyes red n teeth yellowin, smokin since he wuz twelve years old. A Dickens character, a Shakespearian actor in contorted revelation, de truth all over de place, cover it up Rooner, its too much for us te take.

Rooner beclouded in de blocks, stoned, stone mad, hidin in de trees, KO/d on raw whiskey shots on Christmas day, asleep under iz cheap guitar, mop haired, crazy brained. Rooner n me, listen for de notes,

Did ya hear it? Just der, de little note, in de mix?

Yeah, man, dats it man, great mood te it, beautiful flow.

De rest uv de gang look around n laugh, no clue wot wer on about. Rooner n me, know all about de notes in de mix, weve learned te hear a new, n speak a secret language, all nods n nudges, meet ups an stay backs unknown te de rest.

Words all whispered n dreams all shared in de 3 am stony haze. We saunter n throw shapes de same way. We walk de way Achilles n Odysseus wud. De poor boys in de block chained te de walls wit cans in der hands laugh n snort, make funny comments wen we pass,

Look at de boys, hah, get yer hair cut will yiz.

Poor boys, afraid uv another boys hair. Look at der chains, deyre in love wit der own chains. Look at dem rattlin it. Rooner n me walk de length uv Dublin inte every block te find hash, speed, Es.

Rooner cant stand te stay in de Browns anymore, iz head is killinum, iz brain is burnin, iz paranoia is perfect, in iz mind he is murderin everyone who annoys him.

Hes ripin out livers an eaten dem, hes smashin heads off walls, hes pullin off fingernails wit a pliars.

I have te get out Kenny, I need te breathe again, Im suffocatin here man.

Rooner n me traipse around Dublin for a day te find iz social worker, n we do, n Rooner finds iz way out uv ODevaney, te a nice new house in Phibsboro wer await him more unruly n unloved boys te talk, dream n fight wit.

Rooner who left me lonely in de blocks.

De rain uv a June shower turns te a light drizzle, fallin on our heads, were wearin black *Levi* jeans n *Gortex* jackets, Rooner has iz hood pulled up on iz head, Im wearin a black woolly hat wit a *Liverpool FC* crest on it. We march fast, throwin shapes tewards Broom Bridge in Finglas.

Cool its stopped, I/ll take dis hood off me boulder says Rooner.

Freeeeee de big boulder, Ha-ha, better take dis hat off too, less likely te get pulled by de Garda wit it off.

Yeah, ridiculous dat a hat shud get ya pulled over Kenny, but true.

129

Walkin over de bridge I kick an empty plastic Coke bottle as if takin a penalty in de world cup final, aimin for an electricity pole in front uv me. De bottle hits its target.

Yeaaahhh! Good shot Kenny, man.

Ahh, easy enough shot, its a big aul pole, wot does Big Jim want ya te get um out here?

A ten spot.

Take enough for a joint off dat, n de same wit de two deals weve te get for Liam n Tommy, n two deals for us, grand.

Yeah good, ya need a good bita hash wen yer doin de speed.

Yeah, ya do, n we/ll keep sum for de end uv de night te help us sleep.

Dem bits we take off der deals will do for dat, stash dem in yer pocket till de rest uv de lads go home.

Oh, dats wot I intended te do Rooner, dats exactly wot I intend te do, me aul mucker.

Rooner lights iz sixd cigarette uv de journey as we walk tru a tunnel dat leads in te a field wer an assortment off drug dealers, boys on bikes, n gangs uv men drinkin cider from glass bottles er a late 20th century landscape portrait n de sun hangs like a huge fiery red Turneresque cliché in de sky.

Rooner n me tryin te look tuff but casual as we walk over te two dodgey cunts.

Alright lads, have yiz any hash?
Yeah, wot yiz lookin for?
Give us five ten spots, will ya?

130

Five tens, hold on der bud

says, a small fat fella uv about twenty five wit a mousey moustache n greasy brown hair, he bends down n takes up a chunk uv grass dat wuz coverin a hole in de ground filled wit wot looks like hundreds uv deals individually wrapped in tin foil n picks up five uv dem n hands dem te me.

Nice one I say as I hand a fifty pound note over.

Is der any one around wit speed? asks Rooner wit a stern mad look on iz face.

Yeah, Mincer has sum, dya know Mincer?

No.

Eh, wer is eeh? Mincer! Miiinnnceeeeeer! De fat-fuck calls out, lookin around as he does. A tall geezer wit a white *Nike* T-shirt n blue *Adidas* track suit bottoms on, walks out from wunna de small gangs uv men drinkin cider n says,

Wha?

De lads er lookin for de dogs lead, have ya got it?

Yeah, he says as he walks across de field.

How many wraps er yiz after boys? asks mincer.

Six says Rooner.

Mincer takes off wunna iz *Nike air max* n removes de bubble, inside is a bunch uv wraps uv speed packed tightly in cling film. Mincer opens de cling film n starts te count de wraps,

One...Two...Three...Four...Fiiivvee...Six, on de button boys, just wot yizer lookin for.

Cool, cool man says Rooner as he takes out three twenty pound notes from iz back pocket n hands dem te Mincer in exchange for de six wraps, concludin our business transactions for de evenin wit de Finglas drug

131

dealers.

De headstone reads *Paul Sullivan, born: 1972, died: 1991, beloved son,* grass grown long around it n a dead bunch uv roses layin at its foot. Rooner n me er sat between two graves, Rooner lights a joint, Im starin at de headstone, n its startin te get dark.

Only nineteen hah, not a long life was it?

No, but dats it, ya have te go wen ya have te go, Kenny.

True, yid hope te live a lot longer din dat tho?

Depends, sum people want te die dont dey?

Yeah, sum people kill demselves like yer man Duggan dat hung himself at de top uv de stairs up de luxuries, remember he wuz found by iz bird swingin outta de light outside de flat?

Yeah dat wuz mad, poor fucker, sumtimes I get dat feelin, ya know dat Kenny, it goes away after a bit, I dont think Id ever do it or anyting, but, ah, ya know life is tuff sumtimes I ...

Ya better fuckin not man, I know wot ya mean tho, all de shit dat goes on, makes ya feel, like hopeless sumtimes, ahh ya seen me goin nuts wit a few drinks in me, rantin n ragin n fightin n shit, dats wot it does te me sumtimes ya know? But man, I feel like Im gettin tru all dat since I start writin down words, de poems n lyrics, n music it fills me up, makes me feel strong, ya know?

Yeah man, fuck yeah, dats good, cool, cool man, yeah, cool, yeah I love dat shit, de writin, its good shit man.

I know man, n ya have de guitar, yer gettin better man, all we need te do is keep doin wot wer doin get better n better, den get sum more people involved n dats it, get a band together n blow dis fuckin town away, fuckin give it te dem all straight man, wot dya think?

Yeah man, yeah, sounds good te me, but we need te break away from all de rest uv dem, Im tellin ya Kenny, dey dont think like dis, n dem flats, we have te get out uv der n den we can do it, den we can make sumting, do sumting, fuck dem, heh-heh.

Neither uv us says anyting for a moment, both lost in a day dream about bein rock stars, n showin everybody dat wer not worthless, dat in fact wer great men uv genius n style.

De joint gets passed back n forth, Rooner reaches inte iz inside pocket n takes out de wraps uv speed, smilin, he looks at dem den at me,

Dya wanna do one a dese now?

Yeah, fuck it why not? Drop one each, cant snort it here?

Yeah, yeah man, drop one each, have ya anyting left in dat bottle a Coke te wash it down wit?

Yeah, wers iiittttt, ah, der she is.

Takin two wraps n placin dem on de grave, Rooner den very carefully takes two cigarette papers sticks dem tegether vertically, den pours de contents uv one wrap inte de papers, rolls it inte a ball n licks n sticks it tegether makin a homemade tablet, iz dark eyes widen as he drops it inte iz mouth n swallows it wit de help uv sum *Coca Cola*. Repeatin de operation he hands de speedball te me n I gladly down it finishin off de bottle uv Coke.

Drizzly rain starts te fall on our heads n Rooner pulls iz hood over iz large head, I take me black woolly hat out uv me pocket n put it on.

We walk fast towards de gate uv Glasnevin cemetery tramplin on de graves uv de dead wit speedballs eruptin inside our stomachs n slowly releasin elation inte our thin swaggerin bodies.

Rooner who left me in dis lonely block, but wud come again te me, we still had de same dream.

Once, I wrote a song called in de heart uv de city. It wuz de first ting dat really blazed n burned others, it burned Rooner more din de others. It wud burn inte a song wit music played in rehearsal studios, back den it wuz a few words on a page in a note pad, waitin, waitin te burn. I wuz waitin te burn wit de word, Rooner wuz burnin all de time.

Voices from de Blocks

Name: Rooner.
Year: 1998.
Place: Bedroom uv de Byrnes Flat in ODevaney Gardens.

I need hash. I ugh. I fuckin need te get hash now. All dese thoughts n feelins er not good for me. Me Da aniz hands aniz cruel face. Me Ma, I love her but...

Shes just not able te be der for me. Fuckin families. Hmmh. Dont think about it Luke. Just let it go Luke. Dats wot people tell ya. But dey dont know. Hmmh. Dey dont know. Wot its like te see yer Ma so drunk she cant get up off de floor, so drunk she pisses herself, heh-heh.

Wot its like te be held down on de ground n yer Da, yer own Da, stomps on ya. Smashes ya wit iz boot. Breaks yer collar bone. Yer Da smackin de fuck outta yer sisters n brothers, Ugghh. A smoke ill have te do for now. Music. Wers de guitar. Wers joooeeesss guitar. Heh-heh-heh.

Wer er dey? Kenny n Georgie, takin ages te get back from Dinkos. Probably sittin down der, drinkin tea n smokin joints. Smokin joints off uv a deal dat I gave money te. Ahh no bother Luke, no bother dats grand. Just sit here smokin fuckin *John Player* blues n bitin yer nails. Humph. Kenny, hes sound. Hes a bit different, like me. Not sure about dat Georgie fella.

135

Little fucker, looks at me weird sumtimes wit iz squinty eyes. Ha-ha-ha. Yer bein paranoid Luke. Hmmh.

Luke, its Kenny n Georgie at de door for ya, will I send dem in te ya?
Yeah Joe, send dem in.
Lovely. About time. Heh-heh. Time te get stoned.
Alright Lads? Did yiz get it? Course yiz did, look at de eyes on yiz.
Ha-ha, here ya mad yoke ya Rooner, get a nice five skinner tegether outta dat man.

Skins. Licked. Smoke ripped. Hash burned n spread. Roll n stick. Roach placed gently. Toke. Puff. Pass. Toke. Puff. Pass. High. Smoke. Fumes. Giggles. Music. Laugh...

De Spider n Liam

Georgie saw it first. Black, eight legged ting, crawlin along de bedroom floor.

He picked up de football from beside iz foot n bounced it in front uv de tiny arachnid, frightenin it te death, de body intact n motinless.

Ha-ha-ha! Georgie laughed n pointed at de spider.
Fuckin hell I said. How dya do dat?
Dont know, dats mad dat is.
Georgie picked up de dead spider carefully, n delicately placed it on top uv an old Tea-kwon-do trophy I had, wer de little fighter had broken off. De spider hung der, de spoils uv Georgies hunt.

Im not sure if it wuz me or Georgie who came up wit de idea, but we both agreed it wud be hilarious if we put de spider inte sumones cup uv tea later on. After sum deliberation we narrowed it down te Jimmy n Liam as both uv dem took three sugars in der tea, n we reasoned dat it wud be good te pile de sugar on top uv de body n stop it floatin te de top.

De decidin factor wuz Jimmys temper, heed go mad n have a little hissy fit.

It wuz poor Liam for de dreadful deed te be played on. Georgie took de spider n put it in an empty match box.

We wer all at de usual bedroom antics: Darts, joints, cards, music, slaggin. Den it wuz de time for de first cup uv tea uv de night. I lost de card game n had te make de tea, Georgie got off wit it. Georgie slyly handed me de match box coffin.

I made de cups uv tea as per de way everyone liked ders, den got te Liams, I opened de match box n toppled de body inte de cup, mounded de three sugars on top n den de tea bag, poured de water on gently, let it brew a little den poured in de milk, I wuz careful te just stir de top, leavin de sugar mound on de remains, I noticed a leg float te de top uv de tea, I pressed it wit me finger n it went back down in de tea.

Everyone wuz slurpin away n chattin n smokin. Liam wuz half way tru iz tea, wen he spit out de leg n said
Ders a hair in me tea.
Georgie busted out laughin n dis made me laugh too.
Wot er yiz up te? said Liam
Nutting.
Nutting, its just de way ya said it.
He took another sup uv iz tea n de carcass rose te de surface like a washed up victim uv de sea n touched Liams lips, he spat n shouted
Wot de fuck is dat? Ya fucker ya he said as he pointed at me.
Its a dead spider, aggghhhhhhaaaaahhhhahahahah said Georgie loudly.
It wuzzen just me Liam, He killedum, it wuz iz idea as well, I swear.
Yer two pricks yiz er.

138

Jimmy n Rooner erupted inte howls n ugghs, n noways, n looked in de cup at de dead body bobin in de small bit uv tea. Liam calmed down n did laugh at de horrible boyish joke, claimin heed get us back sum how, tho he never did.

For weeks, everyone checked der tea before drinkin it, just in case dey may be drinkin dead insect flavoured Lyons tea.

Doyler

Summer, de sun is covered by indigo clouds in de sky above de blocks. A tall, skinny, red haired, charismatic on n off Junkie named Tommy Doyle is on a robbed push bike cyclin inte de block.

Im hangin around de stairs uv de block wit Georgie, Jimmy n Liam. Tommy hooshes de bike onte iz shoulder n trecks up de stairs headin for iz sisters flat on de top balcony. He smells de joint n stops te chat te us, asks us who has de nice blow around here. We share a few contacts witum n pass de joint around, token n chatin shit, he entertains us wit crime n junk fuelled stories.

Dis is how it went for a few weeks until eventually Doyler wuz wunna de gang. A different kind uv member. He wuz a little older, had a girlfriend, a kid n a heroin problem. Been in jail a few times. Looked tuff n scary wit iz tightly cropped hair n tattoos. Gave our little crew more street cred din before.

He loved music n hash like us, every member abided by dose two rules. He came inte me wit bags

139

uv cash one day n said

Hide dat for me Kenny will ya?

No problem, wer did ya get it?

Robbed it outta de hotel Im workin as a kitchen porter in, I took de key te de safe n

brought it in n got a copy made up, den I put the other back inte de office de next day.

So yuv a key te de safe, te get in take wot ya want?

Yep.

Fuckin deadly man.

For a halycon forthnight we had all de cans, hash n pills we cud consume, until Doyler wuz called inte de managers office n serched n he had de key on him, dat wuz dat, Tommy got de boot n wuz back on de dole, only reason de manager didden shop him te de Garda wuz becuz Tommys Ma worked in de hotel for years n de dope felt sorry for her.

Tommy wuz livin in iz sister Lindas wit her anner boyfriend Markey n der kids. Markey wuz a seventeen stone bull, who had a job in *Bargingtown* furniture shop. Markey didden take drugs like de rest uv us. Wuz a wind-up merchant who took pleasure in eatin peoples food off der plate wen they wernt lookin or heed whack de lads in de job hard on de knukles wen dey wer carryin a sofa or coffe table out te a customers car or de back uv a truck, n all manner uv cruelties n practical jokes, fartin in yer face, flikin de back uv yer ear, hidin yer smokes or lighter on ya. He wuz generous, if ever ya needed a lend uv money or a Video or CD, heed have it, n give it, no rush in payin back either, n he wuz a handy man te know if tings got a bit out uv hand on a night out in de boozer, or back-up wuz needed in a scrap. Big Marky Connolly. A stand up guy. Markey n me got inte a few punch-ups in de blocks wit drunk neighbours n wannaby hardmen, even went for each other once or twice, all in good jest or wit strong drink took.

Tommy Doyle sits on de toilet in iz home in Drumalee. Iz Da bangs a fist on de door.

Tommy, wot de fuck er ya doin in der, come on will ya, I need te take a shit,
Wot do ya think Im doin, yer fuckin curry from last night runnin out de both uv our arses.
Tommy finds de vain he wuz lookin for. Punches in de spike, n draws blood n wham de gear hits n Tommys out uv de blocks, no Da bangin on de door te have a shit, no job loss, no girlfriend dumpin him for bein a prick, no young daughter te think about, no six sisters n two brothers, no Ma worried sick, no gang uv mates in ODevaney, no charges hangin over him, nutting, just de solace n non doin uv untime.
Tommy, Tommy, come on will ya.
Eyes open, drool wiped. Cold water splash.
Yeah, yeah da, ready now.
Flush toilet. Mirror look. Eyes pinned. Head te de flats, head te Kennys gaff.

Tommy Doyle walks tru de blocks brown powder in iz blood, hoody on, arms n legs all swingin n dancin. A John player blue in iz mouth, brand new *Nike* runners on. He stops te talk te everyone he

141

meets, he jokes, he smiles, iz voice is like gravel, iz eyes er blue like me Das wer, iz lips er thin, hes a fuckin wingless seraphim lost in a jungle full uv mangy cats n strung out monkeys.

Voices from de Blocks

Name: Mary n Alice.
Year: 1999.
Place: Balcony uv one uv de blocks in O Devaney Gardens.

Giz a light Mary will ya?

Here ya go Alice love. Hows tings wit ya dis mornin?

Ah thanks, not too bad Mary love, dya want wunna dese?

Ah, thanks. Not bad ehh. Hows yer back?

A bit sore, gettin better. Keeps him off me wen hes drunk.

Blessin in disguise so, wha?

Too bleedin right it is. Fat old drunken bastard dat he is, God forgive me.

Its de one ting I dont miss about my Fred te be honest wit ya.

Ah, God rest iz soul, aul Fred. Good man he wuz.

He wuz, he wuz. But sure de lord takes us all wen he wants us Alice.

Oh, he does Mary, dat he does,

Jaysus, I wish heed hurry up n take dat bollix in der.

Ah, Alice, dont say dat now love, ya be sorry if he did now, ya wud.

Sorry, ya must be jokin, Id get de insurance money n off te Benidorm Id go, might get meself a nice Spanish youngfella one night.

Alice Breen, yer a bloody looper so ya er.

Ah here, look who it is, miss la di da, herself, out washin her new windows.

Why duzzen she just move out uv de block, if she can afford new windows n him workin all de hours god sends him, makin a mint so he is, car an all, hmm.

Too mean te move dey er.

Think I/ll treat meself te a snackbox latter for dinner.

I/ll get little Pauly te go up for ya, give me a shout, wen ya need him.

Ah, god bless him, I/ll give him de money for a bag a chips for himself.

Ya will not Mary Burke. He gets enough out uv ya as it is.

N why not, sure isnt he me best neighbours little boy, n a good boy he is, a bag a chips wont break de bank Alice love.

Spoilt ya have him. Spoilt.

Oh, here he is, Whacker Byrne, stumblin in after been out all night.

Shell bate de bleedin head off um, watch.

Oh, dont ya know she will. Screamin match now in a minuet.

Fights like a man, her.

Strong as one too, remember Id dat run in wit her, years ago.

Didden talk te her for two years.

Made up eventually, didden yiz?

144

Yeah, after de little fella died on her.

Ah, yeah, uv course. Poor little ting. De Leukaemia got him didden it?

Awful dat wuz. De little white coffin. Very sad. God takes dose he loves de most de earliest. Ya see, n ya wish death on yer man inside. Be careful wot ya wish for.

Ah I know Mary. Hes an awful man, but de kids love him.

So do you Alice, sure ya wudden have married him if ya didden now wud ya?

Ders Tracy goin te de shops for her smokes. Nice couple her anner man.

Dey are. Tho I heard a little whisper about him de other day.

Did ya? Well spill de beans Alice love, have te keep up on de goss now dont I?

Well, nutting too bad, heard he sells a bit uv smoke ya know?

Smoke?

De hash Mary, ya know de bit uv hash.

Oh right, ahh as long as its not de hard stuff now, I dont mind. Dat other stuff turns dem inte zombies n rob de eyes out yer head dey wud.

Ah, yer right der Mary, we cudden have dat in our block, Id march on iz door meself.

So wud I Alice. So wud I. Weed need yer man in der den wudden we?

Suppose we wud. Ah der handy for sumtings ha-ha.

Wot time is it Alice?

Half one.

Oh, I better go in, Goin for Gold is startin.
Ah go on so. See ya now Mary love.
See ya Alice Love.
Dont forget te give me a shout for Pauly te go for de snaxbox.
I will do. Thanks.

Drug bedroom block

Speed n Es wer de drugs I fell in love wit next. A wrap uv speed swallowed or snorted n yer at it for hours. 7:30 am n were still up. Drinkin de last uv de duty free cans uv *Fosters* lager dat we bought six for a fiver from Tony around de next block. Smokin de last joint te brin us down. Sweatin in de dawn. Horse voiced from singin songs n chaterboxin all night. Den de Es came in n we wer hooked, every weekend we wud get a few pills each, a bag uv cans n a lump uv hash between us. Georgie, Jimmy, Rooner, Tommy aniz brother Stewie n me cramped inte de bedroom:

De stereo booms out De Doors, De Stone Roses, De Verve, REM. No tops on, dancin like natives in a ring in de small space, smoke all around, huggin n cheek kissin. I fuckin love yiz I do. Deepest conversations ya ever had in yer life n right den in de middle uv de most profound moment bang ya forget wot ya wer on about n its gone n ya dont care, ya just spark up another splif n heavens in de room. De world outside duzzen matter, wars dont matter, poverty dont matter, sex dont matter, only dis room n dese people n dis music matters. Cans all over de room, on de bookshelf, on de floor, on de stool, on the arm uv de chair, on de chest uv draws, sum open, sum empty, sum wit a sup taken n left te sit for hrs, noone knows whos drinkin which can, noone cares. Ders joints burnin in de ashtrays, sumones takin twenty mins te get skins together, cant find de lighter, den ya get handed four at once, everyone wants te help, sumone drinks from a can dat has smoke butts n ash in it, they run te bathroom te get sick, everyone gets a bit freaked out for a moment till de pucker walks back in n is fine, everyone checks dat everyone is alright, is everyone buzzin, is everyone up? CDs keep gettin changed before der finished, everyone wants der song played, pls lads put me song on, I need dat tune right now. Time is meaninless. Pain is an illusion.

De come down is a slump in a chair, a jumper on n a jacket zipped up te yer eyes n yogic stillness. Silence like de bottom uv de Universe. Sleep comes up from ya inte yer limbs n tru yer eyes n wraps ya in its embrace. No dreams. No movement. No Blocks.

***

De smoke is thick, three joints er burnin n bein passed around. Cans uv *Dutch Gold* er scattered about: De bookshelf, de floor, de chest uv drawers, Tommy Doyle is drinkin from one n sittin on wunna de green armchairs. Bob Dylans *Subterranean homesick blues* blasts loud tru de air, Im singin

Johnnys in de basement mixin up de medicine, Im on de pavement thinkin bout de government.

I throw a dart at de board it hits de rim uv de bulls-eye bounces back n lands stuck in de floor beside Georgies foot,

Wooahhh! Dat nearly stuck in me foot again!

Rooners playin tab on iz guitar along te Dylans song, iz face intensely concentrated like a gladiator about te deliver a death blow te a fallin opponent, speed runnin tru iz body like Redrum at de Grand National. Liams round face is red n makes iz head look like a big hairy cherry wit a joint comin out uv it, he smiles drunkenly wit a sweet innocence.

De door opens slowly, de head uv a small five year old boy wit blonde almost white hair n blue eyes pops in,

Im comin in, let us in Kenny.

He walks in wearin *Spiderman* pyjamas aniz belly showin.

Alright Charlo! Say Georgie n Rooner.

Smokin de hash ar yiz?

Yeah we ar, now get out, ya cant be in here.

No Kenny let me stay for five minutes.

Only five minutes, go n sit on de bed, up de top wer Rooner is.

Charlo sprints n jumps on de bed, sits down n grabs a lighter dats lyin on it.

Give me dat ya crazy little fucker, Rooner snatches de lighter from um.

Messin all ready, dats it, out, OUT!

Charlo grabs at de head board as I take him by de waist.

Charlo kicks, twists, grabs shouts NO! NO! NO! struggles wit me like an unwanted cat about te be drowned by its owner. He hangs der n sees Georgies head upside down sayin

See ya later Charlo.

A rap on de window brins Georgie te iz feet n he goes te answer it, an enormous cloud uv smoke floats out uv de open door in te de hall. I walk back inte de room drinkin from a just opened can uv *Dutch Gold*, followed by Georgie aniz cousin Shaun who sways inte de room n says

Gis a blow a wunna dem joints will yiz?

Everyone starts te laugh n holler n yeahhhhearrhhh!

Sit down der Shaun, de ya wanna a can?

No, Im a bollix, I wiz down in *De Furry Glen*, had about nine pints, just came up te say ello n get a blow uv a joint, before I go up n go te bed for work in de mornin.

Shaun parks himself onte de stool, rockin silightly from side te side like a buoy.

Here make one n light it up Rooner says as he hands Shaun de hash box.

After two failed attempts Shaun sticks de skins, den closes one eye n slowly breaks a smoke n crumbles de tobacco inte de skins, n finally spreds de hash in, burnin iz thumb in de process, he puts de joint in de side uv iz gob, lights it up n looks like *Popeye* gettin mashed. We all chukle n Georgie says

De bleedin head on ya.

Wot, its de only head I have ya bollix ya, cud be worse cud have a head like you, ya blind curly cunt ya, hah!

More chuklin.

I stand over de stereo trancin for thirty seconds thinkin wot te put on next, press de eject button den change de CD, de disk spins n de first drumbeat uv *Oasis, Live Forever* comes tru de speakers, heads lift, fingers twitch n er placed on imaginary guitar strings,

150

throats er cleared, n everyone sings

Mayyyyyyyybbbbbbeeeeeeeeee I dont really wanna know how yer garden grows, cuz I just wanna fly...

Music Block

De music uv Oasis, der first two albums *Defiantly Maybe* n *Wots De Story Morning Glory* wer de big entry points inte rock music for me n de boys.

De progression tru it wuz fast: De Stone Roses, De Verve, De Beatles, Bob Dylan, De Doors n uv course Bob Marley.

Jimmy wuz hugely inte Reggae, loved all dis ragga dance hall stuff-Shabba Ranks, Chaka Demus n Pliers-He wud bug us all de time te play it wen we wer on speed or yokes, weed play it for half an hour n den wunuv us wud say

Enough, I cant take anymore.

N wud turn it off before a meltdown ensued.

Dis musical education wuz a big part uv me first artistic development stage, it changed everyting about me over a two year period uv intense daily immersion, a derangement uv de senses as laid down by Rimbaud: Te get every album by de bands ya love n de singles, know all de b-sides n de live stuff, n de bootleg tapes. Try out every band, singer-songwriter n movement from de sixties te de nineties. Sum sound good for a bit n den fall by de way side, sum make no impression, sum ya like one album or song, sum ya hate, sum stay wit ya forever n change yer life. Read

151

all de books n de bios ya can, watch de MTV docs n unplugged sessions, learn all de lyrics n wen de drums kick in, n feel de solos in yer solar plexus, play everyting fuckin loud so de whole block knows wot ya like. Music is de language uv de soul, de sound uv God singin. Music saves lives, it took me out uv de dirt n inte de sky, it gave me a stance, a way te be n think n talk. It made me love meself n others a little more.

I grew me hair wild n curly, stopped wearin track suits, only jeans, shirts, t-shirts, *Gortex* or leather jackets. Drugs, drugs, drugs, always de drugs, speed, Es, hash, beer, wine, whiskey, phy pills, D5s, D10s, D20s. Me mind changed, me body morphed, me spirit woke up tru de music n de writin uv de poems n lyrics. Confidence grew in me te de point dat I became cocky n full uv it or as one might say den, mad for it. De same IT dat Dean Moriarty searched for n spoke uv in *On De Road* a novel I wud come te love later.

I finally knew wot I wanted te be n it wuzzen a fuckin plumber, I wanted te be a fuckin rock star n Rooner wanted it too. He had de guitar he got for Christmas, a shit one, but he bashed at it, played till de fingers bled, literally, one night on speed he played along te de radio all night, aniz fingers wer red raw n bled out on te de guitar strings, stigmata for de holy spirit uv tablature. N just like I wrote n wrote, n filled dose notebooks, he strummed n picked, he too felt de pull uv art. It wuz music dat wud get us out uv de blocks, we wer sure uv it, we wer full uv IT.

So Rooner n me became closer n made a pact one night, we wer different din de others, we had art, style n balls, we had de hair, de walk, de words n de strings, we wer gonna make it baby. As a result uv dis Georgie n me drifted a bit from one an other n in-fact he became a little jealous uv Rooner. Georgie by now wuz drinkin all de time, de dark clouds came frequent n heavy.

He wuz fallin closer te Hades everyday. Tommy n him just like Rooner n me wer drawn te each other threw de allure uv hard drugs n Georgies wish for de best high, de ultimate out uv it, de most danger, Tommys failed relationship, iz heartache n sadness n addiction, n soon dey wer brothers uv de black spoon n tin foil n overdoses in filthy flats.

Fat Liam n Jimmy, who wer both a little younger naturally became de other twosum, goin te de snooker hall n smokin tegether, playin football manager on de P.C in de warmth uv Liams bedroom, dreams uv decent jobs n money on der minds.

Stair standin

Georgie perched on de ledge uv de balcony wit iz back against de wall lookin out at de blocks. Jimmy is sat on de bottom stair lightin a joint up. Liam n me stand flankin him on either side waitin for de joint te get passed around.

De stairs have names n dick pics n love hearts n accusations uv whos a rat or gay sprayed n painted on dem. Sum uv de concrete stairs have large chips n cracks in dem, which have te be avoided by prams or heels. Smoke n joint butts er scattered here n der. A bag uv cans is under Georgie tucked in at de wall.

Me bedroom window is open n *Bob Marleys Legend* album can be heard.

Lucy de junkie who lives on de top balcony uv de block comes up de stairs.
Shes so thin she cud cut cheese. Black hair. Expensive clothes, shop-lifted or bought from de money she makes on de game. She still has her looks for now.

Alright lads, hows it goin?
Howaya Lucy, grand, hows yerself?
Im sound, lads. Here can yiz get any hash around, nunna dem cunts up on de pitch will sell me anyting, dey think Im red hot or sumting, pricks.
Yeah we can go up n get a deal for ya no bother, wot dya want?
Nice one, here get me a ten spot n here get one for yerselves aswell.
She palms a score te Jimmy n walks on up te her flat.
Knock up te me wit it wen ya get it yeah?
No prob Lucy, nice one.

We look at each other n smile as Jimmy hands me

de joint. Wer sorted for another night.
    Lucy
    is
    sorted
    for
    another
    night.

Voices from De Blocks

Name Lucy sings de blues.
Year: 1999.
Place: ODevaney Gardens/Fatima Mansions.

Dats sum nice gear I got over in Fatima offa dat youngfella, he duzzen know how te mix it right, gives me a free bag as well. Well its not free I just have te suckiz little yoke forum, only takes two minutes. Ive a lovely buzz on me now. Lovely.

De first time I had sex, he came inte me room n climbed inte me bed, de smella drink, de first time I felt a hairy body, rough hands.

I wuz fourteen. Had a crush onum. Stephen Brown he wuz me brothers friend, five years older din me. He wuz gentle, tookiz time before he worked it up. It wuzzen bad, he knew wot he wuz doin. De first dick. Since den I had every type uv dick: Long, fat, small, pink, brown, circumcised, uncircumcised, ones dat bent upwards. De dicks, de cum, de taste, de smell, de KY jelly, de group fucks from football teams, de freaks who pay big money in de brothels te get pissed on or shit on, stick yer finger up me arse, suck dat fucker bitch, ya like it hard like dat dont ya bitch, bitch, bitch, bitch, bitch, bitch, bitch, bitch...

BITCH!!!!!

Yeah, dats it, dats it slut, keep it up.

Faster, faster, lash me out uv it.

Yeah, yeah, oh ya dirty little bitch, yeah!

Im fuckin dyin sick have te get sumting inte me
fast. Sweat drippin down me spine, but Im cold. No
money. Ive five blueys take dem te keep me goin.
Ring Tracy n see if shes anyting te lend us till I go out
later n make sum money workin.

Get dese down me neck. A cup a tea, force it inte
me, make dem blues come up on me faster. All me
bones ache, like deyre grindin against one another or
sumting. Look at me face, Im in bits, a dirty junkie
whore is all I am.

Tracy! Tracy! Its me, Lucy, Im dyin sick, Tray,
have ya any money till later?

No, Im broke, Davos here will I askum if he can
do anyting for ya?

Yeah, yeah wotever.

Hold on so.

He said come around n yiz can sort sumting out.

Cool, nice one Tray, I/ll see ya soon.

No prob, see ya wen ya come around.

Dis Davo fellas a prick but hes a prick wit gear.

Give de secret knock te let dem know its me n not
de fuckin *F.B.I*, hah.

Howya Lucy come in, luv.

Alright, Tracy.

De room stinks, ashtrays full uv butts, empty cans,
brown bags from chipper food, smell uv vinegar n
grease.

157

Makes me feel even sicker de smell in here. De state uv Davo. Sittin der wit no top on, not a pick onum, track marks all over um, Indian ink n bad tattoos, iz face just bone wit one layer a skin wrapped around it, greasy hair combed te one side.

Alright Davo,

Wots de story Lucy jaysus, ya look in bits, dyin sick wha?

De cunt knows I am. Sum junkies, especially ones who sell, love seein people sick wen deyre not sick demselves.

Here have a line offa dat Davo says as he hands me a balla tin foil, wit a black hard sticky bita gear on it.

I wuz hopin te get a fuckin turn on outta dis fucker but a smoke ill do for now.

Oh jasus dats better, dat smoke sorted me out, shud stop me fuckin nose from runnin.

Thanks for dat Davo, have ya any bags for sale? On tick till after? I/ll get money out workin.

Dyin fora bleedin TO she is wha? I/ll tell ya wot I/ll do for ya. Ya can have two bags now if ya let me little brother ride ya.

Ah fuck off Davo I/ll give ya money later, tellum will ya Tracy?

Davo stop actin de prick n give de bags te her will ya?

No, me little brother James is in de bedroom, hes only sixteen, hes not strung out or anyting, come on he needsiz hole, give it te um Lucy n ya can have de two

158

bags or else tebe honest ya can fuck off.

Go on so, since hes only a youngfella, wer is he?

In de room I told ya, hold on I/ll go in n tellum wot de story is.

Go on in hes in der in bed, be gentle witum Lucy.

Has he got jonnies in der?

Fuckin right he has, I wudnt letum be wit de likes eh ya witout one.

Wanker, give us de bags first,

I wont use till after Im witum.

Jaysus, hes actually good lookin.

I wuz expectin te find sum mad lookin yoke.

Might even enjoy dis.

Howaya, Im Lucy, James isinit?

Yeah, alright Lucy.

Lovely eyes, green, I love green eyes, n dark hair, great match. A bit shy. I/ll sit down on de bed n relax um.

Youve lovely eyes, dya know dat? So will dis be yer first time?

Ehh, yeah, I got a blow job n a wank uv Sandra Coyle but she wudden let me ride her.

Sandra! Jasus I used te hang around wit er Sister Jenny.

Take off me tracksuit n runners, bend over in front uvum, slide de knickers down slowly, now turn around in de nip, letum see me.

159

Well wot de ya think? Am I nice lookin?

Yeah I thought ya be in bits bein a junkie enall, no offence like.

Im not on it dat long, Im gonna get on de clinic, n get me self clean soon.

Get in beside um, de body onum for sixteen, kissum, soft big lips... Oh... Hands squeezinmetits... agh... Fingers... Grab iz dick... Hard... Oohhhh... Wet... Fuck... Yes... Condom...

Take... Over... Rideim... Yessss... Ohhh... ....hhhhhh.

Well, wuz it as good asya thought it wud be?

Fuckin great, yer a great ride Lucy ehh, I, I, I mean yer deadly in bed.

Ha-ha, thanks yer bleedin deadly yerself.

I likeum. Hes cute, easiest way I ever made two bags in me life. Jaysus, I better bang wunna dem now.

Here, Im just gonna go n have a turn on I/ll come back inte ya, in a bit n we can have a bit more fun if ya want?

Yeah, no prob, Im gonna make a joint.

Dats it, we all get stoned one way or de other Jamesy, huh?

We do around here Lucy, dats for sure.

****

160

Voice from De Blocks witin a voice from de block: Davo, Junk Talk

I fuckin love de gear. Yeah I know, dats not wot yer suppose te say.
Yer suppose te be all whingy, about yer childhood, n its a sickness I have.
Fuck dat shite. Id a bit uv a fucked up childhood like every other cunt in de blocks. But Im tellin ya, I love gettin stoned, loved it from de first joint I smoked, loved it from de first drop uv phy dat Anto Dowing gave me. Wen I first had a turn on, ah man dat wuz it, dat wuz fuckin it pal. Fuck you Bono ya might not have found wot yer lookin for but I have I said te meself. I fuckin hate bein sick, I fuckin hate not bein stoned, I fuckin hate de Garda, de dirty fuckin scumbags, I hate nosey little aulones in de blocks, or in town, lookin down on ya cuz ya have a bit uv a dirty tracksuit on or cuz yer a junkie n ya dont give a fuck who knows. Fuck dem anyway, dey think deyre so clean n good, but wot do dey be doin, smokin all day n night, drinkin der bleedin cans three or four nights a week. Der little poxy bastard kids, runnin around wreckin everyting, scruffy cunts.
I hate stuck-up wankers dat look ya up n down on de street or walk around ya like as if deyll catch de fuckin virus off ya just from breathin close te ya, wit de paper under der arm, addicted te football, rugby, politics n all dat shite. Fuck all dat, load uv me bollix I tell ya. Yeah I fuckin hate all the cunts in de world dat arent fuckin junkies, brazzers, dealers, criminals, or all dem mixed in, ha-ha. Id love te live in a big block full uv

161

junkies n whores. Wer ya just woke-up in de mornin n a nurse had yer first hit uv de day cooked up n de gizmo in her hand, bang in te a nice vein, Good mornin Mr. Crooke enjoy de rest uv de day.

Yeah keep alla us away from alla de fuckin straights n keep them away from us. Just leave us der stoned on de gear, n let us fuckin relax n get out uv it all de time till we fuckin croke it, den fuck the dead body in a big incinerator, ha-ha-ha. Yeah fuck dem all. Here wers dat fuckin works, Im startin te get a bit sober here, fuck dat shit, de worlds too much, too fuckin full, too open, I like bein down, closed, ya know?

****

She had sex. He came inte her room. Standin der in a red G-String, no bra. She felt a hairy body on her skin. Tina Turner album on. She snorted hard. Stephen Brown he wuz her brothers friend. Her red shoes te match. Her bag. Took iz time te get her wet before he worked it up her. A box uv *John Player Blue*.

Slipped it. Every type uv dick, long, fat, skinny, small, pink, brown. She looked in de full length mirror. Dicks dat bent downwards. Dicks dat bent upwards. De football teams. De freaks. Pissed on n shit on. Stick yer finger up me arse. Bitch. Bitch. Bitch. De hot water soothed n invigorated her. Wake up bitch!

Be sure te soap de smell off. Run red painted nails tru it. Ya really no how te do it. Talk de talk. Yer simply de best. Comin out uv a dirty mouth. Lucy swayed her hips, letting de hot water

162

ooohhhoooohhhhhhhhhhhhhhhh yeah baby pump me harder. Lucys thoughts went back te de first time.

Faster, faster, lash me out uv it. Inte her bed, de smell uv drink. De first needle. She dances out de shower, yeah, yeah, yeah. Shes fourteen, has a crush. Do dat swish n tie ting dat women do wit wet hair. Years older din her. At least he wuz gentle. Put out two lines uv coke on de cover. Up her. De first dick. One up each nostril. Her head shot up. Circumcised, uncircumcised, ones dat bent up. Im gonna have a mad one tonight. Horrible fat cunt. De cum. De taste. De smell. Daddys dick, priest dick, dog dick, junkie dick, shy dick, nice dick, good dick, bad dick, young dick, old dick, skinny dick, fat dick, boys dick, mans dick, demon dick, Gods dick, a river uv sperm, Lucy drownin in a river uv white, yellow spunk, seamen, sperm, cum, jiz, balls batter. A monster sized dick in her arse full uv KY jelly.

She put on her little red dress, cut low at de back. Fuck sumone whos awake. Dey pay big money. Bag uv coke, card uv Dolmain. Im about te cum. Yer big dick has me der. Suck dat fucker bitch. Ya like it hard dont ya? Bitch, ya bleedin ride ya. I know it sounds good. Say sum more wit yer big dick. Yer big dick, dicks, cocks, Mickeys, Rogers, penises, willeys, todgers, John Thomases, fucksticks, men n der dirty fuckin smelly cocks, men dirty fuckin men wit der fuckin cocks, its in her hair, on her face. It hurts, its numb. Pull her hair. Gargoyles in a bukkake fest, wit green sperm in her eyes. Blackout.

She lifted her leg n washed de days work from her body. She washed her long black hair.

Tina Turners voice can be heard in de room. Water runs down her hair, shoulders, legs, onte her feet, dat have track marks. Takes a towel te dry. Lucy de junkie, de whore, looks at herself in de mirror n says Ya little ride ya, ya dirty junkie bitch.

She swallows a card uv Dolmain, reads de text from Jamesy one more time:

Yil never get off de gear, Lucy, Im sorry but it wuz just a bit uv fun, a bit uv sex, Davo will go mad if he finds out, I cant have a junkie dats on de game as me bird, ya know? Sorry :(

Fuckum, fuckdem all, de bunch uv pricks, de dirty fuckin bunch uv big pricks.

She finds a vein, puts de works in her groin, draws blood back n shoots de gear inte her body n drifts out uv de blocks inte a memory, den a dream, den silence.

Doylers Gaff

I walk down Anns lane, de gateway from ODevaney te Drumalee, wer Doyler lives wit iz Ma, Da, sisters n brothers. Its fuckin freezin out, so Im wearin a monkey hat n *Gortex* zipped up te de chin. I look bogey.

I knock on de back door dat leads ya inte de kitchen. Doylers Da answers de door.
Yeah.
Is Tommy der?
Tommy? Yeah, who/re ya?-Looks at me tru de glasses, a big Tony Soprano shaped man-
Tell um its Kenny.
Kenny, n wot er ya lookin for?
Nutting, Im just a mate.
He bangs de door shut n gos inte de house te get Tommy.

Tommy opens de door, iz ginger head, n blue eyes starin at me, he smiles
n shouts back inte de house,
Its only Kenny, Da, he thinks yer sum mad yoke lookin for gear or sumting Kenny, hah.
Ahh here fuck off wud ya, tell um Im not like dat, man.
Come in.
Da dis is Kenny Thompson, he lives in ODevaney, across de block from Markey,
hes sound, hes not inte gear or anyting, hes just a

skinny fucker, ha-ha.

De aulfella nods at me,
Thomson huh, I know yer Ma n a few uv yer
uncles. Wot er ya hangin around wit dis waster for?
Dont mind um Kenny, he thinks hes funny.

I laugh at de pair uv dem.

Soon de kitchen fills up wit people comin in n out,
makin tea, eatin ham n cheese sandwiches n gur cakes,
n swissrolls.
De entire house is full up wit people: Tommys
sisters, iz brothers Paddy n Stewie, Stewies girlfriend
a shy, dark, skinny girl named Sabrina, dey have a
young daughter. Ders kids millin in n out, lookin at
me, askin who I am, stuffin der faces wit food, de Da
is cookin dinner for everyone in de house, a massive
pot uv coddle, offers me sum an all. Tommys Ma
comes in n says
A Thomson is it? I know yer Ma very well n yer
uncles n Aunties. Keep dis fella on de straight n
narrow will ya.
I/ll try me best Mrs. Doyle.
Mrs. Doyle! Wer not dat posh, its Mary.
Ok Mary it is so, no prob.

Tommys sister Tara walks inte de kitchen wearin
tight black *Levis* n high heals, brownish red vixen hair
n large beautiful brown eyes, freckles, slim elegant
figure n edible arse, I try not te stare too much.
She looks me up n down, a little smile. Whos dis

166

Tommy?

Kenny, I wuz tellin ya about him, lives across de block from Markey.

Ahh right. Hi Kenny, Im Tara.

Hey.

Hey, is dat all, ya cant be shy around here.

Kennys not shy, far from it.

I smile n say

No Im not, just gettin te know yiz all, ders bleedin loads uv yiz.

Dis is only de start uv us, ders loads more, seeyas later, Tara says

as she walks out de kitchen door.

Seeya.

A spark.

Tommy passes me a cup uv tea n says

Lets go up te de bedroom n smoke a joint wit Stewie.

Yeah, cool.

We walk out de kitchen n up de stairs under de glare uv de Da.

Wer only havin a joint Da.

I didden say anyting Tommy.

Ya dont have te, yer face says it all.

I nod te de Ma n de Da as we walk up de stairs te do de usual in another bedroom on another day in de derangment.

Sleepers n drink wit Tommy

Wanderin de streets again. I had drinks
te celebrate de day.
Smoked a heap uv blow already.
Met wit Tommy, he slid a smile across iz red face as
he handed me de roach pills,
we downed dem wit tea n a splif in me gaff.
We called for de Bull te come out. We had cash n
went te de pub.
Yashudda seen Tommy wit de cash makin sure.
De Bull brought beers. A shot uv paranoia.
I drink me drink, dont acknowledge
de raised eyebrow.
Te hell he says, thin
pink lips n valume voice.
Ders jokin n he gives me de old ya know how it is ya
sold sum shit speech.
De Bull sat down, heavy face brightenin de mood.
He had Chicken curry wit chips
followed by a Mars bar.
We decided te go out n look for a place
dat had de danger signs.
Everywer refused us except one kip, we entered lookin
for a few more rounds uv shit.
Bingo wings n slap heads in de mix.
A couple uv females wit
antenna eyes sat down beside us.
I said hello to one who had a certain sex appeal.
Her friend raised an eyebrow.
Tight figures, like prayin mantis. Tommy leans across
imagines sayin words to her.

168

Den he whispers in me ear wit low valume grunt
A lot uv people in here, a huge plate uv beef.
I raised an eyebrow n de bull smiled.
Slow down, toilet cubicle,
mood faces in de flash bulb light.

I looked around n she wuz gone.
Tommy, De Bull n me swaggered inte a food fight,
spice burgers, vomit vinegar dreams.
De Bull crashed inte a wall n went te sleep wit stars
pulled over him in iz birds bed.
Tommy vanished
aniz spectral voice trailed me home.
A wrinkled wino sang an old Irish ballad,
dogs chased cars,
de Moon spit mucas in me face
n me room wuz a ship in de wine dark sea,
de snot green sea, de roach blue sea, I splashed n
swam n landed on Ithacas shore naked n full uv cum
n heroic lyrics.

Voices from De Blocks

Name: A letter from de Joy from TrevorMad dog
Maddox
Year: 1999
Place: ODevaney Gardens.

Howyiz,
Mad Dog here, I wuz out on TR Last weekend,
interestin weekend, thought Id send yiz dis letter, fill
yiz in on de shenanigans I got up te, so here yiz go.

I phoned up de old man te letum know Id be out for de
weekend.

I/ll get de bed ready in de spare room, he said. Den
he hung up.

If Ma wuz still alive sheed uv cleaned de whole flat,
got in de shoppin, all de biscuits I like, all dat stuff.
Seven years shes dead now me aul Ma. She killed her
self. Said she wuz gonna takea bath, made de dinner
as usual, sat der watched *Coronation Street*, washed
de dishes n put dem away, like dat wuz de most
important ting in de world te do before ya kill yer
fuckin self, hah! Filled de bath, went n got in de bath
wit her clothes on, pair uv black leggins n a black
jumper, like she wuz dressed for her own funeral
mass.

170

Took a razor blade n cut her wrists, hit an artery, lay der n bleed te death.

I wuz out n Da wuz nappin on de couch. He woke up an hour or so later, went te go take a piss. De door wuz locked, he realised she wuz still in der n knew sumting wuz up wen she didden answer. Me Das a big strong bastard, he broke down de door n found iz wife der in de bath full uv red water, razor blade placed neatly beside de shampoo n conditoner.

I found out wen me n de lads heard de siren, den saw de ambulance stop in de block n de paramedics goin up de stairs n inte me gaff. I ran over, we all did, de whole flats wuz out, wen de Garda or an ambulance comes in everyone comes out te see for de gossip or excitement, kids everywer, wen I got der, Da wuz sittin on de armchair, cryin, smokin a cigarette. De paramedics wer puttin Ma on de stretcher. I tried te get te her n see her, but Da grabbed holda me, held me in a bear grip n said
Shes gone, shes gone son, Im sorry, Im so sorry.

I dont remember much from de few days after dat. I like te think dat it wuz a mistake, a cry for help. Dat she wanted te be found, a message for Da n me. But maybe she knew exactly wot she wuz doin, had enough uv her life, married te a waster who drinks almost every night, has no job, shows her no affection, her feelin old, tired, a son gettin inte trouble, cookin n cleanin n watchin poxy soaps on de telly, only leavin de house te go te de shops n back. She gave us a message all right, two useless cunts wuz de message I got. Anyway, Im goin off track here, back te de weekend.

United wer playin Newcastle in de F.A. cup final (yiz probably know dat already), sumone up der must be lookin out for me I said te meself, gettin out on cup final weekend. I planned te run amok for de weekend. Johnny De snake Byrne said heed sort me out for cash, said he had a grand for me. I kept me mouth shut wen de old bill nicked me, never gave iz name, so heed look after me. Besides me own criminal loyalty, ders also de fact dat ya dont fuckin rat on de Snake or ya cud end up wit a ventilation hole in yer head, ya know. Dat wanker Paul Williams christened um de Snake. I met Johnny wen I first got locked up in de Joy.

Twenty one I wuz, he wuz thirty, n he wuz on de way te bein wunna Irelands top criminals. He took a likin te me after I had a scrap wit de Shannon brothers; dey wer supposed te be hard, had a bit uv a reputation for bashin people. Dey came inte me cell lookin for trouble, banged de door shut, I wuz ready. I rammed a pen in te Timmos eye fast n hard, den laid inte de older brother Patsy wit solid digs n a few nice loafs, he hit de deck. Timmos eye wuz gushin blood; I grabbed um, put me thumb in iz other eye n smashed um off de wall, till he wuz in a bad way on de ground. Sat back on me bed, lit a smoke wit de blood dripin off me hands n waitin for de shitkicker screws te come in for me. Johnny wuz impressed, offered me te come inte iz crew. Dish out hidins, collect money, stuff like dat. He made sure der wuz no comeback from de

172

Shannons. So ever since den Ive done work here n der for um, sumtimes on de doors uv pubs n clubs he owned. Not sure how hes gonna react wen I tellum dat Im gonna try go on de straight n narrow, when I get out for good. Im after goin off on one der again, sorry.

Wot a fuckin weekend it turned outta be, crazy. First ting I done wen I got out, went te Johnny Byrnes pub De Old Well, wer Id arranged te pick up de money, not many people know its Johnnys pub, I cudden be seen te meet crims wen Im out on TR. So I go der, walk in, its an early house, barman knows me, Franks iz name, had a bit uv banter wit me, stood me up a pint uv *Bulmers* n gave me de envelope, put it in de sky rocket n I felt a surge uv excitement at havin a nice few bob on me. So I wuz der on de stool, suppin on de beautiful pint uv ice cold *Bulmers*, lookin around de boozer. Hazzen changed in years dat place, old style Dublin pub, wooden interior, dark green colour on de seats n stools, white blinds yellowed by smoke, *Guinness* posters n photos uv Irelands 1990 n 1994 world cup squads n a half *United* half *Celtic* scarf on de walls. A few old boys in de corner, two pints uv stout on de table n a cloud uv tobacco smoke over der heads, A bunch uv younger people dat looked like dey wer up all night wer at another table, laughin, singin along te de jukebox, Bob Marleys *Waitin in vain* wuz gettin murdered. I wuz silent wit pint, bag uv clothes n essentials n de grand in de envelope in me pocket, just thinkin about how de weekend wuz gonna go, I wuz plannin it in me head.

173

After I left De Old Well, I went te de *Kylemore* cafe, had a nice big full Irish breakfast, lovely, n a pot uv tea, smoked about four cigs, I wuz sittin der checkin out de waitress, good lookin little red head, gave me a smile a couple uv times.

I took a taxi te de flats, went inte me Das flat. He wuz drinkin a can uv *Fosters* lager.
Ders a can in de fridge if ya want.
Yeah, nice one.
Dats de way it went, him sat on de sofa, me on de armchair, TV on, afternoon TV, fuckin Goin for gold dat kind uv shite, him answerin de questions as if he knew sumting, drinkin iz cans, me answerin a few, most uv dem wrong, him sayin
No, it wuzzen Joe Louis, it wuz Sugar Ray.
All small talk, small talk n smokin, ya know. I cudden take it for long, so I went n had a wash, put away tings, got dressed, a tracksuit n *United* jersey. Gave de aul fella a hundred quid, he wuz pleased te see it but made a face dat said
Only out uv prison n rollin in cash, wots goin on?
I headed out.
Hadden anywer in particular te go, just went on a ramble around de flats n out inte de city. Just te enjoy de open space, wander in any direction I felt like goin.

I bumped inte Theresa O Leary:
Jaysus, Trevor, wots de story? Wen did dey let ya out?
Only got out dis mornin Theresa, for de weekend, back in Monday,

174

Awh right, how er ya, ya look great, after puttin on a bit uv weight.

Thanks, Im in de gym most days up in de Joy, ya know.

Yeah, er ya gonna go on de rip over de weekend?

Fuckin right I am, gonna enjoy meself, how ya doing dese days, lookin well I have te say.

Thanks Trevor, Im doin great, Ive a part time job, cleanin offices n I get de book as well.

N de little fella, hows he?

Hes grand, hes in school. No trouble at all.

Id noticed dat Theresa looked fine, like I told her, lost a bit uv weight anner hair wuz cut short, looked sexy. She has a good body, always had, nice face too, a good solid womans body, big pair uv tits n an arse ya can hold on te, ya know.

Theresa n me wer wit each other for about a month back in de day. I had te ask, wot I really wanted te know now, wuz she still wit Dano?

Wots de crack wit Dano, hows he doin?

Hes a prick, de same as he always wuz, Im not witum anymore, had enough uv iz crap, broke up witum about two months ago.

Ah, sorry te here dat.

Dont be, Im better off.

So its just yerself n de youngfella is it?

Yeah, Im fancy free again, ha-ha.

Lovely I said te meself, cud be a little action here for de weekend.

I/ll be down in De Oak later tonight if yer around.

Yeah, I/ll get me Ma te baby-sit, we/ll have a drink n a chat.

175

Alright, I/ll see ya der so.

Fatso, Yonkers n Tazzer came over te de flat te see me n we had a good chat, N we arranged te meet down De Oak later on. It wuz great te see me mates an all, Fatsos me best pal since we wer chislers n I/ll always loveum, but Yonkers n Tazzer, sumting wuz missin der. Dey hadnt grown up much since we wer teenagers, ya know, two absolute headbangers, sum laugh n I do love dem but I noticed a gap between us since Ive bein locked up dis time, growin apart n all dat bollix. Had an hours kip, den a smoked cod n chips for dinner.

Wen I wuz shavin in de bathroom I felt dis cold feelin around me hands, den it moved along me arms, on te me face n head. I looked at de bath, de same bath Ma killed herself in, de stain uv blood on de corner dat wont go away. Da must have painted over it twenty times, I swear. It wont go, always der te remind ya, ya know? I got lost for a second n cut meself, just a nic under de jawbone, more blood dropped inte de sink. I fuckin hate dat poxy bathroom.

I went down te De Oak, met up wit Fats n de boys. Drinks wer flowin n goin down de hatch, havin a bit uv crack. Der wuz a few nosey neighbourhood watch types, givin me de look, ya know de one, Look whos out, scumbag. Wudden dare te say it te yer face tho.

A few heads came over te shake me hand, n told me wuz good te see me, all dat shit. About ten, Theresa

176

walked in wit her mates, two sisters, Mags n Mary Duggan, two mad bitches. I walked over te de bar n got dem drinks, invited dem te come n celebrate wit me n de lads. Mags said

Celebrate, I thought ya said heed be back in on Monday Theresa?

Shut up, ya thick ya, hes celebratin bein out for de weekend after been locked up for a year an a half Theresa said.

So I knew she wuz talkin about me te her mates, good sign. Weed a great night, sum laugh it wuz, drinkin pints, shots, doubles, wreckin it on de dance floor, de lot. Der wuz a DJ on n its a late bar on Fridays, half two, fuckin out time.

Ar yiz right der folks? Have ya no homes te go te?

De sisters wer pissed. Fatso headed te de curry shop for a three in one n home te bed te de missus. Yonkers n Tazzer went te a party in Finglas, asked me if I wanted te come.

No, its been a long day I havin been up dis late in ages, I/ll see ya tomorrow for de match I says.

Outside havin a smoke wit Theresa, weed been flirtin all night, she said te me

Ive a bottle uv Vodka in de gaff, dya wanna come back n have one or two, cuz me Ma has little Thomas n Im not in de humour uv goin te bed yet n dem other two er goin te de party wit de lads?

Yeah, I/ll come back wit ya for one or two, thanks, I said, knowin full well wat wuz on de menu.

She only lives five mins away, so we walked te her flat.

177

I wuz sittin der on de two seater, a black leather one. She poured two large Vodka an cokes, n sat down beside me.

I have te take off dese bleedin shoes, feet er killin me she says n off came de heels.

She wuz wearin a pair uv skin tight black jeans, low cut top, dat full womans body wuz burstin te get out. We chated a bit while drinkin de Vodka an Cokes, she put her hand on me leg. Well, dat wuz it, invitation excepted. I kissed her, n bang it wuz wunna dem, de tension dats been buildin up all night snaps, we started kissin each other, drunk sloppy kissin, clothes pulled off, me jersy on de ground, her jeans half off, ya know, around one foot, bra flung across de room, n she started suckin me dick, me head rolled back n den jerked forward. I got her by de hair n pulled her up, struggled te get de tight jeans off her foot, she/d a black G-string on, dis really got me goin, I got de mouth n tongue on dem big tits, den went down on her wit me fingers n tongue, n I banged her over de back off de chair, den wit her sittin on top uv me, we ended up on de floor, a year n a half uv sexual frustration rushed out uv me, I pulled out n came on her belly, den we went te bed n slept till mornin.

I woke up at nine, me internal prison clock woke me later din usual, cuz uv de alcohol. Id a bad hangover. Looked at Theresa out cold under de duvet, hair all over de place, pulled up de duvet te have a peek at her naked, fine strong body. Made a cup uv tea n smoked a cigarette. Dat made me feel a bit sick. De feelin uv coldness in me hands started again, de

178

kitchen seemed fake, like de walls wud fall down n I wud be back in me cell, hidden camera show, ha-ha.

I shook dat off n went back inte de bedroom, Theresa lifted her head up n said

Mornin, wot er ya doin up so early, Im bleedin dyin here.

Ahh, ya get used te wakin up early in jail, listen Im gonna shoot off, de aul fella will be up soon, dont want um te think I got inte any trouble, I/ll see ya later on, or wotever, I says te her.

Yeah, all right, come ere, last night wuz great, thanks she said n pulled me in te her.

We had a little kiss, she tasted like stale beer n smoke butts, so did I. Walkin around te me block, de sun wuz bright in de clear sky, ya cud tell it wuz gonna be a lovely day. I sat down on wunna de small bollards surroundin de block n had another smoke, I wuz sittin there thinkin te me self how fuckin easy it is te fall back inte tings in de blocks. Hopefully wen I get out for good I dont fall back inte all me old bad habits.

Ah, sure we/ll wait n see.

Talk te yiz soon,

yours *Trevor*.

Violence block

Me hands wer red.

It went all de way up te me elbows. De blood. New Years Eve. Doyler, Markey n Me wer out for a few drinks. We ended up in a place wer we wernt wanted.

One too many *Southern Comforts* n me dancin on tables makin a show, n man Jokes n wind-ups n two other blokes at our table, one a notorious bully. He wuz at me for de night makin comments about me hair, me clothes, pickin up me block uv hash wen I wuz tryin te make a quick joint witout bein seein, te which I took great offence, ya just dont touch a young, fiery, mad, drunk mans drugs, so I told um

Give it back or I/ll give ya belt uv dis ashtray in de head. I picked up de glass pub ashtray wit intent te do damage.

It wuz all cooled down by de others at de table, n apologies wer exchanged but de demon lingered in de lounge. De night progressed, converstions wit Auburn haired women, more shots, more slaggin, more spite, red waves uv danger in de chamber.

At the twelve bells de Bully head butted me, wen I offered me hand te shake, he took it, n wit me unprepared he pulled me forward n crashed iz head inte me nose, a real sneak attack by a real bully, blindin light, pain, rage, alcohol. A ruckus uv fists n chairs n grabbin ended wit Tommy, Markey n me gettin put out uv de pub. Bully aniz pal wer regulars, so dey wer allowed te stay n finish der drinks n fun.

180

Outside I wuz spittin n fumin, rage tremors in me spirit.

It wuz comin down from me nose. De Blood.

The Bully lived across de block from me. I wuz drunk, dangerous, fatherless, fed-up, furious, unhealthy, bloodied. I waited for him in de flats n as he plodded in drunk n wuz walkin up de stairs, I heard a whisper from de gloopting
Hit him in his fat fuckin head.
I came up n hitum wit a leg from a wooden table dat we had stashed in me room for such occasions.
One,
Two,
Three,
Four,
Five times, I swung n hit um a few times, pingin open iz head a couple uv times.
He swung an arm at me n de weapon fell, we tangled, rolled on de hard ground,
I landed on top, n layed inte iz head n face wit punches, as he tried te get at me wit a few badly aimed swipes, dis time it wuz me who struck de blows uv revenge.

Well in my time of dyin, dont want nobody te moan,
All I want for you te do is take my body home,
Well, well, well, so I can die easy,
Well, well, well, so I can die easy,
Jesus gonna make up, Jesus gonna make up
Jesus gonna make up my dyin bed.

181

De gargoyles rose up n flapped der wings in delight, de roar echoed in de halls n me head n de glooptings drooled in de darkness n de block wuz alive wit its dark energy in de nightime, all hail de new year.

Iz wife n kids stood der watchin, de wife picked up de table leg n wuz about te smash me skull wit it, wen Doyler snatched it from her, n grabbed me,

Come on Kenny lets get out uv here.

Ten minutes later, de bully knocked on Markey n Doylers door, swingin a snooker cue heed gotten from iz flat, iz shirt wuz torn n blood trickled down iz face n head, iz forehead wuz bruised purple n slashed red.

Doyler blocked de swingin cue wit one hand, n struck de poor fucker clean in de middle uv de head wit a large wrench, bang! He went down, n dis time he stayed down, der wuz blood all over iz face now from de wounds Id given him from de table leg, n one big gash from de spanner dat opened iz head, put him clean out n left him twitchin on de balcony.

Well, well, well, so I can die easy,
Well, well, well, so I can die easy,

We looked at um layin der on de balcony, blood oozin out from de wounds, iz face a red wash, breathin heavy, de snooker cue by iz side, an angel came out from de blackness wit fierce throbbin energy n stood above him, huge n blazin in violet, n did point its flashin sliver sword n say wit great spiritual authority as blue lightinin burst from her eyes,

182

He will live n you will survive too, but know this poet, this is not your role, this is ordinary, this is not the way out, this is deeper in the muck, this is the mind forged manacles of the blocks in dire action, be warned, be careful, be smarter, be better or be damned. '

Me eyes n ears burned wit elation n horror.

Tommy n me ran as we heard de sirens n neighbours screams n hollers n we left Marky der holdin de guys hand n prayin dat de bullyin fuck wazzen gonna die outside de door in de cold January mornin.

I wept.
Doyler wept.
We contemplated takin a boat te England, hid de wrench, washed de blood from our hands n faces, smoked sum more joints n drank sum whisky n fell inte a nervous sleep.
De next day we heard bully boy wuz alive, tho he had sum scars. Scars, Ive a few, so has Doyler, Sure hasnt everybody. Im glad he lived, for iz kids, iz wife, himself, Doyler, Me. For de angel. We wer all blest as de sayin goes. Whose fault wud it uv been if he did die? Doylers n mine for our act uv drunken stupid revenge? De bully for iz cowardly assault in a bar full uv iz mates on a drunk Teenager? De hedonistic openins filled wit de Glooptings urgins? De drinks companies n pub landlords? De Rules uv de blocks? *Dont let anyone get smart wit ya. Dont let anyone hit*

ya, hit dem back harder din dey hit ya. Wuz it de blocks dat wrote de bloody tale uv de New Years Eve fight? Will de tearin down uv de blocks bring us peaceful teachers?

Will it be alright? Is it alright my Angel? Yes its alright. Its alright bully. Its alright Markey. Its alright Tommy Doyle. Its alright Kenny.

Voices from De Blocks

Number: 8

Name: Takin E Bath: Tazzer n Yonkers, Drug Talk.
Year: 2000.
Place: ODevaney Gardens Corner uv de block/
House in Montpellier drive.

We wer all sittin der in de gaff wit de Aunties an uncles. De Ma. De fuckin aul fella an all. Sharons dressed up te de nines for de debs anner fella Jocker is in de suit, wanna see de state uvum hair all gelled back an all, thought he wuz de fuckin bizz he did.

So everyones gettin stuck in te de cans an wer poppin out for splifs in de garden havin a great time. A few uv us dropped a few bumble bees as well. Why not ya know?

Wen de yokes kicked in we wer havin a bleddin cracker uv a time. Dancin wit de aul ones, flirtin wit de youngones, just havin a proper session, like.

Next uv all I look around an cant fuckin see Yonkers anywer n Im askin dem all wer is he? Cuz ya know dat cunt hes always gettin mad outuv it an up te no good. Nobodys seenum in awhile den Jimmy says he went de jacks about twenty minutes ago.

So I says better go up an see wots de fuckin story witum. I goes up de stairs pass de bleedin queue, birds all doin little dances holdin der fannies burstin for a piss.

185

I bangs on de door like n says

Ar ya in der Yonkers?

Yeah pal, be out in a bit.

In a bit, yer in der twenty five minutes ya mad cunt ya, a load a birds out here er pissin demselves.

Be out in a bit pal, dont worry bout dem birds, deyll be grand pal.

Let me in for a sec pal, I need te have a piss come on, ya seen me knob loads a times anyway, ha-ha! Ok pal I/ll let ya in now.

So Im in de fuckin door, locks it behind me an dis mad cunt is in de nip climbin in te de bath. Fuckin steam comin out uv it, ya cant see in de mirror, fuckin sauna like.

He has iz clothes folded nice an neat on de floor an hes just lyin in de bath like nuttings wrong wit it, hes fuckin red raw man, an he says te me

Bit cold in here pal isin it?

A bit fuckin cold is it, here let me runa bit more hot in der for ya so.

De fuckin water is boilin an dis fat cunt is in der like a bleedin lobster sayin its cold ha-ha-ha-ha. Im tryin te explain te em dat wer not in iz gaff, wer in Sharons n er whole familys down stairs but he just duzzen give a bollox ya know? So Im thinkin I have te get em outuv dis bath an down stairs quick. So I says let me give ya a head massage pal datll be lovely wit de bath. Hes gameball for dat. So hes der wit de eyes closed in de fuckin bath, chillin te bits like, an Im massaginum wit one hand an runnin de hot water wit

186

de other till de bath is like fuckin lava or sumting, right?

He fuckin starts pumpin sweat n is goin fuckin redder din a United jersey.

Den I just slaps em in de face real hard te snap um outuv wotever buzz hes on like.

He fuckin jumps up n starts screamin, fukin lookin around de room like wot de fuck am I doin in de bath, like?

Ya wanna seeum gettin out de bath in de nip iz cock wuz red raw, iz legs wer fuckin burnin red, fat arse onum, bleedin gas man.

He just puts on iz clothes an me an him walk out de bathroom an pass all de birds laughin our heads off like nuttings wrong here n him wit a big red tomato head onum.

We get te de end uv de stairs an ya know wot dis mad cunt says te me?

He turns around n says

I feel real fresh now pal, anymore a dem yokes, me buzz is after wearin off a bit over dat bath, ya know?

Wot did I do?

I gave um another two pills didden I?

I mean, wots a mate for ya know like?

Tommy n Georgie shooting up

Have ya got de works Georgie?

Did ya give dem te me?

Yeah, I gave dem te ya dis mornin, remember, in de kitchen?

Ahh yeah, yeah. Hold on... Here de er.

Georgie, sweaty palm, hands de syringes te Tommy. Tommy takes dem n places dem on de table den takes two bags uv gear, de citric acid, two smokes, a spoon, a bottle uv water n a lighter. He gently pulls de filters out from de smokes. De ingredients laid out, Tommy gets te work n cooks up a shot for himself n one for Georgie.

Georgie rolls up iz jumper sleeve, vices iz left arm wit right hand, pumps de arm up n down like hes fistin Aphrodite, a luscious vein offers itself, Tommy caresses de works n wit delicate precision puts de spike in, draws de blood n bangs de shot inte Georgie, who shudders orgasmicly aniz head flops forward, Tommy pulls de works out n places it beside Georgie on de floor.

Tommy cant find a vein so easy dese days. After a ten minute struggle, pumpin like a maniac body builder, slapin iz arm, switchin arms, wrapin de leather *Levi* belt around iz arm he pulls it like he wuz chokin a pitbull n at last a vein rises for de shot n Tommy plunges it in n it feels like de womb, it feels like all de positions uv de *karma Sutra* at once, he goofs n drools on iz chin.

Georgie unslumbers, looks at Tommy n smiles wit a great affection for iz pal. Tommy n Georgie on de floor uv a dark candle lit room in de blocks, curtains closed, one shaft uv holy light comes tru n shines on de works on the floor beside Georgie. Tommy opens iz eyes n says

Hallelujah, hallelujah bud!

Doyler Two

Tommy Doyle a red headed Michael Stipe. A crazy legged loser. A charmer uv women. A poor drug addict, a stealer uv useless tings. A stealer uv money for useless tings. A goofer in a trance, a menace te himself. A product uv de blocks environment. A staunch guy. A worker in every sense. A friend te many. Tommy Doyle a hero uv dis book. A survivor uv it all: Addiction, break ups, beatins, prison, suicide attempts, overdose, underdose. Tommy Doyle a legend in iz own time. Tommy Doyle de thin lipped skinny fool uv me dreams. Member uv de Doyle family, de Da, Ma, sisters n brothers, in laws n aunts n uncles n hundreds uv cousins in every block in Dublin. A raconteur in jail cells, drug dens, pubs, parties, flats, blocks, cars, every street in Dublin.

Tommy Doyle walks like he wuz in Tombstone, like Doc Holiday spitin in de dust. Twinkle in de eyes. Fallin, swayin, drinkin, pissin, singin, dancin, no fear or shame in iz own experience. A drugged out sadhu in dem days uv de blocks. De brother uv me lover. De introducer uv me Love. De brother in de blocks. De love in life.

189

Tommy n me dropped de grey speckled doves n sat waitin for de tremors n wen dey hit it wuz wild. De yellow, red, n green spots on de wall paper danced n blipped. Tommy rollin a joint for de last two hours, it just wont happen. Skins look like bed sheets. De sticky part disappears. De fingers dont work. Den he sits unmoved in a trance for 45 secs, n flickers iz eyes n says te me while lookin at de Bob Marley poster on de wall,

Its yer go man, n hands me a pack uv smokes dat he thinks is a *Playstaion* control pad.

I look at him den de wall n flip inte a convulsion uv laughter.

But dis piece uv stoned art by Tommy is an invitation te join um, te dance n I accept de invitation, whoop, whoop, Im der in de all glow uv magical seein, me younger self appears n says Vision, dats a good word.

Yes little Kenny, it is de word, V I S I O N!

We get de joint tegether n we leave de room, de flat, its all too small. We head for Tara n Denises flat in another block called Fatima.

We brin a bottle uv blue label *Smirnoff Vodka* te sweeten de blow uv our madness n saucer eyes, our sorcerers eyes, our sore eyes.

Even den walkin down dat road in de familiar Dublin rain, I knew dat dis legend wud be writ sumday, it wuz clear te me vision, dat dis wuz art in de makin, I knew life wuz art n art wuz life, I saw meself typin dis den. Im seein meself den as I type dis now.

190

Der wer so many visions dat night, a blur uv colour n sound, Taras smile n hair a vision, her acceptance uv de moment, her joinerinary, de moon a vision, de dark energy dat changed inte a man on de top uv de hill, a vision. De rain a drizzeld vision.

Chasin deer in de Phoenix Park, high n joyful at 4 am, a vision.

Tommy n me, two mad wiry butterflies in de blocks.

Tommy Doyle searchin for veins in de bathrooms n locked bedrooms uv de blocks. Tommy Doyle a Mr. Mojo risin, topless n sweatin, a towel wrapped around iz head in de parties uv de blocks. Tommy cryin drunk wit me as we converse n heal in de blocks. Tommy Doyle loved by everyone he ever sat wit for an hour. Tommy Doyle a pure fuckin idiot in a valume daze in de kitchen makin a scene, aniz Da shakes iz head in anger n throws iz eyes te heaven.

Tommy Doyle who stole one too many times from iz sisters n parents n even Markey, who give um a smack in de mouth n a fight broke out, n so he ended up in me flat, but wuz too much like me Da in iz junk dramas n schemes n scams n Ma said
Go on son, get yer head tegether.
Tommy Doyle, back n forth n here n der n too n fro, n clean n hooked, n just now n again, n off it for three weeks, n only smokin it te come down.

Employed n Unemployed n up n down, n out n in.

Tommy Doyle sold two bags te an undercover Garda n went te Mountjoy again. Tommy Doyle whose younglove dream broke down n died n she found another, who didden go on de nod in de middle uv tings, just like Da did. Tommy Doyle who fought by me side n jammed on iz invisible guitar n played all de great solos wit darin n dash, sweat flyin in all directions, a conjuror uv de imagination if ever der wuz one, n der wuz aniz name is Tommy Doyle n hes a legend in iz own time. Tommy Doyle whos Taras brother, Tara who I saw on de stairs in de block, in a glow like Van Goghs *Sunflowers*, wit an ass dat wuz magnificent. Tommy Doyle who lost a hundred times n won nutting, but got up anyway n said Fuck dis, Im sumbody, Im a man, Im alive, Im Tommy Doyle n Im a legend n dont need any more tinfoil or works or tablets or break ups, or sisters bedrooms, or friends sofas, or on n off, or noddin or jails, or Dublin or de blocks. Tommy Doyle who got clean n went te England te find wot he had lost in little plastic bags n lies n syringes. Oh Tommy Doyle yer a legend in yer own time, a legend in my time n now yer a legend in eternity me friend.

Voices from De Blocks

Number: 9

Name: Mickey Mouse had a house.
Year: 2000.
Place: Flat number 182 ODevaney Gardens.

De little boy sits on de floor dressed in *Power Rangers* pyjamas dat hes been wearin for two weeks. He smells uv stale sweat but he duzzen know it. De room is a mix uv shit brown n uniform grey. Smoke n dust mix in de air.

Mammys drunk again, lyin on de sofa, fag in her mouth. Daddys out wit iz mates at a flat wer dole drunks gather te drone all day n groan de night away.
Tellys on. Childrens TV, cartoons; de cat gets hit on de head n de mouse laughs. De boy laughs n throws a plastic hammer at Mammy.

For fuck sake Billy, me head ya little bastard ya, I told ya, not te be throwin tings at Mammy, didden I? De boy twists iz lip n squints iz eyes den looks back at de telly. Wot fuckin time is it? Half five! Wers dat prick? Suppose te be back by now wit de fuckin cans n de curry.

Mammy lights up a smoke immediately after puttin one out. Her fingers er yellowed wit tobacco stains, she belches loudly n de boy laughs n says Mammy belched, scuse me, scuse me.

Scuse me son, very good, manners isin dat wot we have Billy, manners?

Mammy rubs her arms up n down fast te get heat inte dem n gets up from de sofa, slow n arthritic, limps over te de kitchen n puts on de kettle.

Me hungry Ma, want me dinner, want curry, chicken balls. Ya have te wait till yer Da gets back, de stupid cunt, he has de money. Hungry Ma, want curry. Wot did I say Billy, yer Da has de fuckin money, we have te wait till hes back. Hungry, want dinner now Ma, want chicken balls. ER YA FUCKIN DEAF OR WOT? I SAID WE HAVE TE WAIT TILL YER FUCKIN DA COMES IN WIT DINNER, I CANT MAKE DINNER OUT UV NUTTING CAN I? CAN I YA LITTLE BASTARD YA, STOP FUCKIN WHINGIN OUT UV YA N GIVE ME A BREAK BILLY WILL YA! Bold Mammy, bold Mammy, no shoutin, Mammy a bitch! WOT? WOT DID YA CALL ME? A BITCH? DONT YA BE CHEEKY WIT YER MUDDER YA LITTLE CUNT YA, JUST LIKE YER BLEEDIN DA YA WILL BE, A FUCKIN LITTLE CHEEKY BASTARD!

Mammy goes over te Billy n slaps um hard across de face, reddenin iz cheek.
Billy starts te cry n roll n rock on de floor kickin n caterwaulin in de block.

DATS WOT YA GET FOR CALLIN YER MA DIRTY NAMES LIKE DAT! STOP! STOP DAT! BILLY! BILLY STOP DAT ROLLIN AROUND, DONT HAVE ME TE TELL YER DA ON YA WEN HE GETS IN, BILLY DE YA HEAR ME? DO YA?

Billy, stop, st, stop, come on now, cmere, cmere te me, stop now, come on, come on yer alright, come on it wuz only a little slap, mammys sorry, cmere now, I love ya, Mammy loves ya Billy.

Mother n son cuddle on de floor uv de sittin room as de kettle comes te a boil.

***

Daddy fiddles at de door wit iz key, droppin it te de ground den strugglin te find it n pick it up. He has a takeaway curry in a brown bag under iz arm. He closes one eye n focuses hard on de key hole n finally gets de key in n opens de front door uv de flat. Mammy is sittin on de sofa smokin n drinkin tea.
Billy is asleep on de armchair.

De fuckin state uv ya, wot fuckin time dya call dis? Yer fuckin four hours late ya stupid little prick ya. Is dat de fuckin curry, is it? Yer fuckin child is starvin here n so am I.

Who dya think yer talkin ta? So wot if Im a bit late, had a few drinks wit de lads, heres yer fuckin curry, ya

195

cudda made em toast or summtin ya lazy fuckin cunt ya. Give yer mouth a rest for once will ya.

GIVE ME MOUTH A REST, FUCK YOU YA DIRTY FUCKIN CUNT YA, WERS ME CANS AS WELL YA SILLY BASTARD YA? TOAST, FUCKIN TOAST, OUTTA WOT? MAKE TOAST OUTTA ME HOLE WILL I? YA NEED FUCKIN BREAD TE MAKE TOAST YA FUCKIN DOPE YA.
DONT START YER SHOUTIN AT ME YA FUCKIN BITCH YA, IM TELLIN YA I/LL PUNCH DE FUCKIN HEAD OFF YA I WILL.

Dinner, Daddys home, dinner, curry, Mammy bold, Daddy bold, chicken balls?

LOOK WOT YA DONE NOW, SHUT YER GOB N GIVE ME DE FUCKIN DINNER FOR YER SON WILL YA, YA STUPID THICK CUNT YA N WERS ME FUCKIN CANS I SAID?
HERE, DE YA WANT YER DINNER DO YA, HERE HAVE IT SO N GET YER OWN FUCKIN CANS YA LITTLE SLUT YA!

Daddy throws de takeaway across de room it hits de wall n lands on de floor. A yellow brown splash sprays de wall. Den he takes a crumpled up twenty euro note n hurls it at Mammys face.

YA DIRTY BASTARD YA, YA DIRTY FUCKIN BASTARD YA, GET OUT, GET OUTTA HERE NOW, GO ON FUCK OFF BACK TE YER

FRIENDS BEFORE I GO AROUND N GET ME BROTHERS TE COME AROUND N FUCKIN KILL YA!

AH FUCK YA N YER BROTHERS, IM OUTTA HERE DONT WORRY ABOUT DAT, ENJOY YER CURRY N GET YER CANS YA DIRTY ALCO SLUT YA!

Daddy slams de front door behind him n stumbles off back te iz drinkin buddies.

Billy puts iz finger onte de curry splashed on de wall n den licks iz finger.
Curry, nice, Daddy bold, Daddy fuckin bastard.

Yeah, he is son, yer right he is, ah dont be lickin dat off de wall Billy for fuck sake ya little fucker ya. Jaysus Christ. Here gimme dat fuckin bag, I/ll get plates, fuck dat cunt, well have dis curry all te ourselves.

Mammy n Billy sit tegether on de sofa n eat der curry, stuffin it inte der mouths, sharin from each others plate, curry sauce on der poor faces as dey watch *Coronation Street.*

***

Mammy has te go de shops now Billy te get her cans, ya wait here ill she gets back, I/ll only be five minutes son Ok?

Put on film, wanna watch *Mickey Mouse*, put it on Mammy.

Ok son, I/ll put *Mickey Mouse* on for ya, ya just sit up der on de sofa Baby,
    n mammy ill put dat on for ya, n den I/ll go n get me cans for de night OK?

Ok Mammy, Mammy dont be long gettin cans OK?

I wont be long Billy, just goin down te de corner te de shop, back in a few minutes.

Billy sits on de sofa watchin *Mickey Mouse* n smiles, iz belly full, iz head nods up n down as he tries te fight de sleep comin on, eventually de sleep wins n he leans n falls back on de cushion n falls inte dreams wit *Mickey Mouse* n chicken balls.

Mammy comes back in wit a plastic bag uv *Dutch Gold* lager n looks at her son. She covers um wit a dirty blanket dat used te be white but is now a creamy yellow. She sits down in front uv de telly, opens her first can, takes a long satisfyin sup n den lights a smoke up n laughs at *Mickey Mouse*.
    She remembers wen she wuz a kid, her friends n her used te sing
Mickey Mouse had a house which number wuz it?
Mickey Mouse had a house...
    Wotever number ya picked de others wud say dats how many kids yer gonna have wen yer older, n she

used te think itd be great te grow up n get a fella n have a kid. Tears start te come from Mammys bloodshot eyes n she wipes dem away, turns off *Mickey Mouse* n turns on *De Late Late Show*, Sinead O Connor is on it talkin about herself n people in de audience er laughin.

De girls

De girls came inte de story sumwer in wit all de drugs n violence.

Across de block dey wud stand n stare n giggle. Jemma, we called her Jem n Tommys Sisters: Philo n Tara. It starts wit looks, den chats n teasin. Jem n Jimm wer de first te fall, de first te kiss, de first te make it wit each other, Jimmy stays wit Jem more din wit de boys now, dats how it goes n always will.

Philo n Georgie wer a doomed couplin. Philo wuz shy, hunched shouldered, wit de Doyle red hair n freckles, very cute. Georgie, older, scared her wit iz overbearin love, too intense, too quick, he just cudden play it cool. Iz arm around her too tightly. Iz kiss too feverous. He even stopped drinkin, for a week, he skipped in te de blocks. It wuz all over in a fortnight n he broke in so many pieces like a hammerd in window, he wuz broken already n cud not be mended by any hand, or word or act.

He wudden give it up tho, he doted on her, he followed her. Begged n harassed her.

No good wud come uv it, I toldum.

Two weeks, we said,

Come on how can ya be in love in two weeks?

So love brought out de blades, n walls n poles got hit wit broken fists. So lack uv love brought out de dark energies, te swarm about little Georgie Teeling, who sat on de edge uv de blocks wit only de Gargoyles te weep wit, tegether in agony, amen.

Jem wuz short blonde n big boobed, witty n sharp. Jem n Jimmy, a mini love story in de blocks. My love came in de blindin white named Tara, brown earth mother eyes, rose pink eyelids, most beautiful flower in dis legend. We looked, we stared, we bummed cigarettes n skins, we smoked spliffs, we drank n danced, we sang songs, we talked about music n which bands we loved n hated, I (unshirted n high on E) made Tea, in her flat in Fatima Mansions wer she lived wit her best mate Denise.

We armlinked goin te snooker. Still no kiss. Still no mention uv wot all cud see. Tommy, one day has enough uv dis n comes te me door.

Kenny, get dressed up, yer goin out wit Tara, tonight, yeah?

Ehh, yeah, cool, deadly.

Tommy went te Tara.

Get dressed yer goin out wit Kenny tonight.

Tommy Doyle, match maker, trouble starter, junkie cupid shootin syringes full uv love in our arms. De girls.

Tara came in n as usual I made her wait. She sat wit Ma n Charlo.

Ar ya Kennys Girlfriend asked Charlo.

Makin Tara blush. De date wuz in *De Top Uv De Hill* pub on Thomas street. Taras

Ma n Da wer der anner mate Denise, de Da taken de piss out me shirt, de Ma tellin um te shut iz face. It ended wit me buyin chips for Tara n me n goin back te her flat, wer she let me sleep beside her in bed, but made me leave me clothes on, still no kiss.

201

De next day we walked together from Fatima te Houston station n we stood der, her slender hand in mine, n she said

Ar ya gonna kiss me or wot?

N I answerin.

Yeah, I, I wuz waitnin for yer..

N finally, we kissed, n it wuzzen sloppy or dumb, or drunkbreathed or awkward like de other kisses I had, it wuz tender, light, succulent.

I had butterflies in me belly n den I transformed inte one, a white butterfly n flew above de blocks in de vast Lapis blue sky.

De girls, love, lack love. Dramas. De great loosenin uv regular sex, real love sex, not just drunken bad porn fuckin.

Again I wuz metamorphosied. I remembered how de angel boomed de word Poet.

Wuz I dat?

Tara n me, naked n full uv Ovid n Neruda poems in de blocks. Charlo runs inte de room, jumps on de bed n gets under de covers n says

Ar ya sexin in here, Kenny?

Tara turns away n covers her face wit de blanket, embarrassed. I laugh n say, Will ya get outta here ya little nutter ya?

Charlo, blonde hair, belly stuck out like a Chinese Buddha hee-heein in de blocks.

De writers got iz writers eye opened all de time. It never blinks. It even watches de writer, click, click, click. It records all uv life, turns it inte scripture. Dats holy.

De details er holy. De first girl I fucked, Natalie, she left her purple knickers behind. Dats Holy. De first girl I kissed, Alice Connolly, lived on de same balcony as me in de blocks. Used te send me love letters. I kissed her on de bed, she giggled girlishly so I stopped n thought, dis is stupid. Dats holy.

De great love uv me life Tara. De first n only woman I've made love wit. Dats holy, de hair, de reddish brown hair. Dats holy. Taras hair I take in me hands. Dats holy. Brown eyes dat I kiss. Holy. Thin body dat I love. Holy. Tara whose scent is made uv Hosannas n nectarines, whose flesh floods me wit desire, whose pores release holy water, Tara on whose lips I drop a kiss dat turns in te a prayer, Tara I wrap a rosary uv apologies around yer neck, I write poems on yer breasts, I conduct orchestras on yer thighs, I sprinkle rainbows on de backs uv yer knees, Tara I build wings uv gold on yer shoulders, Tara coducts a mass outta me, Tara de chrysalis who Butterflied me, Tara ripest apple in me garden, head on me pint, manna in de dessert, last bottle uv beer in de fridge, Tara de hi note in dis song! Tara my Helen, my Venus, my Empress.

Poetry about girls. Dats holy. Girls in night clubs dancin in de flash uv strobe lights on ecstasy. Holy. Girls bangin up H in de boarded up flats in de blocks. Dats holy. Girls pissin in de lanes uv de city. Dats holy. Girls cryin in der beds for de lover gone in de mornin. Holy. Girls, all done up te de nines n smokin on corners. Holy. All de girls in all de blocks. Dats holy. Philo n Georgie holy. Jem n Jimmy Holy. Tara n me holy. Edel n Frankie holy. Tara n me wer almost always tegether den, so much so I woke up one day n quit me job dat I hated in *Bargintown* dat Markey had gotten for me. Ma wuzzen happy about dis. I left any job I had after a few months. Rock stars dont work in factories or buildin sites, or clean hospitals or madhouses as I wud do in a future job. De angel said poet. At dis time Ma n me didden get on, she didden see a poet or a rock star, she saw a lazy bollix. It wuz time for me te leave de ODevaney blocks, te leave little Charlo wit Edel n Ma. N go te de Fatima blocks n live wit de girls. I packed me bags n felt free a little while.

Jimmy follows Georgie
out uv de blocks

Jimmy had it all goin well for him for awhile, in a lovin relationship wit a beautiful girl, he got a job in a sweet factory, he had money for iz hash n smokes, a couple uv snooker nights a week wit Liam n another friend uv iz called Tim, who Jimmy lived wit for a few years instead uv at either uv iz parents homes, Tim wuz a dumb, innocent, slightly annoyin but good hearted bloke, Jimmy n him wer close, Tim wuz sumone who wuz a part time member uv our gang, n once let us all write on iz face wit a permanent marker, a black eye, a beard n a skull tattoo, it took three days n ten washes to remove it, de poor holy fool.

Jimmy wuz in dis good place until Georgie died, den de small but good tings werent enough te keep de rage contained. De grief bored a vile tunnel in iz heart. Georgie n him altho dey fought like all brothers, wer very attached, deyd been tru so much tegether, wit one gone de other lost a big ally in dis world, in dese blocks. So Jimmy smoked joints constantly, den him n Tim n a few other heads started te get real heavy on de Es, even taken dem durin de week, on afternoons sittin in a cold bedroom sumtimes wit me n Tommy n Rooner on de weekends at parties, at other times he wud take dem on iz own. Jem got pregnant n dis pulled him outta de pits, he wuz a glow wit dreams uv a little family, he cut down bigtime on de drugs, turned up for work at de factory on time everyday,

205

started savin money, bought a pram. But again tragedy. Again Jimmy Teeling spit on by de Gods, kicked in de balls by faith, shanked in de belly by life, babtised in blood by de Dullahan. Jem miscarried. He carried around a picture uv de baby in iz pocket, a distorted, blackish frightenin picture, but he didden see dat, he saw iz beautiful unlived son, now dead, witout a chance te even breathe a breath, dead like iz brother. De vengfull drugs came back in, all de time, all day, all night, de job wuz lost, n soon de relationship, de cudda been little dream family wuz broken for good, de difficulties wer too much for dem n Jem n Jimmy split, iz nightmare now unendin, blood soaked, deathsheaded, full uv corpses n pills n de rattle uv a bonewheeled coach.

Iz life from der became filled wit drugs, takin dem, buyin dem, sellin dem. Ya cud see de pain in iz face, it took on a bony death quality n greenish white color, he lost two stone, n he looked for sumone te blame for all iz troubles, he had many targets, Tommy n Stewie, anyone who sold H becuz it killed iz bro, de system, de blocks, de world. Finally one night in iz flat, abysmal n alone, he made a noose from iz soiled bed sheets, hung it from de damp white celin, climbed on a rikety chair n dropped out uv de blocks, lookin for iz brother or son, or no thoughts, or de light, or peace n I hope he found sumting der, I hope dat he knows now dat hes loved. In a dream de other night he smiled at me.

After Jimmy died, I didden see dat much uv Liam, he lost sum weight stopped smokin hash n went te collage as he always planed te. He found new mates der Im sure. Ones dat wer more suited te de life he wuz lookin for n we drifted as ya do.

I sat in Fatima in me new flat, in a new block. Tommy gone te England. Rooner moved away n headin for isolation rather din friends.

Georgie n Jimmy Dead. Tara n me madly in love n all over n inte each other but I had lost all me male friends. I still had a copy, a pen, n a dream.

De angel in de room at night stood over Tara n me in bed. I woke n she lay der unwoken, de angel wit great golden immortal light body bent, its face beamed on mine n it said

Poet, see that this is but another door, see that the blocks are but the mind, get up poet n sing.

I saw Georgie in de light, iz baseball cap on, iz eyes no longer squinted. Sing he said, sing,

so I did. I began te sing.

BLOCK C
BANDS, BREAK-UPS & POETIC ESCAPE

*To sing you must first open your mouth. You must
have a pair of lungs, and a little knowledge of music.
It is not necessary to have an accordion, or a guitar.
The essential thing is to want to sing.
This then is a song. I am singing.*

—Henry Miller.

Bed Block

Its two in de afternoon. Tara n me er lyin in bed awake, drinkin tea, n smokin a joint.

Ya know de way we have a spare bedroom now dat Denise is moved out?
Yeah?
Well, me cousin Jason wants te move out uv iz Mas, n needs a place te stay till he can get iz own place.
Yeaaahhh, but isin it good dat we have dis place te ourselves, ya know, so we can do as we please, like?
Yeah, we/ll still be able te do as we please, we/ll just have a bit more company.
Yeah, cool, wotever. Jason, I met um before, didden I? Hes cool, he plays de guitar duzzen he?
Yeah, ya met um here before, yizill get on great, he writes poems n songs like you… Wait, hold on, Im not sure if dis is a good Idea, two poets in me flat, ha-ha.
No, no, ya said it now, yeah dats a great idea, poetry all over de gaff, now

Jason

Jason Jones wuz born in de blocks, Fatima.
Another who called himself poet in de blocks. Jason
Jones or JJ as he wuz called by us most uv de time.
Kenny n Jason, double-trouble-poets tegether. Jason
Jones, paddy hat turned backwards, white shirt n black
leather jacket, ladies man, charmer, wild man wen
drunk, turner uv tables. Brought us bands like
Nirvana, Live n Pearljam.

Jason Jones, eatin iz finger nails te de quick wit iz
nerves, constant cigarette smoker, coffee drinker,
book reader, lover uv black tings. Singer uv a million
songs, poet clown in de parties uv de blocks.

Jason Jones, lover uv Bob Dylan songs, just like
me. Busker in de streets uv Ireland. Man uv a hundred
hairstyles, shaved, long, straight, half shaved, dyed,
pony-tailed. Man uv many jobs, cleaner, security
guard, picture framer, insomniac stayin awake for
three days n sleepin for two days under de gloop uv a
hangover. Jason Jones, once I took a black Knight
chess piece n put it in yer bed while ya slept n a note
sayin *I putta horses head in yer bed*, tomato sauce as
de blood.

Jason Jones once called himself *Devils Heart* n
pierced iz own nipple wit a safety pin n de nipple got
infected n puss oozed from it. Dichotomy uv serial-
killer biography reader n romantic poet. Takes an E
an locks himself in de bedroom n talks tru de door te
me. Trashes de sittin room wen pissed on spirits.
Loves batter burgers from de chipper. Warts on iz

hands. Watches American TV shows, *Cops* n *Friends* n *C.S.I.*

Jason Jones, cold turkied himself clean at de age uv sixteen. Jason Jones wit iz stolen *Takamine* guitar, bought on de streets for um by iz drug dealer brother. Jason Jones, gothic, grungy, sensitive. Jason Jones, cousin uv Tommy n Tara Doyle. Jason Jones me grunge brother, fire breather, seducer, song bird.

Jason Jones n me in de flat in Fatima:

He read me poems n lyrics n said,
Man, dey told me ya wrote, but I didden think yid be dis good, dis is really good stuff, Ken.

Den he played me sum songs uv iz own n a few covers uv Dylan n Paul Simon. He looked me right in de eyes wen he sang, no shame or fear n he cud sing n played enough cords te impress me, ya only need three-six te be in a band anyway right?
Lets start a band I said.
Weve got de lyrics, melody n cords, we can share de vocals n I know a guy named Luke Rooney who can play lead guitar, I can give um a ring, wot do ya think?
Yeah, man, give um a call, it sounds good te me Ken. Jason Jones, me right hand rhythm man.
Rooner got back in touch a few weeks before, he came down te ODevaney, left a ph number wit Ma.

212

I called him up n he came over te Fatima de next day wit iz guitar over iz shoulder n small *Marshal* amp in iz hand.

We jammed, JJ on vocals n rhythm guitar, Rooner on lead n me n JJ on vocals. We looked tru me notebooks n picked out sum lyrics, de boys got a simple three cord melody goin n our first song got created, I dont remember wot it wuz called or wot it souded like, becuz it wuz probably shit. De joints wer blowin n de wine wuz flowin. Tara wuz in bed, work in de mornin. We jammed n talked n put on sum tapes, got well n truly zonked n came up wit a name for de band.

De Urban Gorillas wer formed.

Jason Jones, Rooner n me, gonna break out uv de blocks wit songs.

De Urban Gorillas

De Urban Gorillas rehearsals n song writin sessions wer started wit de enthusism uv a television aerobics instructer.

Dey wer full uv *Blossom Hill* red wine n soapbar hash by de block. We wrote fifty songs n learned covers uv Bob Dylans *Forever Young* n *All Along De watchtower,* Paul Simons *Me n Julio down by de schoolyard,* Christy Moores *Lisstoonvarna.*

De song writin wuz done either by me n JJ tegether usually wit my street poet lyrics n him supplyin de simple melody n basic cords, occasionally wit a joint effort on de lyrics JJ wud add a touch uv romance, den weed turn it over te Rooner n he wud add indie rock

213

lead guitar n refine de melody, sumtimes turnin de strumed cords inte a riff, or Rooner n me wud write tegether, me on vocals n words, him on de music, dese wud be more intricate pieces, de words n licks in conversation n JJ wud come in on backin vocals n play sum rhythm, sumtimes JJ wud come up wit iz own songs n bring dem te Rooner n me, weed put sum backin vocals n lead over dem, usually Id add or change sum lyrics for um.

I started te learn sum basic cords, C, D, G, E, n de minors, I played on sum uv JJs two or three cord songs lettin um go out front n feelin exposed witout iz guitar. Most uv de early songs we came up wit wer melodic sing alongs, social critique songs wit two/three verses a simple chorus n a rock solo in de middle. De flat wuz full uv guitars, amps, leads, mics, stands, cord books, copies, pens, tuners, distortion pedals, strings, string winders, tambourines, rattles n music n de beginin uv songs.

De front room wer JJ slept: Its cold n cramped, Rooner sits on a turned up crate, cheap electric guitar strapped on, lettin de tablature rip, JJ smoke in mouth, ponytailed hair, strummin de acoustic, Im standin, mic clentched in one hand, hand writen page uv lyrics in de other, JJ n me sing in harmony wit each other.

We needed a drummer n found one by word uv mouth. Iz name wuz Keith, he lived in Cabra, blonde curly hair, one eye a bit wonky, worked in the corpo n wuz pretty average on de drums n pretty average in personality, stories da wen nower, Roy chubby Brown jokes dat noone laughed at, opinons passed down te um from iz Da, but he had a car n cud play just enough te hold a steady beat wit no frills n no drumrolls for dat matter, n so we had drums te brin our songs te life wit a backbeat n dat for now wuz enough.

We moved out uv de block bedroom n on te de rehearsal rooms uv de city.

Weed book *Temple Bar Music Centre* wen we had money, *Apple Rock Studios* wen we had less (which wuz most uv de time) n *De Underground Rehearsal Studio* on Aimen Street (across form de petrol station I once worked at) wen we had even less, it wuz a smelly, dirty place wit cheap equipment, but we wer cheap n a little dirty too.

We went der twice a week n tings started te take shape in de band, roles emerged, positions wer took n moves wer made.

A set list emerged over a six month period uv twelve songs dat we liked n we discarded de rest, seven songs composed by Rooner n me, three by JJ n me n only two uv JJs solo songs. Covers wer all out, cept as warm ups or fun interludes, dis wuz at my insistence, I wanted us te perfect our own songs n model our approch on De Stone Roses who didden do any covers.

De songs dat wer left had progressed te be louder, less sentimental, sumtimes long raucous tunes. De lyrical content had grown from just social critique songs te songs about Elizabeth Bathory de Hungarian Countess who wud bade in her victims blood in hope uv stayin young, big rousin rock songs wit thumpin repeatin choruses about individualism, freedom, Blues songs about whores n drinkin.

I stand tense at de mic, power n anger n mysticism all convergin inside me, I take a long drag from a joint n pass it on te Rooner, den spit in te a plastic bag dats on de ground n wait. Rooner takes de joint, a few quick pulls on it den places it on de amp dat he wuz sittin on, he stands wit de electric second hand *Stratocaster* hangin from de strap, he looks cool as fuck, cool enough te be in Joy Divison n mad as Raskolnikov wit iz axe, he starts te play de intro n looks at J.J n nods, J.J takes de nod on, n effeminately flicks iz long straggly hair back, hes wearin a T-shirt wit a pair uv lips on it dat says *Kiss me baby*, he comes wit de rhythm cords, playin steady on iz stolen semi-acoustic *Takamine* guitar, iz head does a little David Gray side te side ting, de tune has begun, Keith, wearin shades te hide iz madeye, comes in loud wit iz basic rock beat number one n wer off, de melody comes back around an I start te sing de verse in a sort uv part Liam Gallagher part Dublin punk part Dylan style.

De chorus is big enough te fill de room n loud enough te break inte de other rooms in de buildin n shouty like Slade n descends inte a long energetic jam wit me bashin a tambourine wit me hand, den on de cymbal uv Keiths kit n hollerin de chorus again, it ends wit all uv us goin crazy n playin hard as we can n I kick over de mic stand n Rooner jumps up in de air n lands lettin a long note scream in de room as if we wer De fuckin Who at de Isle uv White, n we look at each other smilin, high n sweaty, emptied uv all concepts or dilemmas.

Next, we needed te find a bass player, n we put up ads in de music shops n rehearsal rooms, but got no calls or if we did dey wud ask lots uv questions,
Who er yer influences?
Der on de add, mate.
Wer er yiz from?
De Inner-City.
Any gigs lined up, any payed gigs?
Ehh, noooo.
Will der be chicks at de rehersals?
Fuck, no der wont be mate.
N dey never call us back or answer wen we called dem.

Rooner, JJ n me started workin as industrial cleaners for a Kilkenny man called Alan. We wer paid a fiver an hour te clean buildin sites (we wer de lowest on de wrung, even lower din de labours), hospitals n insane asylums. Real horrible, honest work. It paid de bills n for rehearsals, strings n drugs.
Dis went on for six months, de three uv us workin in de same job, in a band tegether, n JJ livin in de flat

wit me n Tara. Rooner practically lived wit us as he wuz der almost everyday n sleepin on de couch three times a week n sleepin at me mas (wer he paid rent) de other four, he ran away from de house uv young, broken boys, after one fella who he became pals wit killed himself in de middle uv de night after a heavy drinkin session, Rooner found de poor cunt on de back uv de door wit a belt around iz neck, iz arm locked in place aniz fingers gripin de belt, so Rooner ended up back in de block in me Mas flat, in de back bedroom wit de glooptings n de noise uv the other flats, n de blocksounds n de brown family around de next block, sniggerin under der breath at whose back in de blocks again.

So, der we wer, Jason Jones, Rooner n me, playin our songs, snappin strings, arguin, watchin movies, drinkin red wine, smokin splifs, cleanin shit, buffin floors, writin tunes, listenin te music on de radio, eatin out uv chippers or home made stews or fry-ups, walkin te rehershals, readin books about Indians n serial killers n rockbands.

Rooner had been tryin te get us te listen te Led Zeppelin but JJ cudden really get inte dem n neither cud I at first, but after Taras da gave us a tape wit Led-Zep three n four on it n I really listened te it, -De craftmanship n virtuoso skills uv every member in de band n de power n depth uv de songs- I thought it wuz de best music Id heard since De Doors, Rooner n me decided dat we wanted te go heavier, we wanted te be like De Doors, Led-Zep, Jimi Hendrix n we had te move out anyting too light or stuff dat started in de key uv G(De Happy Hippy cord we called it), we wanted songs in de bluesy key uv E or moody serious e minor or weird F keyed trippy stuff.

Becuz uv dis Jasons songs n input became less n less. Den de tension n trials set in n its all: JJ cant play dat its too difficult, I cant sing dat melody n say Fuck buskin dats a load uv bollix not art, Rooner plays too loud, de drummers not good enough, dis job is shit, Im not cleanin mad mans shit off de floor for a fuckin fiver an hour, yer fuckin mush again, clean de fire out or go de shop, buy sum fuckin food, Tara in work, Tara n me in bed bein quiet, Tara sick uv men n der smelly feet everywer, washin windows in hospitals, help Im fucked, I hate dat cunt, hes fucked up, hes mad, hes too much, lyrics er shit, late again, drunk again, fucked-up de song again n finally JJ comes in one night a few beers on um,
Lads, Ive sumting te tell yiz.
We sit down n he tells us.
Im leavin de band, boys, Its not de way I thought it wud be, I thought weed be out der giggin, I know, yiz think wer not ready, but I want te just go out n play for people, n anyway, de two uv yiz have de talent n de drive, I dont, its all yer songs we play, n it just works, Kennys words n Lukes music, dont get me wrong I love playin wit yiz n wer still mates, but I dont think I want te do it anymore, Its too much, too intense, I just want te play sum songs for people dats it. I dont want te be de best band in de world or change lives ar anyting ya know?

Rooner looked at um n me n shrugged, iz face yellow, an evil half smile broke out n he said

If dats wot ya want, man, wot can we do?

Wait, hold on now man, we need ya in de band, ya have yer place, we/ll be giggin soon, we just need te get tings soundin right, get a base player, look man, yer drunk, sleep on it n in de mornin see how ya feel yeah? I said.

Honestly Kenny, I know wot I want te do, its just not for me, yiz have te keep goin tho, yiz have it man, yiz have wot it takes te go all de way. Yiz have de passion n drive for it, I, I, I just dont have dat...

In de mornin I asked him once more if he wuz sure n he gave de same answer n dat wuz it, it felt like failure te me, I wuz let down. But I got over it quick.

Rooner didden give a fuck as evident by iz nonchalance de night before n he told me dat he thought JJ wuz right, we didden need um, dat JJ wuzzen good enough n cudden play much or write lyrics anywer near as good as mine, so fuck it n fuckum too.

Its me n you Kenny, wer de ones who have de fire, wer de ones who have de guts, heh-heh.

De Urban Gorillas wer born, burned fast n bright n died young witout ever playin a gig, nevermind recordin an album, de greatest punk band in de world ever, n dat wuz dat, fade-out. Jason Jones it wuz a beautiful trip while it lasted, bud.

De Blocks er full: A Vision

De blocks er corpo flats forty foot high concrete housin estates wit grafftied walls *Fuck de garda Anto wuz here* everyone livin on top, beneath, beside each other, patches uv grass in-between blocks de Backers wer our playin fields as children n teens, arguments about did de ball hit de post or not de post a rolled up jumper, wen de sun shone weed sit in de backers chewin grass n spittin like loafin work-men on brake time in sum American movie weed seen, de smells uv de blocks burnin piss-stained mattresses Sunday dinners chicken corned beef roast potatoes cabbage hash tobacco dog-shit larger, teemin wit de smell uv sex n burnin wood n rubber piss cider shit n vomit buttercups dat grow in de backers coal turf briquettes black smoke from chimneys, teemin wit drugs hash speed roach methadone heroin ecstasy, teemin wit used condoms empty crushed aluminium cans millions uv cigarette butts overflowin bags uv rubbish piled inte large communal bins broken bottles uv Vodka n *Scrumpy Jack* cryin babies barkin dogs drunks singin n fightin notes from a cheap guitar, de blocks er full uv seraphim junkies demons danger, full uv whores n madmen tortured poets wit broken pens painters wit no canvases footballers wit no feet singers witout songs martyrs wit out causes lovers witout heart dead men who dont know deyre dead, full uv wounds n sores, full uv thorns n tears, full uv excrement n seamen, full uv dreams phantoms dark energies, full uv de holy light, full uv life, full uv poetry music dance, full uv words, full uv de creations uv time, full

221

uv de sound behind de world, full er de blocks, full te de brim, I/ll let it all out in wild exuberance, sea-gulls crows n pigeons fight over stale bread in de backers, school boys n school girls eat porridge n toast, full uv tea coffee cigarettes dogs bark at de postman music reggae Bob Marley n UB40 house music bangin in de dawn light rock n roll big guitars cranked up loud sad songs uv suicide n loneliness Rimbaudian youths wit tasselled hair weepin under porch stairs banshee wailin tru de walls lullabies under covers uv moonlit bedrooms lovers n junkies, de blocks er full uv lovers n junkies, *ahh baby dats so good love it wen ya make me feel like dis, Lovely dats fuckin lovely gear man, Im feelin dat now er you, do it te me babe, do it babe, put it in stick it right in, Hit dat vein, punch it hard, Make me hard, Get me wet, Suck on dat ting,*
Suck dat H right up,
Yes no do it do it yes no
ahhhhhhhhhhhhhhhhhhhhwwwwwwwwwwwwwhhhhh
hhhuuuuummmmmmhhhhhh
Sure wer all Junkies for sumting arent we be baby, de vision darkens, vision uv de dark, darken does de vision now, de block blooms open like a black rose, a junkie shows her wound it stinks it spurts, Glooptings in a ring singin a creepy ballad de lyrics blow in de wind n land in de ears uv children n make dem bash each other wit sticks n stones sticks n stones will break yer bones but poems will never hurt ya, blocks tremble in dese lines, boys in gangs topless punchin each other in de loins greasy hair n bad tattoos slice each other wit broken bottles put cigarettes out on der arms, girls run tru de block screamin wit blood drippin

222

from der vaginas n arses, dogs growl at cars, rats bite baby fingers off, river uv vomit runs tru de middle uv de block a troupe uv winos row a galleon a top it piss stains all over dem dey mumble n fight wit de pigeons who swoop at dem, dead children play ball *Queenie I oh who has de ball is she big or is she small*, de block cracks open a huge cavern crawlin wit syringes guns n Glooptings drinkin hooch joy riders wit mutilated faces suicide victims hangin from trees crucified on crosses made from Mack 3 razors, giant snake wit red eyes rares up n swallows de blocks writhes on its back n spits de blocks out like venom, de blocks er supermarket shelves wer de poor er stacked tegether yellow pack people brand X flats n brand X lives, de blocks wer gargoyles perch on de edges, wer de dark entities cry in de cracks uv reality poor wretched tings whisperin on de shoulders uv addicts n predators full uv pain wot do dey want who er dey wer do dey come from who bore dese bastdards, oh my God wot has become uv yer children in dis garden uv black flowers, de block is dark de walls dark n oozin a black goo, a gang uv youths drinkin cans n bottles uv Budweiser smoking Joints n sniffin coke *Gis a blow uv dat will ya*
Dats lovely stuff
Waitll I seeim Im gonna smash iz head in
PrickDopeSniffCuntLovelyDeadly
Yeah yerMa
How much
Fifty bag
Scoreblock

any skins bud
Wanker
Cunt
InbitsIam
Imtellingyadatsdewayhesaidit
Itsmadisinit
Sniffloadabollix
Sniffwotsdat
Sniff,Garda
Sniff,wendidyagetout
SniffRingmeyeah
SniffDeadishe
Ishedead
Dead,Sniff, Who is
Wotsdatendewall,
de sun comes up over de block
a bloodshot eye weepin on de boys
de virgin Mary stands on top uv her stone pillar arms
out by her sides
round here dey say dey seen her move
not a mark on her immaculate grotto
de football pitch dat faces her is striped wit tyre tracks
from handbrake turns
small black patches on de grass from fires lit te warm
bodies
dat wud rather stand n drink cans uv cider in de cold
din listen te girlfriends whingin kids cryin parents
fights
a child throws a stone at de number ten bus drivin pass
under gaze uv de virgin

if she can move whys she still here
if she cant move well at least shes got plenty te watch
over
de blocks er de corpo flats that grow in de heroin
ecstasy teemin wit stone blocks uv memorytime
poetry wit drugs millions uv cigarette butts overflowin
bags uv light n blocks uv empty crushed aluminium
broken bottles uv smack a book that I write piled inte
large community n fightin notes from a cheap guitar
babies barkin n dogs drunk demons full uv danger
whores n families uv single parent blocks full uv
seraphim junk canvases thorns full uv excrement n
boots pullin hair tears full uv dreams music full uv me
n de sound behind de world is full full full full sirens
wailin ambulance uv bones flicks lighters words uv
blocks burnin piss stained steel n concrete shakin
nights blocks uv roast potatoes cabbage hash tobacco
sounds n everyone livin n fightin couples moan uv
orgasm wind blown young mens arms burn punches
between blocks dreamin de blocks er teemin wit
works blood comin from make believe pitches uv
teenage boys fuck ya tru de veins uv junkies fuck ya
inte joints cheap cider smells in de backers chewin her
head in sum American movie were de blocks goof
Sunday dinners Infected HIV runnin dogshit sounds n
smells uv sex burnin wood rubber n piss uv life space
n time blocks rolled inte mornin a blessin bleedin God
forgive me be honest,
I sit top floor uv me apartment in a modern block n de
wind is blown Novemberly at me window in a winter
mornin in Dublin n I smile Hildegard Von Bigens
Music n Visions plays loud as I tap de keys wit me

fingers once more te tell de tale uv how I rose in de blocks.

Zorro

Zorro strolled inte de story at dis time. He wuz an old shoplifter friend uv Tommy Doyles. Scored hash wit us a few times n after sum good chats n goofs, he passed de unvoiced operatin rules uv de Rooner/Kenny friendship n we became a new kind uv band in de blocks.

Zorro, wit iz whispy moustache n long brown ponied hair, iz low drawl, iz facts about world war I n II n Vietnam n Korea n the Boer war n the battle uv Bannockburn, UFO sightins, Samurai warriors n Ninjas, iz philosophies on drug culture n political ideologies n literature, he always had a book or two on um n a can uv *Mace* or a blade just in case sum fucker tried te start on him or a drug deal took a dangerous turn.

Zorro, weird in de extreme, former stroker uv *Lynx*, *Gillette* Razors n *Domestos* from newsagents n *Man U* n *Liverpool* kits from sports shops, cannabis connoisseur full uv conspiracies n cosmologies, lean n wirey, dressed in green combats n green hemp jumpers n black *Docs* n black hoodys.

Zorro, maker uv de most powerfully noxious joints in Ireland, abstainer uv alcohol, told us dat white bread wuz bad for us n full uv e numbers, be careful uv too much sugar or salt or red meat.

Zorro fades like old silent movies into de night, lives wit iz Ma an old crazy lady dat never left de house n had wild unwashed Einstein hair. Zorro n me talkin about poetry, Orwell, Huxley, Tim Leary, Marx n Socrates.

Zorro de zonked. Zorro de strange. Zorro de chilled. Zorro de starved.

Zorro on de dole forever, a madman drifter sage, a loner, a mystery te be solved by noone, a shy prophet, a freak in de old n wonderful sense uv de word. Zorro, who introduced trippin n mushrooms n sumtimes silence n contemplation n sumtimes long drawn out talks inte de blocks dawn.

Zoro, part time Yogi, guitar carrier, part time rodie, rage buried far in iz mind, iz Da dead from self-defenestration, dead like my Da, dead like Rooners Da who got Cancer n went witout an apolgy, went witout a word, almost.

Zorro, de fantastic liar whose anger wud erupt volcanic from iz mouth aniz face wud go lava red, Zorro de mad monk uv de blocks, de stranger in de party, de man at de back uv de room, de carrier uv tools, de back pack uv hidden tings, de voice dat came from de back uv iz throat in a low mumble, de shy, de embarrassed, de unsexed, de floater, de uncontactable, de muddy, de melancholy, de buzzer, de hungry, de Dosteveskian, de sufferin, de heroic, de one, de only El Zorro uv de blocks.

Education

De flat in Fatima: Its night, its bitter cold, its late autumn. Taras downstairs in her sister Mandys flat, drinkin wit de girls.

Jason has been evicted for none payment uv rent, drunken loutishness, leavin de band n spoofin about wages, iz contribution te de cause at de zero point, iz hook gettin slung turned out te be good for um in de end, it awoke him te iz procratinatin n forced him te be commited at last te sumting, iz own life.

Rooner n Zorro er off on a hunt in de concrete Dublin jungle for sum drug or other.

Im alone, searchin, I need more answers, Im sinkin back te de primordial me. Ive a pen n a copy on me lap n on de table is a cupa tea. De rooms atmosphere shifts,

ITS here again, I know time boy, I remember dat pasture witout want wer we used te saunter upon, way back before time. De light enters tru de slit, a sound, a low perfect pitched whistle comes from de spare bedroom, a callin. I rise reverently n ease inte de room wer de angel sits on de bed wit wings enfolded n green eyes ablaze, androgynous face n statuesque physique, points wit marbled finger at a small tattered book on de floor.

This is a key, poet, read it n unlock the gate you seek.

I look at de book: *Songs uv Innocence n uv experience* by William Blake,

a drawin uv an angel n a child on de cover. Angels in de trees, angels in de blocks, angels in me n you my ancient guru aul Willy Blake, my poet saint. De angel stands, unfolds its bright wings, electrons shimmerin, razes de roof n soars. I pick up de book n turn de pages thinkin,

A key!

De first Trip

De first trip is de essential one.

Der wuz a drought on, Rooner, Jason Jones, Zorro n me cudden get any hash anywer in Dublin, all contacts wer out. El Zorro had enough for two Joints on um. We gave up de search n decided te buy sum alcohol wit de cash we had. Jason bought a bottle uv California red *Blossom Hill* wine, a customary tipple for de time. Zorro, no alcohol for him. Rooner n me purchased a large bottle uv *Jack Daniels* Tennessee whiskey, de fireiest demon drink ya can buy!

We wer listenin te music, playin *Fifa football* on de *Playstaion*, jammin on guitars, Rooner n me swiggin on raw shots uv whiskey n drinkin it in a glass mixed wit *Coca Cola*, Jason sippin on iz Homeric dark wine. De two joints wer made n smoked quickly. Yeah think fast-cut cool British Gangster moive style.

Can ya smoke mushrooms? I think I read sumwer dat ya can.

I think ya might be right der Kenny, ehm, I think it wuz Kerouac, in *On de Road*, ehm, in Mexico at de end uv de book, Zorro said in iz monotone droll way.

I dont think it wuz Kerouac, might uv been Castaneda n Don Juan who smoked de mushrooms in a pipe?

Yeah, dat might be wot Im thinkin uv, altho its generaly belived dat ol Carlos wuz makin up half de shit in de Don Juan books, but ya never know?

Fuck it lets try it, n find out if de Don wuz talkin shit or not.

Zorro got out de skins n made a joint wit tobacco n fifty dried out n chopped up shrooms. All four uv us hit de splif like de filthy fucks we wer.

I dont advise it. Absolutely foul taste n putrid smell. Hard not te vomit after a few drags. I imagine it wud be like smokin shit, but den dey do come from cow n sheep shit (Holy shit is wot it is). Der wuz a light trippy effect, giggles, a lightnin uv atmosphere, brightenin uv colours but not much else, certainly no big visions or revelations like Id been let te believe. No squidgey for de third eye just yet.

As de night progressed we got louder n rowdier, singin blues songs, jamin out tunes on de guitars. No hash. JJs wine all gone n de bottle uv JD down te de last couple uv shots, mad Rooner n me wernt ready for sleep.

Fuck it we said n decided it wuz time te take sum mushrooms.

Zorro had divided dem inte packets containin a hundred each. A packet wuz opened, handfuls wer taken n washed down wit de last uv de whiskey, de anxiety n excitement n anticipation uv a new drug mixin in our psyche, ders always dat feelin, a new experience is comin down de line n ya never get it again after de first time.

Give us sum more a dem.

Im gettin nutting outta dem.

Id relax on, eh, dem, der, emh if I wuz you lads, said de more experienced Zorro.

But like de radical experimentalers dat we wer, we consumed wunna de packets between us n let de laboratory uv or bodies await de results.

Playin away on de *Playstaion* n chattin, an old bootleg tape uv Oasis wuz playin on de stereo, Rooner n me started te sing along, standin up wit our hands behind our backs, chins stickin out, puttin on our best Liam Gallagher voice,

Ya can wait for a lifetime, te spend yer days in de sunshhinneeee.

Laughin our heads off. We opened another pack, n started te gobble sum more. Jason n Zorro looked at us wit worry n admiration. Deyd triped before. Rooner n me figured, wot de fuck, we done plenty uv speed n ecstasy, hash, alcohol, n mixed all dese on occasion. Rooner n Zorro had picked a thousand uv de little sons a bitchs, up on ol Mushy mountain out in Tallaght, n used my gaff te dry de fungi under de grill n bag dem, so Rooner n me had claim enough te munch away all we wanted te n dat wuz dat.

So der we wer, two hundred downed between de two uv us, de bottle uv JD emptied. I wuz tryin te play a match against Jason on de fifa game, wen I got de first tingle, de TV screen looked an odd shape, de picture kept goin out uv focus, hand te eye coordination all over de place n Im gettin hammerd by JJ n hes shite at de game.

I cant play dis ting anymore, man.

De terracotta orange walls wer glowin at me.

Im feelin a buzz comin on me now, er you? I said te Rooner, who wuz sittin in an armchair eyes fixed on de wall, real quiet.

Yeah, wuz all he said.

Zorro seein de onset uv de trip, asked if it wuz ok te go inte de spare room n go te sleep for de night.

Yeah, just leave us sum more uv dem shrooms.

He threw two packs on de table n left de room.

I/ll do sum if yiz dont mind lads? said Jason,

Yeah man, go for it.

Jason opened a pack, poured out about seventy mushies in iz hand, popped dem inte iz gob n washed dem down wit a glass uv water n bobs yer Brujo. By den Rooner n me wer on it, notin de curvature uv objects in de room, like two Huxleys wit de doors clensed, seein everyting wit intense vibrancy, de aliveness uv tings, everting wuz real yet unreal, distortions uv space n time. De room widenin in a flash, den ya close n open yer eyes n its shrunk back down, fuckin wonderland effects. Rooner got dis big power trip goin, talkin about himself as a God n I join in,

Yeah man, dats it we/re de Gods, we control er own destiny, fuck!

Den we start te pick on Jason, cuz he left de band.

Yer a soft little shit, dya know dat?

A scared little boy, afraid uv a bit uv hard graft make it, wot ya gonna do now, work for de rest uv yer life in a factory or buskin for hand outs on de streets?

I wuz half windin him up, Rooner wuz really layin inte um n ya cud see in Rooners eyes de flames, de hate spittin out, he glared sadisticly n bared iz teeth at JJ.

Jason just got up, left, witout a word n went home. After heed gone Rooner n me wer shocked at our own behaviour.

Wot de fuck did we do dat for? I said.

I don't know man, shit, he took a load uv dem, an hes gone off on iz own.

Weed find out later dat Jason had iz own trip on which he wuz accompanied by iz friend de Orange dat he held in iz hand for five hours, he drew a smiley face on it in black marker n spoke te it, on occasion it spoke back te um or so he claimed, it wuz mashed in iz palm, juice n rind all over iz fingers wen he arrived at iz brother Pauls house at six in de mornin lookin for a smoke n a bed.

Rooner n me shared an identical experience.
We stood up n felt like we had grown two feet taller. Investigatin de room n everytin in it.

Dis is deadly.

Look at de plant.

Dat TV is huge, man, ha-ha.

Heh-heh-heh.

We went te de kitchen, made a cup uv tea, took fifty more each, te really crank it up te ten warp speed, hyper reality. De old yellow n white checked curtains started te sway from side te side, den melt inte de surroundins, sumting inexplicable called us towards dem, we opened dem, wow, de clouds dark n masive.

Outside, oneuv us said.

We grabbed de cups uv tea, headed for de balcony, two newborns, mad te see de world for de first time. Out on de balcony our other eyes opened wide, de walls wer fizzin up, de sky a spiritual idigo n violet, clouds right in front uv us pulsatin wit atomic energy, ya cud reach out an touch dem if ya dared, we wer transfixed by de wonder uv existence, de wonder uv bein. Me cup uv tea wuz placed on de ledge uv de balcony n wen I tried te pick it up, it wuz stuck, like it wuz part uv de balcony, real heavy. De world became a great paintin by Turner or Blake. De Ancient uv days reachin down from de vastness te mock our desire n grief.

A girl came from de other side uv de block, down four flights uv stairs, across de block n out uv it, like Sonic de fuckin hedgehog, woof! Dis astounded us so much dat exclamation marks popped out uv our minds, we clasped each others hand n we fled back inte de safety uv de flat fearin de crazy computer game scene we just witnessed.

Back inside craziness abounded. Me demandin more, Rooner sayin

NO MORE, man, ya had enough.

Lookin at mushrooms in our hands, talkin te dem

Ya little bastards, how can ya do dis?

Eatin dem off de floor, from de packet dat Jason

had left on de table, sumtimes it wud be a bit uv dirt dat looked like a shroom. Both uv us amazed at de size uv Rooners hands, dey looked like two giant spades te me, he kept lookin at dem, turnin over iz palms, holdin dem up te de light n smilin. Hours uv hulcinatory weirdness passed by. De sun rose n it wuz bright out. It wuz time te go out n explore de outside world again, time for a walk around de city te see its hidden pasagess.

We creeped inte de bedroom te tell Tara dat we wer out uv our heads, n goin te go for a walk in de city.

I know yiz mad cunts, its de third time yiz told me, fuck off out, please, I have te get up for work soon she said, bless her.

Sorry, did we, oh shit, sorry,
we said.

Next we barged inte de spare room n tried te rouse Zorro, te try get more mushrooms, but he just lay der n wudden answer, even wen we kicked um a few times. Bug eyed, open sould, tripedo maniacs tegether Rooner n me, we ventured off te see our Dublin town.

Down in de block a stray mongrel dog walked about ten feet around us slowly, starin right inte our eyes. Never blinkin or taken iz eyes off us, as we walked out uv de block. Like two wise old men we looked at each other n said

He knows, he knows n noded at each other n de dog.

Walkin down pass James St flats, tru de vast area

owned by *Guinness*, a feelin uv utter contentedness took over. We strolled, talked loudly, speculatin dat we wer in a different dimension, another side uv reality. We wer Gods in our own creation, we wer infinite love on a stroll tru itself. Everyting wuz sublime, perfect, nutting mattered, everyting wuz alright, n it always wud be. Tings wer never born n never died, life had no purpose but itself, blisshood in de blocks.

As we came te *Christ Church*, de bells rang out, n announced de modern city te us. Moloch stood starin at us wit iz blind windows aniz industry. Insect People swarmin around, buzzin n zippin te mundane jobs n schools dat cud never teach wot we had been thought tonight. De machinery uv de city wuz a monster made uv trucks, cranes, buses, taxis, lights, shops, Garda cars, ambulances. Dark satanic mills, spectres everywer, Glooptings on many shoulders, devils strokin de hair uv drunk girls, angels in de trees, a huge black metalic hand in de sky revealed a terrifyin toxic fume reality n wen it hit us it made us heave from our bowles te our mouths. I nearly got run over by wunna de trucks. De dirty rubber tire a spinnin death mask, Rooners giant hand pulled me by de shoulder te safety, I stood still n closed me eyes, cudda bein for an hr, n inhaled a gulp uv air, n den two more n sighed out, calmness entered de long dream den.

Our last truly inspirational vision uv de blessed night happened wen we laid eyes on a beautiful black girl uv about fourteen or fifteen, she wuz stood at de bus stop in her school uniform. She completely wowed us. Not in any sexual way, but a pure angel, visionary beauty. A cosmic glow came from her. I know now dat it wuz innocence.

We wer enthralled by her innocence. We frightened her by gawkin. A black man came from sumwer, maybe her brother or Da n looked at us like we wer two perverts. We walked away exhausted n cold. Rooner puked a puddle uv white lumpy sick in de street. It wuz gettin scary. I needed te piss, so we went te a lane on Thomas st, wer ya cud always go for a piss witout bein seen, Piss Lane we called it. Piss Lane had grown, gotten bigger sumhow. We wer stood der sayin

Dis lane is not dis big.

Holy shit, how can dis lane be dis big?

People walkin by lookin at two men standin in a lane sayin te each other dis lane is not dis big. Turns out, we wer standin in de wrong lane, Piss lane wuz de next one up.

It wuz time te go home, te bed, te sleep, perchance te dream unspeakable dreams.

De Junkyard dogs

De Blake book wuz a key inte Literature, a new n more personal art, in which I cud reach de sublime on me own. All dese books n writers came tru de angels hand: Blakes biography, De Beats—Ginsberg, Kerouac, Burroughs Corso—De Romantics, *Moby Dick, Don Quixote*, Plato, Homer, Ovid, Joyce, Kafka,

Whitman, Shakespeare, Genet, Celine, Rimbaud, *1984*, *Brave New World*, *A Clockwork Orange*, *Trainspottin*, Bukowski, Selbyjr, Dosteyevsky, Yeats, Reinaldo Areneas, Henry Miller. It opened de head up again. De poetry grew deep n broad in me consciousness. I cud hear de wings uv dose white doves in de distance once more.

Rooner n me put an add up in *Waltons* music shop n found a new drummer, a six foot five German, powerhouse named Franz who had enormous hands n feet. Den at last a base player from Switzerland, curley haired, speckled Tomas. De Junkyard Dogs wer born.

A much tighter unit din de Urban Gorillas. Heavier, bigger. Louder. Raw n dark wit a current uv confidence runnin tru. Bluesy, shouty n dirty. *De Underground* wuz ditched for de more professional *Temple Bar* n *Loop* studios. We practised relentlessly. We made lots uv recordins on a cheap *Boss* four track n listened scrupulously te dem while stoned on hash or mushrooms, perfectin every nuance n note till we sat der flaked out, eyes closed, immeresd in our sound, lovin our art, norishin our spirits.

Zorro is sittin on de floor rollin a splif, watchin n listenin, gettin inte de mood. Franz pounds down on de kick drum wit iz massive foot, n powers tru de beat fillin in wit John Bonham style rolls. Rooner wit a smirk on iz face, iz big mop haired head noddin, a nasty, contagious riff blitzes de room, Tomas stands tappin geekishly, iz base rumblin under de riff, I stand cocked te one side, hangin onte de mic n stand, snarlin n spittin, stoned immaculate voice, hollerin on de chorus,

Twenty I/ll suck ya, thirty I/ll fuck ya n eighty five te bring me home, thirtyll do ya, I only wanna screw ya, Im never gonna bring ya home, ahh brinnnnnnnnnnnnnnggg ya home nooowww, I got de Benburb Blues, I got de Benburb blues, I got de benburb Bllllluuuuuuuuuueeeeeeeeeeeeesssssssssssssss yeeeeaaauuuuuuhhhhhhhhhhhhhh!!

A new set made uv ten Rooner n Kenny numbers wuz nailed down. Titles like *Wen De Hour Come, In De Heart uv De City, Suicide Swinger, De Benburb Blues,* de sound wuz a mix uv Led-Zep, De Doors, De Sex Pistols, Pink Floyd, ODevaney Gardens, William Blake, De Blues n Dublins Streets n night time danger. Sum uv de tunes went on for ten minutes, but we wer tight n we wer ready te go out n blow up n be de best fuckin band in de world.

Rooner n me quit de job in de industrial cleanin company. Rooner got in te wunna iz mad dark n paranoid periods, convinced dat Alan wuz rippin him off on wages n tax. De truth wuz he wuz rippin us all off, n we wer rippin him too. Rooner n me wud go into work late n stoned, do ten minutes uv idlin, sweep a bit uv dirt up, clean a room wit de enthusiasm uv a hung over sloth, wipe sum sawdust from a draw, stretch a bit, have a piss, den have our break, Ham or Chicken sandwiches washed down wit milk n den smoke a splif n go back te work bombed.

239

It wuz summer again n wen de sun shone in tru de windows, weed go up on de roof uv de site n lay down wit our tops off n smoke while listenin te de portable radio or weed leave work early n go te de park wit de guitars, a nice lump n Zoro.

Den one day Rooner in iz broodin started inte a rant, yellin, kickin over work tops, fumin, intense paranoia n anger, he looked at iz phone n said

Dis is a piece uv shit,

n hurled it against de wall smashin it te bits, den stood on it, de phone crushed n bits broken all over de room, den he just walked off n left de job. I lasted about a month witout um before I quit, de monotony wuz too much.

We wer free te be rock stars n stoners, good old loafin, like de flowers do, like monks do, like de Apostils did, stoned out Whitmans me n you Luke Rooney, ya wild, black eyed wonderful maniac ya. Tara n me still great lovers, love grown older n deeper, de fights come te sort out de differences n glitches, ya iron out sum uv each others neuroses, as has always been, but love is a root dat grows deep in de soil wen watered with care n tended wit affection.

De junkyard dogs found n lost a bass player just as quick. Tomas wuz sacked for lack uv communication skills, not bein able te keep up n play wit de skill uv Franz or Rooner, n a generaly awkward dispositon, he looked like a member uv Blur who walked inte de Oasis rehersal room, another one dat didden fit wit us.

De first gig came in de back room uv a smelly pub on de quays, wit a bunch uv other bands no one ever heard uv or wud hear uv, each band wuz givin twenty tickets te sell, 80/20 split in favour uv de promoters, we sold eleven tickets.

JJ, Tara, Zoro n Edel wer out in de crowd. Rooner on guitar, Franz on drums n me out front.

We dropped half an E n drank two pints each. De half a pill kicked in n loosened us up a bit, calmed de nerves, we wer still intense fuckers tho, lookin at de other bands like dey wer enemies, stalkin around de pub, lookin like trouble, we got on stage n I had de sound guy put a touch uv echo n reverb on de mic, we started te play, de first big riff fired out by Rooner, Franz came wit de thunder God stomp n roll n people wer interested, heads turned. I wuz givin de fuckin rock star posses n half shoutin half singin, Iggy Pop glare, de groove flowin nice between de boys, first song went down good, applause from de crowd, second song n wer gettin in te it n Rooner snapped a string, Franz pointed at him as if te say Ah shit, Rooner took it as Look wot ya done, ya stupid cunt n looked at Franz wit utter hate, afterwards he complained te me about

De big German fucker, like who de fuck does he think he is?

Rooner threatened te bash sumone in de crowd wen dey heckled him. I stared down inte de crowd like a man eatin tiger, threatenin anyone else te say sumting, dey didden. We played fast n loud wit intimidatin faces n punk fulled power, ended wit a rousin repeated chorus n monster riff, n left de stage in a feedback storm. We got a few compliments afterwards, an old rock roddie wit a patch over one eye, sailor tattoos n grey pony tailed hair said te me dat me lyrics had a lot uv depth for a youngfella. I felt high on de beer, pills n adrenalin, it felt like weed made another step forward on de way.

De promoters uv de gig wanted us te come back n play again. Der wuz sum tension between Rooner n Franz followin de string incident, but in de next few rehersals we sounded great. It wuz December 2003. 2004 wud be our year we wer certain uv it.

Franz went back te Germany for Christmas holidays. He never came back te Ireland again. We got a letter from him about three months later, he claimed te have been in sum nut house, after havin a nervous breakdown n dat iz parents said rock music n bands n drugs wer te blame, dat he wuz te rest n den get back te real life, a proper job wit a carer. He cud have been tellin de truth about de sickness, but we didden believe him, anyway he still listened te wot iz parents had te say, rockstar, noway, de boy cud play de drums like a monster but he wuz just one more muppet who didden have de guts te be an artist, so fuck him too. We cudden bare it tho, it deflated us badly, knocked us right back down de ladder te de bottom again, no bass, no drums, no gigs, no jobs, no fuckin band even, fuck it, fuck it all.

It wuz back te me n Rooner wit one guitar n Zoro as stoner fan n encourger. We went on courageously. One guitar n a voice. Played a few acoustic sets at open mics n didden like it, we wanted te sound big, obnoxiously loud, ya cant get dat from a voice n acoustic guitar. We retreated te de bedroom n wrote n recorded epics uv sound dat Rooner worked on endlessly n lyrics spoken or sung over dem by me, we felt they wer as good as anyting we listened te n we wer such harsh judges uv music den dat we only listened te a select few: Led-Zep, Pink Floyd, De Doors, De Stone Roses, De Who, Jimi Hendrix, De Beatles last four albums, a bit uv punk, de blues n ourselves.

Rooner at de 4-track, breath heavy, ear phones on, twistin knobs n dials, blendin tracks n over dubbin, me sittin on de bed rollin a joint.

Wots it sound like now man?

Wot? he takes off de ear phones.

Wots it like, any good?

Fuckin class Kenny, really good wit dat beat I made on it, here have a listen.

He hooks de 4-track up te de fender amp n presses play, de song comes on, layers uv intricate guitar parts, a dark hypnotic beat, me voice soundin more mature den ever, a little bit uv pain, a little bit uv wisdom, lyrics about war, power, sex, freedom. We listen wit maximum concentration, we enter de song, nutting else exists only de song. We look at each other at de end n nod yes, confirmin te each other dat dis is de real shit, dis is de best fuckin song in de world right now n only de two uv us know it, but we do know it. We play it for Zoro later n he agrees.

Its a soild piece uv art, lads.

Wer in de flat in Fatima, its late October. Rooner, Zoror n me er talkin about dead pigeons, n De metaphysical meanin uv churches, trees n outlines uv tings. Rooner n me er drinkin *Smirnoff Vodka* n all three uv us have taken a small but potent dose uv mushrooms. We slump back into our chairs, n put on the appropriate music, De Doors *The End,* Pink Floyds *Darkside Uv De Moon* we get absorbed in the tunes, feelin each note --the gaps between beats--after an epoch uv silence, we merge wit the loss. We merge wit sadness. We merge wit each other. We merge wit the Godessance in an Epiphany uv cords n melody n den BANG heartburn from the Vodka for me n vomitin from the mushrooms for Rooner n Zoro sits smokin a spliff sayin

Ehm, Im grand boys, Im, eh, grand, ya shudden mix alcohol wit mushies lads.

Tryin te get back te dat state we wer in de first night we done em with de JD man,
dat wuz fuckin class, I know ders sumting for me der, an answer te me questions, says Rooner.

Man I dont think wer ever gonna get back te dat place, it wuz a one off, wer gettin hung up n dat experience man, we got wot we needed from it, fuck it, lets move in de journey, lets not recreate but seek de new, seek de next epiphany, wer ever it may be, I

244

said n lay back n closed me eyes n saw flashes uv rainbow lights.

Yeah, yizer probably right, fuck it, heh-heh.

Everyone in de blocks laughed, dey said we shud give it up. Dey said Rooner had talent, he shud be in a band. Hes gonna make it. Dey thought I shud get a job. Dey knew fuck all about art anyway I said.

Rooner started te hate everyone barr Zorro, Tara n me. Iz broodin got deeper, longer, iz comedy darker, iz anger explosive, iz paranoia extreme, he felt he cudden trust people, heard tings that werent said, iz language more sinister, iz threats more violent n sadistic, heed come up wit torture scenarios dat he heed like te do te Dole officer, Taxman, a person dat bumped in te um, boybands, girlbands, Garda, anyone who pissed um off,

Id love te fuckin get de cunts head n put it in vice n just keep squeesin till iz head popped or smash de fucker wit a lump hammer, crack iz fuckin skull open like an egg I wud, I swear I fuckin wud Kenny.

We fought more n more. Zorro n he became, Rooner n Zorro as dey wer both single n dey wud go off tegether te give Tara n me space. I still had Tara n she still had me. Rooner cursed de government, iz family, de dole office, me Mas dog Max for iz incessant barkin, de weather as if it wuz only him dat got pissed on, de price uv smokes, de blandness uv TV, de opinions uv everyone, if iz tea wuz too hot, if he cudden get hash it wuz becuz

God hated um or de universe wuz conspirin te get um.

He stayed in me flat till 4 am, went home n came back throwin stones at de windows n yellin, wit a trail uv slime, a head like a barbarian n an army uv dark energies around him at ten in de mornin. Sumtimes Id pretend not te be in, just for a break. Heed go te Zorros n get no answer der either, n Rooner wud curse us all out, why wer we doin dis te him? Dublin became an never endin ghost ride, n expandin horror house full uv ghouls n zombies n tormenters out te get um at every turn, he had te run again, he had te get out.

He decided te go n find iz Ma, she wuz livin in limerick wit her fella. Tara n me even went down once te stay der for a weekend witum. We played a Junkyard dogs acoustic gig in a pub it ended wit me topless on stage, all skin n bones n faux danger, Rooner behind me in iz own world uv tablature n notes. He said we shud move down der, get a band goin, I said Limerick wuz too small, had nutting dat Dublin hadden got more uv, a smaller block wer weed have strange accents. De paranoia got stronger. De accusations against one n other bigger. De silent periods longer. Weeks n months went by, no music, no new songs, no recordins, no desire. Books became much more interestin te me din Rooner or Zorro or singin songs.

Tara wuz in work, I wuz cleanin out de fire, n weed no hash(Id been goin on periodic bouts uv givin it up anyway, but Rooner witout hash, wuz wen de demons in him reared der horned heads n spoke loudest in der awful tongues), Rooner tromped around de flat like a starvin animal, moanin, complainin, Id begun te write more n more by den for me own pleasure, not thinkin will Rooner n Zorro like dis, n wuz practisin wit magickal or mind/brain change techniques: Mediation, Hypnotherapy, NLP, Creative visualisation, Trance Drummin n me vision wuz growin again, me art wuz movin in new directions. I felt like I didden know who dis guy Rooner wuz anymore, he changed too, did I like wot heed become, did I want or need him around me? He felt de same about me n he wanted out, he wanted te do wot hes always done, n only knew how te do, n really cudden help but do, n dat wuz te run.

A huge fight engineered by de both uv us broke out, me at de fire wit a bucket uv ashes n a shovel, Rooner standin over me shoutin down, I stood up, we went face te face, it all came out uv us, a torrent uv abuse, a tirade uv resentment buld up over months, a table got broken by Rooner wen he kicked it in a rage fit, I told him te get de fuck out uv me gaff now n fuck off. Rooner went out de door wit iz second hand *Les Paul* guitar over one shoulder, iz back pack full uv pedals, wires, tapes, tuners, aniz *Fender* amp in iz hand, n De Junkyard Dogs just like der predecessors De Urban Gorillas, wer finished. It wuz low, it wuz heavy, it wuz lousy n it wuz over.

Rooner came n went from Dublin te Limerick n Galway, found girlfriends who wer madder din him, one who drank beer from cans she found on de street, n ate left over food in cafes, another who wuz intimate wit de Glooptings n every dark entity in de shadows n smelled uv death he told me.

We saw each other every so often, heed come n visit, no apologies wer ever made, sumtimes we talked uv gettin back tegether, but it wuz never de same after dat day, n I wuz done wit music anyway n eventually Rooner n I lost contact.

He stopped visitin, Zorro n him now best mates, runnin around de country, goin from one block te de next, lookin for highs n bands for Rooner te play in n Zorro te hang out wit n carry de guitars, n roll de joints. A pair uv mad outsider vagabonds. We made sum fuckin magic tunes tegether Rooner, we had trips tegether dat noone cud ever know de depth uv, we had de same dream once didden we Luke Rooney?

Voices from De Blocks

Number:10

Name: Spin De Wheel: Yonkers ONeil, drug talk.
Year: 2004.
Place: Flat 264 ODevaney Gardens.

I wuz sittin on de bed right an de fuckin K just kicks in bang like. I just threw de joint at lambo, says Here get dat away from me like. Next uv all me legs er just fuckin heavy, me arms flopped down mad heavy like. I wuz like fukin mala or sumting ya know? Fukin bombed outta it.

So Im der stuck te de fuckin bed right? Cant fuckin move like. So I try te talk te de rest a dem, nutting comes out just bleedin mumbles n grumbles, me tongue is rollin in me bleedin head, sos me eyes like ya know? Right, so Im der stuck te de bed in fuckin bits like an I can hear dem all askin me if Im alright n dat ya know? Tazzers breakin iz shite laughin at me de prick.

All I do is sort a roll an rock like a fuckin baby on de bed right. So next uv all, it gets even fuckin madder like. I look up n ders fuckin Tazzer, Lambo, Jacinta, Pauly, Gar, Louise an all in de fukin *Lotto* show, ya know de bleedin three stars yoke on de telly like? Marty fuckin Whelan man, like holy shit like.

Deyre all runnin round de room playin fuckin games an de crowds cheerin an all, an dis poor cunt here is stuck te de bed rollin around like a bleedin dope. All Im thinkin is Id love te be on de fuckin

249

show. I manage te let out a shout Gwan Tazzer spin dat fuckin wheel I says. So he dose he goes up n spins de fuckin wheel right. De cunt only wins de 250,000 n Marty hands um de cheque. All dem goin mad jumpin around de room an me rollin on de bed imaginin all de weed, gargle, pills an special K ya cud get for 250 grand like, ya know wot I mean like?

I wuz on dat bed for three fuckin hours man, pissed on me self a little bit an all I did. Tewards de end uv it Lambo said I finally just sprang up n sat der an looked at um an says Man dats deadly dat ya won all dat cash isin it pal, wha we gonna do wit it? He hadden a fuckin clue wot I wuz on about ya know? So dats why ever since den man I cant stop buyin fuckin scratch cards. I dont even care if I win cash on dem, its nice like dont get me wrong now but I really, really want te get on de fuckin show ya know? I cant fuckin get de idea out me head since dat fuckin night ya know like? Anyways Im off, gonna go collect me dole n get a few scratch cards. Never know might get de three stars n get on an spin de fuckin wheel.

Typical type block uv dat time

Saturday night in Fatima, in de blocks, Shane MacGowans voice fills de room
N a rovin, a rovin, a rovin, I/ll go for a pair uv brown eyes, for a pair uv brown eyes.

I pour a tall glass uv *Blossom Hill White Zinfandel*, hock n spit a demon inte de bin. I raise me glass high inte de air n say
Te me brothers who have fallen.
I Kiss de glass n take a swig uv de sweet wine.
Now Shane sings
I met me love by de gasworks wall, dreamed a dream by de old canal.
Out on de balcony I look up at Dublins cloudless, indigo, summer night sky. Three tracksuited, airmacked youngfellas walk by underneath, throwin shapes n hollerin, across de road two arm linked lovers stroll, here comes a *Dominos* Pizza delevery man, n two Garda walkin de beat lookin for sumone te nick.

N de band played Waltzin Matilda.

I pour me second glass uv wine, raise me glass n drink te Dublin,
Dublin yer a wimpperin bitch, yer a made up whore, yer a dirty swine, yer a mountain flower, yer a fake diamond, ahh Dublin yer me wild love.
De music has changed now: De Righteous Brothers, *Youve lost dat lovin feelin*

Marvin Gaye, *I heard it tru de grapevine*. I let me voice free n sing, no concern for neighbours, its Saturday night, let me sing, let dem sing, let everyone sing, tru music we fall in love wit ourselves. I top up me glass, n empty de bottle, I raise it te meself dis time, as Satchmo sings,
N I think te myself wot a wonderful world.
I read aloud Allen Ginzbergs *Howl*, selections from Lorcas *Poet In New York* n Rimbauds *A season in Hell*.

Ders a party on de way, Tara is comin home wit a gang in taxis from pubs n clubs. Ah! Let de celebration begin...

Here dey er: Tara, Linda, Philo, Catty, Andy, Rose, Jacinta, Yonkers, Tazzer, Paddy n Brenda. Dey brin crates uv alcohol, *Miller* n *Bulmers*, bottles uv *Smirnoff* Vodka n a oner bag uv coke.

Hugs n handshakes, we dance te Prince n Amy Winehouse, sing *Dirty Old Town*, talk n talk n talk about kids, relationships, drugs, poetry, football, fights, money, all kinds uv drug bullshit, everyone tryin te out do de last story. Bulgin eyes, red faces, roarin laughs, wolfe smiles, glass smashin, Tara moppin up spills, joints, smokes, backslaps, knee rubs, bangin tunes, Shane MacGowan, Amy Winehouse, grindin teeth, headlock love, sweaty handshakes, sly snorts, gum rubs, drinkin de wrong can, burnin shots, violent thoughts, sexual thoughts, splifs shared, bullshit brains, Taxi home, n Tara n me er last up, everyones gone, its 9.am wer still drinkin, sharin de last bottles uv beer, de sun is rayin in tru de blinds n me hand reaches for de inside uv her thigh, Tara yer soft wettin thigh, here we ar still throwin love inte de mix uv chemicals, dust n music. Music like a slow piano tune played in a dream, music in a dream I had.

I wuz now truly experienced by me time in de blocks. De mornin wuz a war in me eyes.

A Poet at Last

I wuz still mired in de blocks, a twenty six year old man now, no job, no band, still livin n lovin wit Tara, who worked as a sales assistant in a clothes shop in de *Ilac Centre*, n me dream uv roackstardom dead as me Da, Jimmy n Georgie wer. Dead as me friendships wit Rooner, J.J n Zorro wer. Charlo wud stay over n weed play *FIFA* n watch Premiership football matches n Kung-Fu n action movies. A dullness had set in, de parties werent fun, de drug highs cudden match de music, pubs were full uv shite talk, gossip n bluster, de guitar lay aganist de wall inside its case, me creative heartbeat slowin down, me art on de ropes, de exit music fadin out, de audience fillin out de door.

I wuz in de flat in Fatima alone, Tara wuz at work. I looked at de bookshelf n remembered dat de angel said poet not rock star, not singer, poet, fuckin poet n I went te de window n looked at de Autumn Dublin sky, tangerine n pinkish clouds, de sun settin above de blocks, a paintin is all it is I thought, wer in dis mad playground, an illusion dats all, a game dat feels real, ders a way, I know ders a fuckin way out I said, n den I dropped it, de rockstar dream, de band stuff, de infamy seekin n said fuck it anyway, I gave it a shot, I

253

tried te make it wit dem, maybe its not suposed te be wit a group? Maybe destiny had planed it all out dis way? Before de blocks, before people, n planets n suns, before time, I thought uv de tree dat spoke in me childhood, I thought uv de Angels words, I picked up a book uv Blakes poems n read de words *Te see a world in a grain uv sand n heaven in a wild flower...*n heard de epic voice uv Whitman come rollin down de mountain n along de river Liffy n tru de city streets te me sittin room in de top floor flat uv de blocks sayin *I Celebrate myself, and sing myself...* n I felt at home, relaxed, wer gods in our own creation, little gods only growin up I muttered n saw de shape uv a huge bird in de distance, as it came closer I saw it wuz a dove, de biggest dove I ever saw, it came swoopin down from de sky, a ten foot supernatural wing span, brilliant Himalayan snow white feathers wit de sun shinin offa dem, gold dazzilin me eyes n de dove shattered tru de glass uv de window n dropped inte me open arms a *Brother* electric typewriter from its enormous claws n spoke

Write poet, type poet, sing de song uv Kenny Thomson de angel uv de flats, be de hero uv de blocks n do thou will in dis world, witout fear.

N de typewriter landed at me feet wit a kerchin n a whirin.

De dove swooped up n out uv de blocks, inte de tangerine sun dat wuz gowin down over Dublin. I picked up de typewriter placed it on me desk n began te hit de keys n heard de greatest music I ever played.

254

Exorcism block

Tara saw de seven foot tall ugly Gloopting shiver across de hall n go inte our bedroom. Her belly twisted in fear, her face wax, her skin cold. I got up from de sofa, n calmly walked in te de bedroom after it. I no longer feared any dark tings in de blocks. I entered de room n de Gloopting stood der, red eyes n black smoke, a large shadowy gunk. I stuck out me chest n howled in iz face, showed me tigers smile n it shrank in te de corner. I called on de great spirit, on all me ancestors, on de friends in de land uv de dead te fill me wit power. A young man appeared before me. A tall, skinny junkie. He had a works in iz arm. I asked um who he wuz n wot he wanted.

Te be free he said.

I want te get out uv de blocks but he wont let me.

He pointed at de Gloop in de corner.

I died here in Fatima, on de stairs, Od/d, n dat ting locked on te me, has me under its slimy grip. Me names Terry.

De last two weeks we had sum problems in de flat. We fought. We over slept. We felt coldness. Terry said it wuz him, tryin te get me attention. He knew I had de sight, de vision, de experience needed te help him release from de blocks.

I called out again te de great spirit. De dead. De angel I called. De light I called. N it all came tegether. It opened up de ceilin uv de room, a ladder uv stars leadin te a band uv angels, swirlin electric blue, crimson, emerald, a million glowin hands, a massive fatbellied laughin Buddha, n I picked up Terrys light spirit wit both hands, up over me head n pushed him up n inte de lights, up out uv de room n out uv de blocks. Den I turned te de Gloopting in de corner, n I caught it by its slippery dark neck, n I looked at it, squirmin, it dropped te de ground its shawl n wailed. It wuzzen evil, it wuz pathetic. I picked it up by de back uv its neck n hurled it out uv me room, out uv me flat, out uv Fatima, out uv de blocks in te de lights n glowin hands n it turned inte a beautiful blackbird n de angels n Terry dropped lilacs n carnations down on me n de fat Buddha opened iz mouth n chuckled forth a tidal wave uv pink lotuses dat covered de room n de whole flat, n de buildin n de blocks wer covered in pink lotuses n lilacs n carnations n all wuz light in me eyes n behind dem, all wuz light. De dark tings wer light too. How very strange I thought.

De strangest life Ive ever know.

Kennys Jobs: A List

1. Forecourt attendant: Lasted two months. Age:17. Pros: Free Chocolate, time te sit n listen te *Sony Walkman*. Cons: Borin, low paid.

2. *Bargintown* furniture shop: Lasted three months. Age 21. Pros: Able te hide down in de basement n sleep on a stack uv mattresses. Cons: Annoyin work mates, late hrs.

3. *3com* computers. Lasted four months. Age: 22. Pros: High income rate, lots uv other smokers in de factory. Cons: Weekend n night time 12 hr shifts.

4. Industrial cleaner: Lasted two years on n off. Age 23-25. Pros: Had friends workin wit me, cud smoke joints on de job. Cons: Low income, fights wit bosses n co-workers.

5. Stage production wit MCD. Lasted six months. Age: 25. Pros: Workin in music industry, free passes te gigs, lots uv drugs around. Cons: Back breakin work wit heavy liftin, lots uv old worn out heads, hippies n rockers.

6. Writer: Started at birth says Genet, cud be before, in de Bardo? In de time before time?
Lasted for as long as breath flows n beyond. Pros: Followin ones vision n true will. Cons N/A.

De world opens its arms

Wit de death uv de band, de guitars n amps out n de electric typewriter n a desk installed, me life as an independent artist began. Pictures uv Jack Kerouac, William Blake n Walt Whitman pinned te de wall above de desk. I gathered up me copies n pgs dat had song lyrics in dem, n put dem in a pot n burned dem, I watched as de pages engulfed de past, smoke billowin inte de air n den I took te embers n ashes n flung dem over de balcony te de wind, de ritual complete. Only de few real poems remained, I typed dem up, printed dem n put dem in manilla folder marked wit the header Poetry n den I sat down everyday n wrote poem after poem, n read n re-read all me favourite poets n sum new ones too, solitaryhood n practice only broken by visits by Charlo n livin wit Tara. Eventually I had ten poems I wuz proud uv.

After a year or two uv livin like dat, I upgraded de *Brother* Typewriter te a PC n got online n on te *Myspace*, n on der I found other poets my age, n dey wer here in Dublin n a few uv dem had a forthnightly poetry n song night in a small bar on Camden st across from *Whelens*, de name uv de night wuz *Naked Lunch* after de William Burroughs novel. Holy shit, der wer others out der waitin for me. So on de night uv me birthday Tara n me went te *Naked Lunch*.

I wuz nervous n excited but cocky n drunk by de time me name got called out on de open mic. I read two poems, one short concise image-mystic ting n a longer Beat-Gen inspired one da got de crowd on der feet n cheerin, I wuz hooked in te de feelin uv bein on stage on me own. Dis wuz it, no fuckin tryin te stay in tune, no music way too loud over me voice, no arguments about de material, no endless rehearsals, no ego clashin. Just me on stage wit me art, me body, meself expressin me own human experience for a crowd dat related te it n gave me praise n encouragement.

Over de next twelve months I made a bunch uv new friends, n lots uv dem wer poets, performin poets, poets who wer uv de same time, de same generation, de same enthusiasm as me n we wer in de same space tegether, doin it tegether: De *Naked Lunch* host Mark Tello, a gay, skinny, whisky drinkin, Irish beat poet, a banker by day n foppish, stroppy, cravat wearin, hair-tossed-poet at night. De Americans, Clint Hanmann, a charmin, smart, well read, friendly, Kentucky man in a matrix leather coat, aniz friend Crow (Surname dropped), an African American, cool as fuck, tender, perceptive, sumtime hip-hopper, I learned a lot about stage work n performin by oneself, n memorisin yer work, n deliverin it tru de body as well as de voice, by watchin dem two on stage. Andy kavor wuz our Rimabaudian youth, a sixteen year old, Croatian Irish, tall, vampire-good-lookin poet, wit a smooth voice n smooth stanzas too. Seamus Smith, de big unpretentious, *Guinness* swillin Dubliner, intense performer n hard grafter, who went on te start up de *Glor Sessions* in *de International bar*, dat wud become a legendary weekly event wer de live poetry scene really tuk off, n Dan Jordan, short, stout, imposin, loud, brilliant, blazin brained, west corkman, winner uv a Kavanagh award, n de only wunna us at dat time te have a book published n any sort uv recognition uv iz work, tho he liked te come n hang around wit us, n wuz indeed wunna us, over de years me friendship witum wud grow te be wunna de great bromantic love affairs in all uv Irish letters, de Shams te me Rumi, de Tu-Fu te me Li-po, de Byron te me Shelley.

De first ting he ever said te me wuz typical uv him, I wuz on stage before him, n wen I finished I went n sat down, he came n sat beside me n said

Jaysus yer a hard act te follow boy, dats sum great shtuff, but here I tell ye wot ye dont always have te bate dem over de head ye know?

A complement n den sum good advice, dats wot he gave me n I knew he wuz de real deal der n den. In dose days der wer no female performin poets, all de women wer friends or girlfriends, a lot uv dem came wit de singers n bands.

Later on wen de whole spoken word movement took off lots uv brilliant n talented woman poets came n energised n broadened de scene n nights like *Naked Lunch* started popin up all over Dublin n de country.

One day I received a copy uv *Revival* literary journal in de post wit a poem uv mine published in it. De first publication is a joyous experience, ya take de journal n go straight te yer poem n look at on de page n read it n ders yer name on de end uv it, den ya go te de back n look at de profiles uv all de writers in it, n ya have one or two who ya admire in der n others wit three books published n PhDs n yer in der wit dem n it

260

feels fuckin nice n ya show it te yer family n all yer friends, carryin it around in yer pocket for weeks, takin it out wen yer drunk n lookin at it again. De same day I got an Email from wunna de new Cabaret nights around de town, dey wanted me te be a featured poet on de next monthly show, it wuz called *De Brown Bread Mixtape*, music, comedy n poetry, no open mic all features, hosted by a bald, rambunctious, fun, chubby, part Scandinavian part Irish, spoken word artist named Knut Moore.

De angel said

Poet that is what you are, be ready, for it is not for everyone, it is risk, it is folly, it is the most glorious enterprise in this holy life. I sat meditatin on de words n smiled as I saw laid out before me de way uv de writer, de one true honourable way uv me destiny, n I walked inte it wit steps light as barefooted Adam on a sunny mornin in Eden.

EPILOGUE

In a wakin dream I see Georgie, Jimmy n me Da playin heads n volleys in de park, up at de pitches by de Popes cross, de air hums wit joyful odes, de ruby sun is perfect in de faultless sky, I stand pitchside n wave at dem, dey stop playin, turn te me, smile n wave, finally safe in de land uv de dead...

Tommy Doyle is sittin on iz posh black leather sofa wit iz wife n young daughter, hes just come home from a days work in de *Swan Youth Centre*, iz red hair has grey in it, iz blue eyes still a glint, he looks n feels healthier din ever, a sense uv belongin runs tru iz body, aniz soul is calm in de Dublin night...

Jason Jones is playin wit iz two children aniz dogs out in de backyard uv iz family home in Roscommon, ders a chicken in de oven n vegetables cookin on de stove, iz girlfriend is just about te dish it all up. A guitar is on a stand in de bedroom, hes come a long way from de blocks n de drugs n de alcohol n de muck...

Ma is drinkin tea n watchin telly in de sittin room uv de flat in ODevaney, Edel is on de phone talkin loudly te a friend as dey organise a girls night out, enjoyin her singlehood te de maximum, Frankie havin gone tru heroin addicton n prison n come out de other side is wit iz new girlfriend, setteld n a full time drug councillor, Charlo comes in te de room wearin Belvedere football kit wit a trainin bag over iz

263

shoulder, hes grown te be stocky n fit, iz blonde hair has sum muck in it, he takes off de bag n drops it in de middle uv de room on de floor n sits on de sofa,

Wots for dinner nanny? Im starvin.

Ahh yeah, just drop de bag in de middle uv de floor dats it, dinner is

chips, beans n fish.

Fish, nice one Nanny, Ma er ya goin out tonight?

Yeah I am, why?

Cuz if ya er Im ringin Kenny te see can I stay wit Tara n him tonight, bring me *Playstation* over, deadly.

Ringum so, after yer dinner.

Friday night in de blocks...

I bump inte a pair uv ragged misfits in de street, its Rooner n Zoro out buskin.

Rooners hair shaggy n greyed, face hollow, teeth yellow n brown. De fire turned more embers now, n Zorro still ponytailed, conspiratorial, cannabis idolatry spewin from de thin lips. Both caught up in de cracks uv de city, stuck in de blocks, dark in der reveries...

Rooner says hes been drinkin hard for de last two weeks, a joint in iz mouth, he asks if I want a pull, I decline. Standin on de pavement uv Grafton Street, Rooner, still de supreme musician. Funky, bluesy, de easiness uv it. De artful hands. De crowd mesmerised. I tell Zorro uv de comin soon uv me first published book uv poems n me new writer friends, Dan Jordans manuscript uv darkmagic stories in me bag, I tell dem dat Im straight edged dese days, no smoke, no

264

alcohol, just vision, n writin. I shake hands wit dem n wish dem all de best, see ya around lads, I walk away from dem n get in a taxi dat takes me te de Phoenix Park...

I pay de fare n get out...

I hear house music, Bum, ba, dum, ba, dum, ba, dum, dum...

Im a recordin angel under grey clouds.. White winged Butterfly flits in de sky, above junkies wit tattoos, wearin navy pyjama bottoms...

De enormous white dove is in de sky n laughs, arg, ga, gar, gar, gar, gar, ga ck... Now Im park sittin again...Wer de boys n me played football... Wer we climbed trees n smoked joints... Dan Carr hangin from a branch, fear struck gettin down only two feet from de ground... Georgie n me laughin... Wer we sniffed bags uv glue in de night... I sit wit de serene butter cups n daffodils n I am like de lilies, I neither toil nor spin... N I look around at beech, oak, foilage, faunna, roses, children, sparows, crows, n I see de essence everywer in de ancient land...

An insect... De sky... Dirt on de ground... A kid throwin a Frisbee... A dog...

A giant talkin bee... A gloopting... De doves... De barbed wire on de fence... Georgie, Tommy, Jimmy, Rooner, Tara, Edel, Ma, Da, Charlo, Me, everyone, everyting... De Wicklow moutains... De river Liffey... De Phoenix Park...De Blocks...Dublin City... Ireland...

All Earth de essence... De glorious sun...If I just shut up, sit down n be...

Itll all unfold its self before me... If I just accept it, all de pain n pleasure n loss... De whole tale will come... itll roll all over me in waves uv ecstasy... Itll enflame me dis eternal essence... N Im burnin wit it...I am de essence, n dats all der is te it... Godessence.

A flock uv doves glide gracefully in de blue grey sky above me de Godessence in der wings... Wit words Im breakin out... Im writin me way out... Im burnin wit de word... I lie in de grass n know dat de universe is a novel dat writes its self... A symphony composed n conducted by all sentient beins tegether... De great Orator recitin de pome uv us all... I see de Tao winkin back... I write wot comes or is given... I record de essence... I transmute de muck inte glory... I walk back home now te de blocks...

De Godessence in de concrete uv de blocks... De Godessence in every face in de blocks... De Godessence everywer... Im burnin wit de Godessence n de word... Finally I am out uv de blocks tru de writin uv dis here book called *The Blocks* n I am free, thank you.

Acknowledgements

Thanks to Tash, Ma, Elaine, Shane, Dave for your support, friendship and love.

Thanks to Rob Doyle, Kevin Curran and Alan McMonagle for reading the manuscript and for the blurbs.

Thanks to Dave Lordan for his help with the editing and help with the many drafts of this book.

Thanks to James and New Binary Press for publishing this wild book.

Excerpts from this book were published on bogmanscannon.com and a playlist, a soundtrack to *The Blocks*, can also be found there.

Karl Parkinson is a writer from inner-city Dublin. *The Blocks* is his début novel. In 2013 Wurmpress published his début poetry collection, *Litany of the City and Other Poems*, and his second poetry collection, *Butterflies of a Bad Summer*, was published by Salmon in 2016. His work has appeared in the anthologies, *New Planet Cabaret* (New Island Press) and *If Ever You Go: A Map of Dublin in Poetry and Song* (Dedalus Press), as well as in several journals, including *The Stinging Fly, The Poetry Bus, Penduline, Colony, Can Can, The Pickled Body, The Bohemyth, The Incubator, Revival* and *Wordlegs.*

Karl is one of Ireland's most acclaimed live literature performers and has read by invitation at festivals and events in Ireland, the UK, the US and Canada. His work has been broadcast on RTE1's Arena Arts show many times. In 2015, he featured on the Setanta Ireland live TV New Year's Eve show. Karl is also one half of the spoken word/electro music duo, *The King Mob*, and a creative writing workshop and course leader, teaching in schools, festivals, youth clubs and adult learning centres in Ireland.

He is a facilitating editor and regular contributor for Irelands leading alt-lit, multi-media online hub, bogmanscannon.com.

karlparkinson7@yahoo.ie
@kparkspoet

Hidden Track
We Deal In Dreams

Fatima, 2014

Tony stands at de wall wit de presence uv a mountain Gorilla. Its windy n de rain is dat drizzly kind dat pebbles ya all over. Rain n wind wudden keep Big T off de street. Hes got te be out der doing iz work.

Iz hood is pulled up. He smokes a joint n looks out at de street thinkin about de *BMW* hes gonna buy wen he saves up de cash, hes got five grand in a shoe box in iz mas house.

Big T sees a buyer coming iz way. Scrawny n broken. Legs n arms like *Mc Donalds* fries.

Story T, have ya anyting on ya, bud?

No Im just standin here for de good a me health, course Ive sumting on me, ya dope ya n Im not yer bud, de ya hear me?

Ehh, ye, yah, alright T, no bother bu, em, yeah, give us two bags will ya?

Two bags, no bother, give me de cash, go over te him, an he/ll give ya de bags n den fuck off outta here, yer bleedin red hot ya ar.

Grand, cool T, nice one, dont worry Im outta here, quick as I can, get dem bags in te me ya know, cya later bu...

De junkie hands big T de cash n walks across de street te collect de bags from a fourteen year old boy who spits on de ground n has iz hands shoved down de front uv iz tracksuit bottoms. De deal is done. De Junkie lightens up n hurrys out uv de block. De boy tips iz head tewards Big T n leans against de wall one foot raised. Big T nods back at de boy n stuffs de cash in iz pocket.

Big T eats a large batter burger n chips wit loads uv salt n vinegar on de chips.
Big T whistles n glares at de girls dressed up for a night out gettin in te a taxi in de block.
Big T smokes cigarettes n joints, coughs in fits, spits out green flem on de ground.
Big T sniffs coke out uv a plastic bag n sniffs n rubs iz nose, iz gums er numb.
Big T kicks a dog in de arse as it walks by n barks at um.
Big T goes inte iz flat n has a wank while watchin *YouPorn*.
Big T back in de block on de street sellin product te iz loyal customers.
Big T drives around in a silver *BMW* wit tinted windows, in iz dreams.

Its 2:30am, cold n quiet in de block. Big T is about te retire from iz days work,
wen he sees a car drive slowly inte de block. He looks at it n a thinks nice motor,
Silver *BMW* just like de one Big T wants te get.

De *BMW* stops in front uv Big T n de tinted black window rolls down.
Here Bigman, any stuff?

Yeah, wot er ya lookin for, Brown or white?

Oh no brown for me Bigman, I like de white, te keep me up n goin,

ya know wot I mean man?

Hah, yeah, I know wot ya mean, like me self, how many bags?

Ive three hundred, wot can ya give me for dat?

Three hundred, tell ya wot I/ll give ya all de bags Ive left, dats about eight, ok?

Here bring me over dem bags, ya have, yeah, bring dem all over, all dem I said ya little prick ya, have te keep dese little fuckers on der toes ya know, like?

Indeed I do bigman, indeed I do.

De boy comes over n gives Big T all de bags he has n stands der gawkin at de car.

Wot er ya standin der for, fuck off outta here, go on yer finished for de night.

De boy shrugs n turns n walks off down de street.

Big T hands de bags te de man n takes de cash from um, leanin in te de *BMW*. Lovely motor ya have der, Im gettin one meself soon.

Yeah, dya ya like it?

Fuckin luvit pal, here if yer lookin for anymore white, ya can find me or wunna de boys here anytime, I/ll sort ya out, alright pal?

Sound, sound bud, wots yer name?

Big T, just ask for Big T if Im not around n ya be sorted.

Big T, cool, cool mate, see ya later.

Later bud.

Big T is in iz bed, headphones on, joint in iz mouth, he closes iz eyes.

Big T is in de drivers seat uv de BMW, lookin de woman in de passenger seat over from head te toe. She looks at him at smiles.

Big T leans back inte de brown leather interior uv de seat n closes iz eyes for a second n presses play on de stereo.

Tupacs *Picture me Rollin* comes on n Big T smiles as he pulls a wheelspin drivin out uv de block.